HEATING UP

They sat in the truck's cab for a few seconds. She rubbed her hands together.

"Cold?" He took her hands and sandwiched them between his larger ones, instantly warming them.

They locked eyes and he leaned across the center console, capturing her mouth with his. A shot of heat went through her. His lips were warm and pliable, and he tasted a little of beer. She twined her arms around his neck and closed her eyes, letting him take the kiss deeper. He cupped the back of her head and explored her mouth with his tongue.

Her tongue met his and the kiss became more fervent. More sensual. She couldn't remember a kiss that had roused her this much. He lowered her onto the seat and moved over her. She arched up, pressing against his chest, wanting the rest of him...

Books by Stacy Finz

The Nugget Series
GOING HOME
FINDING HOPE
SECOND CHANCES
STARTING OVER
GETTING LUCKY
BORROWING TROUBLE
HEATING UP
RIDING HIGH
FALLING HARD
HOPE FOR CHRISTMAS
TEMPTING FATE
CHOOSING YOU
HOLDING ON

The Garner Brothers
NEED YOU
WANT YOU
LOVE YOU

Dry Creek Ranch
COWBOY UP
COWBOY TOUGH
COWBOY STRONG
COWBOY PROUD

Published by Kensington Publishing Corp.

Cowboy Proud

Stacy Finz

LYRICAL PRESS
Kensington Publishing Corp.
www.kensingtonbooks.com

LYRICAL PRESS BOOKS are published by

Kensington Publishing Corp.
119 West 40th Street
New York, NY 10018

All Kensington titles, imprints, and distributed lines are available at special quantity discounts for bulk purchases for sales promotion, premiums, fund-raising, educational, or institutional use.

Special book excerpts or customized printings can also be created to fit specific needs. For details, write or phone the office of the Kensington Sales Manager: Kensington Publishing Corp., 119 West 40th Street, New York, NY 10018. Attn. Sales Department. Phone: 1-800-221-2647.

Lyrical Press and Lyrical Press logo Reg. U.S. Pat. & TM Off.

First Electronic Edition: November 2021
ISBN: 978-1-5161-1123-7 (ebook)

First Print Edition: March 2021
ISBN: 978-1-5161-1124-4

Printed in the United States of America

A big thanks to all my readers. This is the book you asked for. I hope I did Angie proud.

Chapter 1

Dry Creek Ranch was even more beautiful than Angela remembered. Everything was so green. The pine and oak trees. The pastures. The surrounding Sierra foothills.

And the creek, which ran heavy, was crystal clear. Angie was sure that if she stared into the water, she could see her own reflection. She didn't of course, afraid that she wouldn't recognize the person she saw. The person she'd been stripped of and forced to reinvent like the Hollywood stars her parents represented.

This will be good, she sighed. Here, she could get her bearings, figure out what she wanted to do with the rest of her life, and bury Katherine Moore, a woman she never much cared for, anyway.

That's why she'd chosen the ranch over her native Los Angeles, a city that traded in role playing. On Dry Creek she could be herself again. But first, she had to find out who that was.

Even before she'd become Katherine, she'd been searching for so long. Traveling the world, joining up with any movement or group that caught her fancy, and falling for men who played her like a chess piece.

That's what got me into trouble in the first place. She let out another sigh and continued to stare out over the mountains.

Tap. Tap.

Her head jerked up to find a man leaning over the side of a horse, knocking on her car window. Angie reached for the can of pepper spray she kept in her glove box, then chided herself for being ridiculous. He was probably a ranch hand.

She unrolled her window a crack, letting in a rush of cold air.

"You lost?" He pulled down the brim of his cowboy hat to keep from squinting into the sun. "The shops and restaurant are that way." He pointed in the direction of her late grandfather's old barn.

"Actually, I'm looking for Sawyer Dalton's house." She hadn't been here…well, it had to be at least six or seven years. Not since Christmas when Grandpa Dalton was still alive and everyone gathered at the ranch to celebrate holidays.

The cowboy straightened in his saddle. He was tall. Over six feet, judging by the size of his horse and the length his legs had to travel until his boots rested in a tooled set of stirrups. Broad, too, like he spent a lot of time lifting hay bales. His face was sun worn and there were crinkles around his eyes that made him look like he was smiling even when he wasn't. But it was his eyes. A rich mahogany that reminded Angie of good leather.

"He expecting you?" His voice was a deep rumble with a hint of a drawl. Not Texas but definitely not California. Somewhere West, though.

She considered the question. There was no short way to answer it, so she lied. "He is."

He leaned down again, giving Angie the impression that he was dubious. One look at her Dalton blue eyes—the unusual color of cobalt—and his expression changed. "About a mile past that copse of trees and the big ranch house on the right. Continue up the hill until you see what used to be a barn and now looks like something…architectural. That's Sawyer and Gina's place."

Angie smiled to herself. Leave it to Sawyer to reinvent one of Grandpa Dalton's livestock buildings.

"Thank you." She started to close her window.

"I'm Ted…my friends call me Tuff." He stuck out his hand and she opened the window wider to shake it.

"I'm Kath…Angela," she said, letting her name—her real name—linger on her tongue, reveling in the taste of it. The taste of freedom. "My friends call me Angie. Angie Dalton."

"Welcome to Dry Creek Ranch, Miz Dalton." He tipped his hat.

She watched him ride away, then pulled off the shoulder, back onto the road. As she passed the ranch house, she considered stopping. There'd been so many happy times in the wonderful rambler when her grandparents were alive. Now, she knew her cousin Jace and his family lived there. Even from a distance, she'd kept tabs on the doings of the ranch and on the Daltons.

She would see Jace later. First, Sawyer. Angie had missed her family with an ache so painful, there were times she thought she would die from it. Most of all, she had missed her brother. Sawyer had never stopped searching for her. He'd never stopped believing in her. And because of that, she'd never stopped believing in herself.

The cowboy...Tuff ...had been right. She parked alongside a Range Rover, killed the engine, and stared up at what used to be a hay loft. She, Sawyer, and their cousins had spent many a summer up there, playing hide-and-seek.

Architectural glass now covered the once weathered wooden windows, and two large industrial-style barn lamps flanked each side of the building. The old hay elevator was still there, but other than the cows that dotted the distant fields, no livestock was in sight. The barn had been transformed into a cross between a trendy farmhouse and an upscale artist's loft.

She got out of her ancient Mercedes—a find off Craig's List—and stretched her legs. After the ten-hour drive from Portland, she felt like a pretzel. She left her suitcase, a Costco closeout holding all her worldly possessions, in the trunk. After a few steps, she stopped, suddenly overwhelmed.

It had been six years. Six whole years since she'd seen her brother in person.

She took a fortifying breath and walked the rest of the way to the front door. Poised to knock, she silently prayed for strength. But before she could act, the door opened. And there stood Sawyer, looking as if he hadn't aged a day. Still her too-handsome-for-his-own-good big brother.

She watched his expression slowly turn from mild annoyance to shock. "Angie?"

She self-consciously touched her hair. "I went red."

"Oh my God, it's you! It's really you." His eyes filled and he swiped at them with his hand before swooping her up in the air. "Holy shit, Ange, there's nothing to you. What...are you out...are you even supposed to be here?"

She clung to him, the lump in her throat making it impossible to respond. All she could do was cry.

"Ah, jeez, Angie, come inside. Come inside."

He pulled her over the threshold and practically carried her up a set of stairs that landed in a huge great room. "Let me look at you." He stepped back and assessed her. "You look great, Angie."

She didn't, but she gave him points for sounding genuine.

"Mom and Dad...Did you call them? Do they know you're here?"

Still choked up, she shook her head. To buy time while she gathered her emotions, she turned in place, surveying the loft. It was an open floor plan with a large kitchen and soaring cathedral ceilings. The old barn's big wooden trusses were still exposed, and again she had a memory of them playing in the loft. "Wow, Sawyer, this is some home."

"Never mind the house. What's going on, Angie? Talk to me."

"It's over." She choked on a sob. "I get to come home."

Sawyer guided her to one of the couches and wrapped her in a throw blanket. That's when she realized she was shaking.

"Let me get you something warm to drink and you can start at the beginning."

"Some tea would be good." She hadn't had anything to eat or drink all day. Her only concern had been getting to Dry Creek Ranch.

Sawyer turned up the thermostat and made his way to the kitchen where he made her a cup of tea. He watched her take a sip, then settled down next to her. "Better?"

"Yes. Thank you."

"I've got a lot of questions, Ange."

She knew he would. He was a successful investigative journalist after all.

"You want a little time? Or should I call Jace and Cash?"

She sucked in a breath. Her cousins were both cops. They too would have a lot of questions. "Call them." She just wanted to get this over with.

Sawyer returned to the kitchen and brought her a slice of banana bread. It was still warm as if it had recently come out of the oven. She took a bite and then devoured it.

"I'll make you a sandwich in a few minutes." He swiped his phone off the center island and disappeared behind a closed door.

She could hear his voice but couldn't make out the conversation. He was probably preparing Jace and Cash.

While he talked on the phone, she went in search of a bathroom. She'd only stopped twice during the drive. Each time, looking over her shoulder as if her life depended on it. When would it stop? Her handlers warned maybe never.

What a way to live? But it sure beat the alternative.

Thirty minutes later, Cash and Jace rushed in while Angie finished her sandwich. They hugged her so hard she was afraid her bones would snap. Even after they let go, they took turns squeezing her shoulder, her knee, her arm. It was as if they wanted to ensure she was real—and not an apparition.

"The US Marshals know you're here, right?" A year ago, Cash, a former FBI agent, had found out through his network of law enforcement friends that Angie had been hidden away in the federal Witness Security Program. Because he'd pulled strings, authorities had allowed her to have a brief conversation with her family remotely.

Until then, they'd believed she'd disappeared off the face of the earth. One day she was living in a commune in New Mexico, and the next day she was gone.

"They know." Three pairs of eyes bored into her from across the coffee table. "Last week, the FBI and ATF arrested the last of the ring. They said I was safe."

"Safe to resume your real identity?" Sawyer watched her closely.

"Yes," though they thought she'd be safer to continue assuming her fake one. But she'd had enough. Enough of living a lie, enough of hiding, and enough of being separated from her family.

"What happened, Angie? How did you get caught up in all this?" Sawyer wanted to know.

She looked at Cash. "How much did your friends in the Bureau tell you?"

He rubbed his hand down his face. "Not a lot. Just that you somehow wound up involved with arms dealers and helped the feds." Cash held her gaze and waited for her to fill in the blanks.

She was so tired. The drive had been a bear. But more than that, the last couple of days had come crashing down around her. After Zane's arrest and the aftermath, she'd taken close stock of her life, including all the mistakes she'd made.

All she'd ever wanted to do was make a difference and change the world for the better. She'd spent most of her adult life drifting from cause to cause, ultimately founding a commune in Taos dedicated to feeding the hungry. Little did she know that it would attract a criminal organization, and that a radical conman would take it over.

"It's a long story." She pinched the bridge of her nose, trying to keep her eyes open. She'd be sharper after a good nap. But judging by their penetrating stares, they didn't want to wait. That's what she got for being related to trained interrogators.

She let out a sigh. "Where do I start?"

"At the beginning," Jace said. The other two nodded in agreement.

The beginning. That would start with the idealist, who left the privileged confines of her parents' Beverly Hills manse right after graduation to do good. But they already knew that story and had watched with wry amusement—and sometimes disapproval—as she traveled the globe, joining up with activist groups, living out of a suitcase.

"I met Zane Johnson six years ago in Kenya," she started. "We were both volunteering for the Water Project. He was the most principled man I'd ever met. Smart, hardworking, a true believer. Or so I thought." Angie swallowed hard. To this day she couldn't decide whether she was a terrible judge of character or if Zane, in his zeal, had metamorphized into a ruthless zealot. "He and a few others from the project decided they wanted to buy land in the US, plant it in crops, and distribute food to the poor. With time, we hoped to branch out, planting everything from deserted fields to urban parks. A giant victory garden to feed the country."

"But it was a scam, right?" Sawyer propped his feet up on the coffee table in a relaxed pose. But Angie knew the studied gesture was anything but relaxed. That's what made him such a good reporter. He was able to put his subjects at ease with casual body language, thereby encouraging people to spill their guts.

"I don't think he started out that way. But I don't know for sure." The fact was she didn't know up from down or right from left anymore. Living in the Witness Protection Program would do that to a person.

"So he bought the land in Taos." Cash got up, grabbed a few water bottles from the fridge and tossed one to Sawyer and one to Jace. She was still nursing her tea, which had gone cold.

Angie nodded. "We all did."

"Who's all?" Jace asked.

"Zane, Rich, Kari and me. The four of us had been in Kenya together and had…money." Well, she had had money. "So we founded The Farm. That's what we called it—The Farm." Looking back on it, the desert hadn't been a particularly smart place to grow food crops. They'd trucked in the water, though, and had made a real go of it.

"But The Farm was a front for an arms dealing operation," Cash said.

Angie slowly nodded her head. "Not at first, though." In the beginning, Zane had been happy farming. But that quickly changed.

"Is Kari the woman I talked to in Santa Fe while I was trying to track you down?" Sawyer watched her over the rim of his water bottle.

"I can't talk about that." Kari had changed her name and had cut all ties with anything having to do with The Farm. And while she hadn't helped the feds in the same way as Angie, Kari continued to be freaked out about her safety. Angie wouldn't do anything to betray her friend, not even to her brother.

"Let's stick to the chronological order of events," Cash said. "We'll circle back to Kari afterward."

Angie let out a breath, girding herself. Even after six years, talking about it made her chest squeeze so tight it cut off her air supply.

She turned to Sawyer. "We bought the land, the yurts, and enough farm equipment to till the fields and plant our first crop. We were less than three months into it when something started to bother me. Suddenly Zane and some of the other men who'd joined our rag-tag group were spending a lot of time behind closed doors. When Kari or I asked about it, they sloughed it off. Just guys talking about sports and women. That sort of thing. For a while, I convinced myself that it was nothing. But something didn't feel right about it. Some of the men made me uncomfortable. Two of them had moved into the commune with girlfriends. The women were meek, too meek. Kari and I began to suspect they were being abused. We went to Zane about it, and he, in so many words, told us to mind our own business, that it wasn't our place to get involved, which was counter to everything we believed in. When we got loud about it, he agreed to talk to the two men. After that, if we still weren't satisfied, he promised to ask them to leave.

"Things got better for a while and the women started to come out of their shells. The four of us formed a nice little group. We worked the fields by day, and in the evenings planned our strategy for distributing the food we grew." She shifted on the couch, feeling wearier than she had before she left Portland.

"And?" Sawyer folded one leg over his knee and signaled for her to continue.

"And…a few weeks later, Diana disappeared."

"One of the women?" Jace asked and Angie nodded. "What do you mean she disappeared?"

"We went to bed one night, and the next morning she was missing. Her and her boyfriend Jacob's VW bus was parked exactly where it was the day before. We searched for her, fearing that she might've gotten up in the middle of the night to use the outhouse and had an accident. But there was no trace of her. Nothing."

Jace straightened up in his chair. "Did you call the cops?"

"Jacob didn't want us to. He said she'd likely hooked up with her ex-boyfriend. He had some crazy story about how Diana had been cheating on him with the ex and that the ex had come to Taos and had probably picked her up from The Farm in the middle of the night. None of it made any sense to me. Or to Kari. There'd been no sign of an ex-boyfriend coming into the picture as far as we could tell. And we were with Diana every day."

"What about the other woman?" Cash asked.

"Leda? After Diana disappeared, Leda went back to being reserved. She stopped hanging out with us and spent her days working in the fields alongside her boyfriend, Ian. In the evenings, she made herself scarce in her yurt, while the men congregated in an old barn on the property."

"After a few days, Kari and I drove into town and reported Diana missing to the Taos Police Department. They took down our information and a photo I'd taken on my phone of the four of us women together. But we got the sense they believed Jacob's version of the story about her running off with her ex. Zane said he'd seen Jacob and her fighting over the other man a couple of days before she went missing. Still, I had a funny feeling about it, and to this day wished I would've pushed harder with the police." There were a lot of things, in hindsight, she wished she would've done differently, like not getting involved with Zane in the first place.

"There probably wasn't much more you could do. She was an adult, and as long as there wasn't anything to suggest she was abducted or the victim of foul play, the police didn't have a case." Jace was the Mill County Sheriff, so he knew how these things worked. Still, Angie had been angry at the time, wishing the police had done more.

She went to the kitchen and turned a flame on under the kettle. Her throat was dry, and she couldn't seem to shake the chill that spread through her like a winter's day.

"Did they ever find her?" Sawyer asked.

"No. The feds think she knew what was going on, was afraid of getting caught up in it, and took off in the middle of the night." It would've been nice if she'd warned the rest of them, but Angie tried not to judge. For all she knew, Diana had been in eminent danger at the time. "She'd been estranged from her family, so there's no telling where she is now." Wherever it was, Angie hoped she found peace.

"After her disappearance, more people came to join our co-op. Not a day went by without one or two people showing up with bedrolls and backpacks, claiming they wanted to be involved in our farm." She let out a mirthless laugh. "These people didn't look anything like farmers. They didn't look anything like the volunteers we'd worked with at the Water Project or Green Peace, or any of the assorted other causes I'd been involved with. No, they were rough and brittle and angry. And truthfully scary. Some of them talked about the government in a way that made me uneasy.

"Once again Kari and I went to Zane and Rich to complain, to say this isn't what we signed up for. They promised to keep the men in line, and in so many words told us we were being snobby. Elitists, who expected everyone to look exactly like us. I tried to see it from their point of view, but my gut told me they were troublemakers. And soon it became apparent that these men intended to take over. First, it was their antiquated belief in gender roles. The women were expected to do all the cooking and cleaning, while the men went into town on mysterious excursions. Kari and I couldn't tell what they were doing. They never returned with provisions, and there were a lot of meetings and secret discussions."

"One day, Kari started to go into town to buy necessities and one of the men stopped her. He said that, from then on, only one of the men would be allowed to do the shopping. When she pushed back, he became belligerent and physically prevented her from taking one of the cars."

"Why didn't you call me, Angie?" Sawyer rocked forward. There was so much anguish in the question that it made her shudder.

She squeezed her eyes shut. "I didn't want to tell you at first because…"

"Because you're the one who put up all the money for this venture, weren't you?"

She wasn't surprised that Cash had guessed the crux of the matter. Her family always thought she was a flake, a young woman who used her wealth and privilege to hook up with fringe groups and join every do-gooder movement she could find. But this time she'd gone too far, ultimately bankrolling what would turn out to be a radical group called the Liberty Fighters.

Angie gave an imperceptible nod. "I didn't want any of you to know about it until we'd gotten the fields planted, until we were established." She wanted her family to be proud of her endeavor, and not appalled that she'd spent every dime of her trust fund on the project. "And then… it was too late."

"How?" Sawyer asked.

"After the incident with Kari and Burt we held a meeting with Rich and Zane. Just the four of us. Kari told them what had happened. Zane said she was overreacting. 'Tell Burt to fuck off,' was Zane's answer. But Rich was pissed. He had witnessed Burt being aggressive with a few of the other women and wanted him to leave. And if Burt refused, Rich said he was going to go to the police. Kari and I told him we would go with him. But by the next day, Rich, just like Diana, was gone. And so was his Jeep Cherokee. Zane's theory was that Rich and Burt got into it and Rich decided to quit and leave the commune."

"Do you believe that?" Jace stood, his hands shoved in his pockets. His anger was palpable.

Angie shook her head. "No. He was a good man. He would've gone to the police, like he'd promised."

"What do you think happened to him?" Cash asked.

"I don't know. The authorities don't know. But whatever it was, it wasn't good." She tried to keep the tremor out of her voice. "We called him repeatedly, but he never answered his cell. So Kari and I decided to go to the police ourselves. When we got to my car, Burt was there, holding an AR-15. He told us we weren't going anywhere and forced us to hand over our phones."

Angie stopped to catch her breath. All three men waited, staring at her raptly.

"That's when we knew we were in trouble."

Chapter 2

Tuff Garrison spent a good part of the morning riding fences. It wasn't his job, but he frequently performed the task. The Daltons had given him a good deal on rent for his living quarters on the ranch, as well as an enviable lease on his work studio and storefront. It was important to him to return their kindness. And he'd been riding fences so long that it didn't make sense to stop now, even if he was making a good living selling custom saddles.

Besides, he enjoyed the solitude. Just him, his gelding Muchacho and 1,500 acres of lush land, majestic mountains, tall pines, and Dry Creek, which wended through the property like a fat snake. The rides spurred his creative juices. And by the time he walked into his workshop, he was raring to go.

Today, there was no sign of the redhead he'd passed on the road a few days ago. But he'd seen her old Mercedes parked at Sawyer's place on his way to the stable. He wondered what the story was with her. Tuff had been living on the ranch for close to a year now and hadn't crossed paths with her before. No question she was a Dalton, though. All of them had those piercing blue eyes. Hers were prettier than her male counterparts. Then again, he'd always been a sucker for a redhead.

He turned Muchacho toward the stable and gave him his head. It was getting late and he had a Zoom meeting with a finicky client on the East Coast. He had two saddles that needed to be packaged and shipped to members of the United States Olympic Equestrian Team and some last-minute alterations to a bridle for a Texas rodeo queen. A full plate.

But setting up shop here on Dry Creek Ranch was the best decision he'd ever made. He was getting too old to be a full-time wrangler. And though he'd never cared much about money, it turned out being a saddler was quite profitable.

Leatherwork had started as a hobby, something to do in a bunkhouse before bedtime. Wranglers, impressed with Tuff's handmade belts, bridles, hackamores, and his eye to detail, began asking him to mend their weathered tack or make them new pieces.

It had been his bunkmates who'd encouraged him to rent a stall at the annual National Finals Rodeo in Vegas and sell the leather boot bags and rope cases he made. That business slowly grew to pro cowboys and wealthy ranchers commissioning him to make tack and luggage with their trademark brands and monograms. The extra income went a long way to holding Tuff over during the lean times.

Soon, word spread, and he was selling four to five custom saddles a year. When the opportunity to have a brick-and-mortar shop fell into Tuff's lap, he took the plunge.

This year, he was looking at a six-figure profit. It was more than he'd ever made in his life. And he was doing what he loved. Sometimes, he had to sock himself in the arm just to believe it was real.

By the time he reached the barn, Muchacho was in a lather. Tuff's own shirt stuck to his back, even in fifty-degree weather. He dismounted, slipped off his saddle and gave his horse a thorough brushing.

It was good of the Daltons to make space in the stable for Muchacho, another perk of living and working on Dry Creek Ranch.

"Hi." Cash's daughter, Ellie, climbed over the fence into her mare's stall. The kid came every morning before school bearing treats for her mare, Sunflower.

"How you doin' Miss Ellie?"

"Good." She scratched Sunflower's head. "My dad says he'll go in half with me for a saddle. I'm babysitting now and the Morgans pay me twelve dollars an hour."

He grinned. "I'm sure we can work something out." Hell, he'd make the kid a free saddle, given all her old man had done for him. But he appreciated Cash instilling the meaning of a buck in his daughter.

Tuff led Muchacho to the paddocks, removed his halter and gave him a slap on the rump. "Have a good day at school, Miss Ellie," he called as he headed home for a quick shower.

His cabin had been Cash's originally, then Sawyer's celebrity chef wife, Gina's. It wasn't anything fancy, just a small two-bedroom cottage with a mostly open floor plan. He'd painted the walls and rebuilt the deck, which had been a whisper away from falling down. And he'd furnished the place with a few good pieces from Jace and Cash's wives' farmhouse store, Refind.

It was the first time he'd ever had a real home, and he was still getting used to laying his head on the same pillow every night. Until now, he'd been a nomad, traversing the country in search of his next job.

He washed away his morning's ride and threw on warm clothes. November in Dry Creek was nippy. His studio and adjoining shop had a woodfire stove. He'd cut enough wood over summer to supply both the cabin and his workspace with heat for the next two years.

Tuff hiked less than a mile to Dry Creek Village, the ranch's business park, a series of Western-style storefronts anchored by Gina DeRose's eponymous restaurant. The Daltons' cattle enterprise hadn't been enough to support the cost of running the ranch. So, they came up with the ingenious idea to turn a small portion of the ranch into a destination shopping center that promoted the region's agricultural products. Besides the restaurant, Refind, and Tuff's Saddlery, there was a large specialty market, a butcher shop, a florist, and a kiosk serving locally made sarsaparilla. Cash's wife, Aubrey, also ran an interior design business from the center, which was headquartered in Refind.

The commercial park had been designed to retain the rugged charm of the ranch, and offered walking trails and picnic areas that took advantage of views of the Sierra foothills and Dry Creek. And it didn't hurt that the parking lot was full of electric charging stations for the visiting Bay Area folk, who made the two-hour trek to soak in the countryside.

In the last week, holiday decorations had started going up, including a huge fir tree that had been trucked in from the other side of the ranch. Lights were strung along the eaves of the buildings, and rows of luminarias lined the walkways. An enormous barn star tacked to the side of Refind lit up at night. If it were up to Tuff, he'd keep the barn star lit up year-round. It was a nice touch.

He unlocked the door to his shop and turned on the light. While contemplating whether to make a fire, he booted up the coffeemaker. He hung his jacket and hat on the deer antler rack the ladies had given him from Refind as a welcome gift.

The storefront was small, just a few displays of saddles and bridles. On one wall was a custom shelving unit with smaller items such as luggage, wallets, handbags, and riding gloves. The tourists gobbled those pieces up as fast as Tuff could make them. In the back, he kept his workshop, which was full of patterns and bolts of leather. A small desk with a computer sat in the corner. The bulk of his retail business was run online. His clients spanned the country, and he'd even started making a few saddles for equestrians abroad.

It was as close to a perfect setup as it got. In addition to a nice place to work with good neighbors, the Daltons had given him and Muchacho the run of the ranch. The men and their wives had been the closest thing to family as Tuff ever got. But at the end of the day, he was still a loner. Nothing would ever change that. Still, it was good to be surrounded by trustworthy people and have a sturdy roof over his head.

He poured himself a cup of coffee, flicked on his computer, and started to scroll through his emails when the bell over his shop door rang. "Howdy," he called to the front of the store.

"Tuff, can I borrow your key to the storage unit? I forgot mine." The storage unit was an old livestock shed where the shopkeepers kept their overflow junk, everything from seasonal décor to excess stock.

He walked up front to find Ava, one of the young co-owners of the floral shop eyeing a toiletry bag. "This is gorgeous. Maybe I should get one for Bryce."

Bryce was Ava's boyfriend and from what Tuff could tell a lazy piece of shit. When Ava and her partner, Winter, first opened the flower shop, Bryce had sat on his ass while the two women ran around, setting everything up. Ava waited on the dude hand and foot.

"Here's the key." He handed her his shop ring. "How's business?"

"Good. Thanksgiving arrangements galore. Two December weddings and the Christmas orders for wreaths and centerpieces have already started coming in. It's crazy."

"Nice." He liked Ava and Winter. They were fresh out of ag school and, except for Ava's taste in men, had good heads on their shoulders. Besides running the shop, they leased a few acres from the Daltons and grew their own flowers.

"Gina's having us do all the holiday florals for the restaurant, which is huge." She sat on the stool by the cash register in no hurry to go. "You have any more of that?" Ava nudged her head at his cup of Joe.

"Let me see if I can scrounge up another mug." He wandered into the back, found a cup from his mismatched set, and scrubbed it out in the bathroom before filling it with coffee. "Here you go."

"You're a prince among men, Tuff Garrison."

If he didn't know better, he'd think she was flirting with him. There was likely an eighteen-year age difference between them. Unlike most of the men he knew, Tuff preferred women his own age. They didn't tend to get ideas in their heads of everlasting love and marriage.

"Did you hear that Sawyer's long-lost sister is here?" Ava took a sip of her coffee and eyed him over the rim of the mug.

He didn't like idle gossip, but admittedly was curious about the redhead. "What do you mean long-lost?"

Ava shrugged. "All I know is she's been out of the picture for six years. Gina mentioned her but didn't say much else. I heard she's moving into Cash and Aubrey's old place. So I guess you'll be neighbors."

That was news to him. Cash, Aubrey, and Ellie had recently moved out of the little cabin across the creek from his place into their newly built home on the other side of the ranch. The new, custom two-story was a showstopper. Tuff wasn't surprised, given that Aubrey was a first-rate decorator. Prior to moving, she'd redone the couple's cabin on the exterior with flowerboxes under the windows and red shutters. It looked a hell of a lot more finished than Tuff's.

"I hadn't heard" was all he said, intentionally leaving out that he'd already met Miz Dalton.

"Gina says she's super nice and might start working in the market."

He pointed at her cup. "You want a warmer on that before you go?" It was a subtle hint that he had a business to run and couldn't stand around talking all day.

"I'm good." Ava hopped down from the stool. "Thanks for the key and the coffee."

"Any time. Just leave the key on the counter when you're done. I've got a Zoom meeting in the back."

"Will do."

After his conference call, he found the final sign-off for a parade saddle in his inbox. He and the client had been going back and forth on the design for nearly a month. Lots of tooling and silver.

To celebrate, he wandered over to Gina's for a late lunch. Usually, he nuked something in his studio's microwave, but why not live large today? Besides, he was curious about Ava's news regarding the redhead being his new neighbor. Best to get it straight from the horse's mouth.

The restaurant was busy for a weekday afternoon. Gina DeRose had her own cooking show on FoodFlicks and a culinary empire that included frozen entrees, baking mixes, and kitchenware. This was her only restaurant, and people flocked from all over to say they'd eaten there.

Tuff asked to be seated at the bar. It made more sense than taking up a whole table for himself. The bartender took his order. He perused his phone for any emails he'd missed while he waited for his food.

Gina came out of the kitchen, caught sight of him, and strolled over. "Hey, stranger. Haven't seen you in a while."

"Been swamped." He stood up and gave her a brief hug, then gazed around the dining room. "From the looks of things so have you."

"Can't complain. Business is good. I'm glad you came in. Sawyer and I have been meaning to come by the cabin."

"Oh yeah." He tensed, hoping they weren't kicking him out. The lease was a month-to-month and had started out as temporary housing until he found something else. But he'd grown rather fond of the place and its bird's-eye view of Dry Creek. Hell, he could fish right off the front porch.

"Sawyer's sister, Angela, is here. We'd like her to stay a while and our place is only a one-bedroom. So, she'll be moving into Cash and Aubrey's old cabin for the time being. We didn't want to just spring a new neighbor on you."

"It's your place. I'm just lucky to get to live in it." He grinned, relieved. It turned out Ava had gotten her facts right.

"We're lucky to have you as a tenant. You'll like Angie. She's great."

He bobbed his head. "I believe we already met. She was on her way to your house and stopped for directions."

Gina cleared her throat. "Sawyer and I were kind of hoping you could look out for her. She's had a rough time of it."

Tuff waited for Gina to explain. But it soon became clear Gina had no intention of saying more on the subject. In his world, a "rough time" could mean a whole host of things. But he wasn't one to pry, not when he had his own secrets.

"Sure," he said. From what he'd seen of Angela Dalton so far, looking after her wouldn't be difficult. She was easy on the eyes. "When is she moving in?"

Gina let out an awkward laugh. "Uh, tonight."

Sure enough, when he got home that evening, the redhead was sitting on the front porch of the cabin, sipping a glass of wine. He waved to her from across the creek. She came to the railing and said something, but he couldn't hear her over the rushing water.

Tuff crossed over on the footbridge and stood a few feet from her porch steps. "Sorry, I didn't catch what you said."

"I said I'm your new neighbor." She stood up and smiled, but it didn't quite reach her blue eyes.

Tuff didn't think it had anything to do with him, more to do with those rough times Gina had mentioned.

At their first meeting, he would've put her somewhere around his age. But now, without a car between them and her hair tied back, he could see she was younger. Thirty maybe. She was slight and not an inch taller than five-five. Her clothes, a dress and high-heeled boots, weren't what you would call ranchwear. But they were sexy without trying. She was sexy without trying.

And too damned young. And sad. She reminded him of a flower waiting for rain.

"Welcome. I'm right over there if you need anything." He aimed his chin across the creek.

"Thank you."

He started to walk away when she asked, "Have you lived here long?"

"'Bout a year. Right when your brother and cousins opened Dry Creek Village. I own Tuff's Saddlery."

"I peeked in the window the other night on our way to Gina's steakhouse for dinner. You do lovely work."

He tipped his hat. "Thank you."

"I used to ride." She looked out over the land and for a few seconds seemed lost in the view. "Back when my grandfather was alive, he kept a horse here for me. I lived in Los Angeles with my family but was here every summer and for the holidays."

Like her, he gazed across the fields to the surrounding mountains. "It's a hell of a place. I've lived on a lot of ranches in my time but nothing like this."

"Where are you from?"

"Oh here, there, and everywhere," he sidestepped.

She started to say something and stopped herself. And for a moment they just stood there.

"I've got dinner waiting for me," he finally said. "Again, welcome to the neighborhood."

He crossed the bridge to his side of the creek. When he turned around, she was still standing there, staring out over the horizon, a haunted look on her face.

Chapter 3

Angie finished her wine and went inside. It had gotten dark and was too cold to sit outside any longer.

The cabin was storybook perfect. The exposed beam ceilings and the pine flooring were nothing like the bland apartment she had in Portland, where the walls were so thin she could hear the flush of her neighbor's toilet.

Here, everything was...cheerful. The kitchen cabinets were painted in a shade of green that reminded Angie of the outdoors. A cowhide rug anchored the living room where two sofas faced each other, and a large antler chandelier hung over the coffee table. There were drapes on the windows and paintings on the walls. Cash and Aubrey had left nearly everything for the next tenant to enjoy. She supposed it was a benefit of being part owner in a furniture store.

It would be a good place to stay while she figured out her future. The open skies, the big trees, and the green hillsides alone were transformative. And while she relished the time to herself, it was a comfort to know Tuff was just across the creek. Sawyer and Gina swore by him. And while he appeared to be a private man, nothing about him came across as threatening. Though she'd proved to be a pretty bad judge of character.

She peeked out the window at the little cabin across the creek. Other than a light on in the living room window, all was quiet. In the kitchen, she made a sandwich and forced herself to eat it. In the last six years, she'd lost a good amount of weight. Funny, because she'd worked as a hostess in a restaurant, surrounded by food.

That was the thing about the Witness Protection Program. They placed you in jobs you'd never done before to further protect your identity. For her it had been easy. She'd never had a real job, so everything was on the table. Except farming. Farms would be the first place Burt, Zane, and their group would look for her.

The other rule was that she couldn't have any contact with friends and family. And making new friends was difficult because everything about her was a lie. Her trumped up history, her fake name, and even her bogus age.

Here, she was liberated at last.

This weekend, her parents were coming. They'd be reunited after six long years. As much as Angie missed them, part of her dreaded the reunion. It was one thing being the family's eccentric free spirit. A whole other to have unwittingly financed a group of violent survivalists.

It would be a long time before she could forgive herself, if ever. So many lives had been ruined by her choices. Diana's, Rich's, Kari's, just to name a few.

She finished her sandwich and called it an early night, only to awaken at five the next morning. The sun was just starting to rise over the mountains, and she stepped out onto the porch to look at the sky and breathe in the clean air.

At first, she thought she was alone. But the sound of a thud in the water caught her attention. Tuff stood on her side of the shore, fishing.

She was just about to slip back inside when he called, "Mornin'."

"Good morning." She went to pull her robe tighter and realized she was only in her nightgown.

"I didn't disturb you, did I?"

"No, not at all." She watched him cast his line, a faint memory playing in the back of her head. "My grandfather used to fish early in the morning, before he rode out to check the cattle and the fences."

"Best time." Tuff grinned, showing off a set of not-quite dimples. He was a good-looking man, no doubt about it.

"Did you catch anything?"

He held up a bucket with a couple of fish. "Dinner."

"Nice." She looked up at the pink and orange striped sky. "You always rise this early?"

"Yep. I usually go for a ride but decided to fish instead. You?"

"I'm a morning person." The fact was she hardly slept at all anymore. "I'm in the midst of making some career decisions." For the world she didn't know why she'd offered that information.

He simply nodded. "This is good place to think. It's meditative."

"You think?" She should've gone inside and put something on. Instead, she sat on the top step and hugged herself.

He gazed across the water at Banner Mountain in the distance and took a deep fortifying breath. "Yeah, I do. Something about nature puts everything in perspective, you know what I mean?"

She didn't. But at least one of them had it figured out. She nodded anyway, though. "When I was a kid, I used to love this place. I'm glad Sawyer, Cash, and Jace figured out a way to keep it going. My grandfather would really be moved."

"It was smart." Tuff reeled his line in and cast it out again. "Ranching ain't what it used to be. Land's worth too much to run cattle. Ranchers sure could take a page out of your brother and cousins' book." He looked up at her. "You weren't involved?"

"No. I mean a quarter of the ranch is mine, but I was...involved in something else when my grandfather passed." She'd missed that too. Grandpa Dalton was one of the most instrumental people in her life, and she hadn't even been there to say goodbye.

"But you're back now."

"I am." At least for the time being, until she figured out her path. "Sawyer and my cousins want me to manage the market. They've got full-time jobs and I happen to be at loose ends right now."

He slid her a sideways glance. "Retail, huh? So that's your background."

She had to keep herself from laughing. "Food service." It was partially true. Her two jobs had consisted of working on The Farm and in a Portland restaurant.

"Not a journalist like your brother, then?"

"Nope. I can't write my way out of a paper bag. Much to my parents' chagrin, neither Sawyer nor I wanted in on the family business. They own a PR firm in LA. How about you? Did you always want to be a saddle maker?"

He blew out a breath of white air, put down his pole, and rubbed his hands together. "I wanted to be a rodeo cowboy. When that didn't work out too well, I became a ranch hand. Somewhere along the line I discovered that I was handy with leather." His eyes fell on her nightgown. "You must be cold."

She got to her feet, tugging the flannel past her knees. "Yeah, I better get inside. Nice talking with you."

"You too." Before she walked away, he called, "I hope you don't mind me using your side of the creek. More fish here in the morning."

"No, of course not."

She turned the heat up in the cabin and started a pot of coffee. When she peeked outside the window, Tuff was gone. She looked down at herself and sighed. Her nightgown was something her grandmother would've worn and her hair was probably a mess. Why it bothered her, she didn't know. Angie had stopped caring about her appearance a long time ago.

With that in mind, she hunted through the closet that now held what few clothes she had. Over the years, she'd learned to travel light. And when she'd fled for her life, she'd taken just the clothes on her back. In Portland, she'd picked up a few things. But on a hostess's salary she'd stuck with practical pieces she could wear to the restaurant. Her only splurge was a pair of designer boots she'd gotten at Nordstrom Rack on deep discount.

Maybe she'd ask her mother to bring clothes. In LA, at her parents' home, she had a closet full of chic outfits. Things she'd gotten on Rodeo Drive a lifetime ago. Very appropriate for Dry Creek Ranch, she laughed to herself. But at least some good jeans and sweaters for the winter.

For now, she laid out a pair of leggings and a tunic top on the bed. By the time she got out of the shower, the coffee was ready. She lingered over a cup, contemplating whether to fry an egg. Perhaps some toast. Gina had stocked the refrigerator. But Angie wasn't hungry. She'd grab something later, she told herself.

It was still early but she decided to hike up to Dry Creek Village anyway. She could explore until the shops opened, maybe drop in on Jace and Charlie to say hello to the boys before they left for school. Angie would find something to do.

The Christmas lights draped from the roofs of the businesses were still on, their glow faint in the morning light. Everything looked so festive. So happy. She followed one of the meandering paths along the creekside, enjoying the tranquility. She didn't know how they managed to do it, but the center worked. It blended right in with the ranch without being too commercial. Or too Knott's Berry Farm. Most of the buildings looked like old barns. And Refind actually was an old barn. Angie remembered it as being a bit ramshackle. Well, not anymore.

She kept moving, wishing she'd worn something warmer. That was the thing about fall in Northern California. One minute it was cold and the next balmy.

As she passed the florist, she caught her reflection in the glass door. Ugh. Her shirt hung on her like a gunny sack. She pressed her nose to the window and looked at the beautiful floral displays in the refrigerated cases. Lots of oranges and greens.

The lights were on in Tuff's Saddlery, so she tried the door.

"In the back," came his deep drawl.

"Oh, hi." She went inside and peeked around the corner where he worked with a piece of leather on a big lighted table. "I wasn't expecting anyone to be here this early."

"I've got a couple of deadlines." He didn't look up, just stayed focused on whatever he was doing.

"I won't disturb you."

"You're not disturbing me."

"You mind if I look around, then?"

"Knock yourself out."

She went back to the front of the store and explored the shelves. On a hook near the cash register was a gorgeous, tooled belt with a silver buckle that made Angie drool. She dared to try it on and moved to the full-length mirror to have a look.

"It's too big on you." Tuff came up behind her and reached around her waist to adjust the belt, sending a wave of warmth through her. "I'd have to lop off about four inches of leather."

She couldn't afford it anyway. There was a time when she would've whipped out one of her gold cards without even glancing at the price. Now, she only had one credit card. It was in Katherine Moore's name, and it didn't have a high enough credit limit to cover the belt.

"It's beautiful." She took it off, brushing against his calloused hands in the process, and hung it back on the hook. "Amazing craftsmanship."

"Thank you. You waiting for the market to open?"

She didn't really know what she was doing. "Uh-huh. Just killing time until then."

"You want some coffee? I just made a pot."

"I had at home. But I appreciate the offer. I really don't want to take up your time. I know you're busy."

"Come on back while I work. If you're bored, you can catalog a bunch of leather samples I haven't had time to unpack."

"I could do that."

He showed her how to inventory each bolt of leather in the computer, and she got to the task, happy for something to do. For a while, they worked in companionable silence.

Occasionally, she'd sneak a glance at him while he concentrated on the pattern he was cutting. His long sleeves were scrunched up to his elbows, showing a pair of heavily veined forearms. On the right one was an intricate tattoo of a lasso. He'd said he used to ride in the rodeo, and she wondered if he was a roper.

His hands were large and rough and his nails neatly trimmed. She watched as they deftly molded the leather as he concentrated on his cuts. There was something sensual about it and she suddenly found herself aroused. Embarrassed, she turned away, fearful that he'd be able to guess what she was thinking.

It was odd because she hadn't wanted to be with a man for a long time. Not since Zane. Now, the thought of Zane made her sick to her stomach.

"How you doin' over there?"

"Good. About halfway done." She entered another bolt number onto the spreadsheet. "Where do you get your leather?"

"All over. I try to stick with American but there's some beautiful leather coming out of Italy and Brazil. India too. Some of my clients specifically request it."

"What about leather from the ranch?" If you were going to slaughter a cow for its meat, Angie thought you should at least make use of the whole animal.

"Jace and I have talked about it. But tanning the hides...it's a process that I don't know either of us has time for."

Angie had no clue what went into converting cow hide into usable leather. It was just a thought.

She plugged in more sample numbers, taking pleasure in being useful. The earthy smell of the cedar shiplap walls combined with the rich scent of leather reminded her of her grandfather for some reason. And listening to the swish of Tuff's knife as he blocked out his pattern was oddly calming. Or maybe it was the efficient way he focused on his task. She was fascinated by him.

And unexpectedly attracted.

The front door chimed with a visitor.

"We're back here," Tuff called to the front.

A few seconds later, Sawyer strode back, carrying a stack of papers. "Hey, Tuff." He did a doubletake when his eyes fell on Angie. "Ange?"

She felt like she'd been caught doing something she shouldn't, which was ridiculous. "I'm helping Tuff inventory his leather while I wait for Daltons to open."

"Oh...Nice." He grabbed one of the stools at Tuff's worktable and dragged it next to her at the computer. "How was your first night in the cabin?"

"Great." She'd actually slept better than she had in months. The sound of the creek had lulled her into a deep, dreamless slumber.

She held Sawyer's gaze, silently imploring him not to say more. Tuff didn't need to know her sordid history. No one did.

Sawyer handed Tuff a flyer from his stack. "We're throwing a dinner at the restaurant for all the shopkeepers the Wednesday before Thanksgiving. You can come, right?"

Tuff gazed at the flyer. "Is Gina cooking?" Sawyer nodded and Tuff said, "Then I wouldn't miss it."

Angie watched Sawyer's expression fill with pride. She never thought she'd see the day when her big brother was crazy in love. And she couldn't be happier for him. Gina was Sawyer's perfect match. According to her family, it had taken Sawyer a while to figure that out. Angie only wished she'd been there to watch her hard-headed brother finally lose his heart.

She'd missed so much, including seeing her little cousins grow up. Well, there was time for that now. Time to make up for all those lost years.

"Deadlines call." Sawyer got to his feet.

Angie pointed at the stack of flyers. "You want me to hand the rest of those out, so you can get to writing?" She had nothing better to do, and it would be a good way to meet some of the other shopkeepers. The center had been her family's way of preserving her grandfather's legacy, instead of losing it to back taxes. The least she could do was help out and get to know some of the merchants.

"Yeah, that would be great. Are you sure you're up for it?"

Ever since she'd returned, her brother and cousins had been treating her with kid gloves, clearly afraid she'd crack like a piece of glass if they asked too much of her.

"Of course." She gave a tight smile as if to remind him Tuff was sitting only a few feet away. Tuff was liable to think Angie had just been released from a mental hospital—not witness protection. The two weren't that dissimilar, she supposed. Four years, hiding in plain view was enough to make anyone crazy.

Sawyer handed her the invitations. "Then I'll be on my way. Take it easy, Tuff. See ya later, Ange."

"Bye."

The bell over the door jingled as Sawyer showed himself out.

Tuff glanced over at Angie. "Don't feel like you have to inventory all the samples." He bobbed his chin at the flyers. "Looks like duty calls."

She laughed and held up the stack. "This will take me less than thirty minutes to deliver, and I've got an hour until the market opens...unless, of course, you want the place to yourself."

"Nope." He grinned and those not-quite dimples reappeared. "I was enjoying the company. But I wouldn't want to hog you for myself."

He winked and she felt a second rush of inexplicable desire course through her. Maybe it was better that she did leave. The last thing she needed was a crush on her new neighbor. One of her vows after everything that had happened was to be ultra-cautious about who she let into her life.

Before, she'd been a revolving door. Not sexually, but she'd been too trusting, too giving, and too open.

Not anymore. She may have brought Angela Dalton back to the living, but there were characteristics of that girl that needed to remain dead.

Chapter 4

Tuff crossed the wooden footbridge, deliberating on whether to leave his package at the door or deliver it in person. He'd put in a long day and the six-pack in his fridge called. But then so did the pretty lady who'd moved in next door.

Bad idea, he told himself. She was too young and way out of his league. And it was pretty clear she was recuperating from…something. A shitty relationship? A nervous breakdown? An illness? Who knew? Whatever it was he wanted to steer clear of it. He'd never been what you would call a reliable friend or a good shoulder to cry on. Just the opposite in fact.

His MO had always been to cut and run at the earliest sign of complications. And Angie Dalton had complicated written all over her. Add in the fact that she was part owner of the land where he'd made his home…Nope. He only had a high school education, but he wasn't stupid.

He was just about to leave the gift on her porch when she opened the door in a pair of exercise pants and one of those short tops that left her midriff exposed. A lot of pale creamy skin. Her red hair was damp and had started to curl around her face. If he'd been tempted by the flannel nightgown, this evening's getup was putting him over the edge. It was time to take a trip to Sacramento where there were plenty of bars and women looking for a one-night stand.

"Hi." Her face flushed. He couldn't tell if it was from her bath or him.

"Hey." He tipped his hat. "Hope I'm not bothering you. I just came by to drop this off." He handed her the package, which he'd wrapped with butcher paper and a piece of string. Not exactly a department store job but it did the trick.

She looked down at it, surprised. "What's this?"

"Just a little something for helping me out today." Hell, he should've offered to pay her, but something told him she would've been offended. And he doubted Angie Dalton needed the money. Everyone knew that her parents were blue chip publicists in Los Angeles, who had recently bought the ranch next door to add land to Dry Creek's cattle operation. Nope, that side of the Dalton clan had plenty of dough.

"Oh." Her blue eyes grew wider as she carefully unwrapped the gift.

"It won't break." He tried to hurry her along, already regretting that he hadn't dropped it off when he knew she wasn't home.

But she took her time, working on the knot on the string instead of just tearing it off. "You didn't have to give me anything. I enjoyed the work."

He didn't see how. Adding numbers to a spreadsheet was one of the more tedious tasks of his business. "Well, I appreciated it. More than likely I wasn't going to get to it for a while, so it's a relief to have it done."

She finally untied the string and began removing the paper. The minute she caught a glimpse of the belt her face lit up and just like that, it fell.

"I made it smaller," he blurted. "It'll fit you now."

"Oh, Tuff." She covered her mouth, then used the same hand to stroke the tooling on the leather. "I can't accept this…it's too much."

"It's exactly worth what I would've paid a bookkeeper," he lied. "Please accept it as my thanks."

She let out a breath. "You're making it difficult for me to say no." She wrapped the belt around the waistband of her pants. "From the second I laid eyes on it I loved it."

He tried to avert his eyes away from her hips and her flat stomach. "I put in a few extra holes, so it'll be more versatile." A lot of his women customers liked to wear belts over their shirts or a sweater. But if she wanted to wear it through her beltloops she'd have options.

"I don't know what to say." She studied the buckle, a sterling silver concho.

"Say nothing. And thanks again for helping me out." He turned, ready to cross back to his side of the creek.

"Come inside for a glass of wine," she said.

It was exactly what he didn't want to do. Yet, he followed her into the cabin. To keep his eyes off the sway of her USDA prime backside he looked around the house. It was identical to his in layout but the rest of it was unrecognizable. Aubrey had obviously put her stamp on the inside of the cabin, too. From the paint colors to the furnishings, the cabin reminded him of the lodgings at a Wyoming dude ranch where he wrangled one summer. Magazine rustic is what he liked to call it.

"Nice place."

"Isn't it lovely?" She swung around to face him. "Aubrey did all this. She and Charlie are so talented. But then so are you." Angie gently laid the belt on the kitchen peninsula. "What's your poison? I've got a Russian River Chardonnay or a Napa Valley Cabernet Sauvignon."

He wouldn't know a red from a white, let alone what appellation it came from. "You got beer?"

The smile fell from her face and she shook her head. "Sorry."

He could've jogged over to his place and grabbed a few bottles from his icebox, but he needed to cut this short. The longer he stayed…well, he knew how it would turn out. And he couldn't afford to let that happen. "Whatever you're having works for me."

"I'll do the Chardonnay then." She cut her gaze to the fireplace. "I tried to start a fire, but the papers kept burning out."

He went over to the hearth. "Why don't you pour the wine and I'll see if I can get it going for you?"

By the time she brought two glasses to the living room, he had a small blaze burning. "You have to give the kindling air." He pointed to how he'd propped up the fatwood tipi style.

"My late grandfather taught me. Guess I'm just out of practice."

It was the perfect opportunity to ask her about herself. Where she was before Dry Creek? What she did for a living? The usual types of questions when two people were getting to know each other. But that was a reciprocal thing and Tuff didn't like talking about himself. And something told him that Angie didn't either. So they both stared into the fire.

"Do you like your wine?" she finally asked.

"It's great."

She raised an eyebrow at his goblet, which he'd hardly touched, and stifled a giggle. "I have juice, water, and some of Laney and Jimmy Ray's sarsaparilla that Gina gave me if you'd prefer."

"I'm fine." He held up his glass and took a long sip. "I can't stay long."

She didn't say anything, but he sensed a sliver of disappointment. Or maybe he imagined it. It wasn't as if she couldn't have the company of a man every night of the week. Just not his.

"I've got a rotisserie chicken from Gina's sitting in my refrigerator. Let me at least send you home with some of it."

"I'm fine." He fidgeted with the stem of his glass. "I've got fish from this morning. Cleaned, deboned and ready to go. I'll bring you over some tomorrow." He should've stopped while he was ahead, but couldn't seem to help himself. It was just that she appeared so lonely. Ridiculous, he reminded himself. Three members of her family lived a mere stone's throw away.

"That would be lovely. I have a great oven-bake recipe for rainbow trout that tastes just like fried. I can make us dinner."

He deliberated, then said, "I've got dinner plans, but I'll leave the fish at your door in the morning."

"Oh, okay."

He got to his feet, took his glass to the sink, and swiped his Stetson off the coffee table. "Thanks for the wine."

She followed him outside. "And thank you for the belt. It really wasn't necessary, Tuff. But I do love it."

He bobbed his head and crossed the bridge to his cabin, patting himself on the back for his strength.

* * * *

The next morning, Angie found two big fish fillets packed in ice on her front porch. She stowed them in the refrigerator and grabbed a quick shower. Today, Jace and Sawyer were walking her through the Dalton Market books. The idea was for her to pick up the task of doing all the buying for the store, a duty her brother and cousins had been sharing. None of them had time for the chore. Cash worked full-time for the California Department of Agriculture as an agent, investigating livestock thefts. Jace had his sheriff's duties. And Sawyer endless deadlines for all the magazines he freelanced for.

Angie had zero retail experience and secretly thought the guys should hire someone who knew what they were doing. Though happy to take it over in the interim, Angie was sorely afraid she'd screw it up. Besides Gina's, the store and the butcher shop were supposed to be the cornerstones of the center. Her family relied on the income the retail operation generated to subsidize the ranch.

Like her late grandfather, Sawyer, Jace, and Cash ran cattle. But ranching was no longer as lucrative as it once was. In order to keep from having to sell off the land to hungry developers, they had to find new and innovative ways to support the ranch.

Angie held a lot of guilt for being MIA while her family scrambled to save their legacy. As well as the ranch, Grandpa Dalton had left his grandkids a hefty property tax bill. Sawyer, Jace, and Cash had been stuck trying to raise the funds. She should've been there to help.

She heard an engine come to life and ran to the window. It was just Tuff, leaving in his pickup. These days, the slightest sound made her jump.

Last night, she'd practically begged Tuff to stay, even though he'd made it plenty clear he had better things to do than babysit Angie.

She wondered what his dinner plans were tonight and who they were with, then mentally slapped herself. It was none of her business. And furthermore, she had no reason to care.

Angie quickly dressed, looping the belt Tuff had given her through her jeans. On her way out, she took a second to admire the leatherwork in the mirror on the back of her bedroom door. It was by far the nicest thing she owned. She shouldn't have accepted the gift. Yet, she had. None of the men she knew outside her family had ever gifted her anything of significance. She'd always been the giver and they'd always been the receivers of her generosity.

The belt had probably meant little to Tuff, whose signature work was saddles. But to her, the gesture had meant the world.

She tugged her down jacket off the hook and crossed the ranch on foot. Though it was chilly outside, the cold felt good. On her way to the center, she spotted a small herd of deer and took a few moments to watch them graze. The smell of pine and manzanita hung in the air and, in the distance, she heard a cow bawling. A rush of memories hit her. It was like being a kid again, back when her family spent every holiday on the ranch. Funny, how she hadn't missed it until now.

She zipped her jacket to her chin and lengthened her stride, not wanting to keep her brother and cousin waiting.

They were in a small alcove in the back of the store when she got there. The space was barely large enough for the two men. But she squished in.

The store itself was fairly large. It was designed to resemble a barn converted into an indoor farm stand. The floors were made from old barnwood planks and the walls were lined with custom shelving. A built-in refrigerator and freezer section held locally brewed craft beer, artisan cheeses, and Gina's frozen entrees. Wooden crates overflowed with produce and old farm tables sagged with jams, jellies and homemade breads and pies. There was even a small kitchenware department, filled with pots, pans and serving pieces from the Gina DeRose collection.

The store was as pleasing to look at it as it was welcoming. Angie had seen a lot of farm stands in her time, but nothing as lovely as this. Unfortunately, sales weren't as good as her family had hoped for.

"Did you eat, Ange?" Sawyer gave her a concerned once over and landed on her belt. "Is that one of Tuff's pieces?"

"Uh-huh." She quickly added, "He gave it to me in exchange for the work I did for him yesterday."

"Nice," Jace said and went back to flipping pages in a large ledger.

Sawyer took another glimpse of the belt, then turned his face to study her. She looked away, pretending to take in the store.

"You ready to do this?" Jace pointed at the books.

"Sure," though she wasn't a numbers person. Her major in college had been human services and community organization.

Sawyer went in search of another chair and Angie took his.

"Jeez." Jace scrubbed his hand under his cowboy hat.

"What?"

"I don't get it. We're getting throngs of visitors each week. Gina's is drawing in people from the Bay Area, Sacramento, even LA. Yet, our numbers for the store and butcher shop suck. I can't figure out what we're doing wrong."

She wondered how Tuff's store was doing but refrained from asking. "What about Refind?"

"Charlie and Aubrey are killing it. Even more reason why we should be seeing better numbers here. Everyone who stops at Dry Creek Village should leave with something from Daltons."

"But they're not?"

"Not enough to make the market profitable. The butcher shop is even worse." He let out a long sigh.

"Maybe we should hire someone who knows about this kind of stuff."

"Yeah, like who? We're in the middle of freaking nowhere. It's not like we can lure away the chief marketing officer of Whole Foods. And even if we could, we couldn't pay her."

"Good point." She chewed the inside of her cheek, knowing it would now be up to her. Kind of a gamble given her lack of expertise in the grocery business.

Sawyer returned with a chair and went back for the thermos of coffee and three cups that he'd brought from home and left at the front of the store. "What do we got?"

"Let's put it this way," Jace said. "Even our cattle enterprise is doing better than this store."

"That bad, huh?"

"Not great, that's for sure."

"I'll schedule a meeting next week and will include Cash and Gina. This is her area of expertise. Maybe she'll know how to improve the situation."

Jace muttered his agreement.

"What do you want me to do in the meantime?"

Jace handed her the ledger book. "Go through this in the next few days and see where we can make adjustments."

"Okay." The binder was heavy in her hands. It was a big store with a lot of stock. "You both realize that I don't have a clue when it comes to these kinds of business decisions?"

"Neither do we," Jace said. "So we're going to have to learn on the fly. In the meantime, can you call Kelly Moore about the refrigeration system? One of the fridges appears to have given up the ghost. We lost three hundred bucks' worth of dairy products."

"Sure." At least making a phone call was something Angie was equipped to handle.

"I'll text you his number." Jace got to his feet. "I've got to get to work."

Jace took his coffee with him. Sawyer hung back, feigning interest in the nut display. Ever since she'd returned to the ranch, he'd been walking on eggshells around her, afraid she'd break.

"You holding up okay?" he finally asked.

"Everything is fine, Sawyer. The cabin is lovely. The ranch is perfect. Very restful. And I'm looking forward to seeing Mom and Dad." A slight exaggeration. She was scared to death to face them after all the pain she'd caused. All the money she'd cost them on private investigators. There were just so many damn mistakes.

"You don't look like you're eating."

"I am. Stop worrying. I'm home now. This is supposed to be a celebration."

His eyes teared up and he reached for her. "To have you back…it's everything to me, Ange." He stood quietly, trying to compose himself. "I want nothing but happiness for you. You know that, right?"

She rested her head against his chest. "Of course I do. I'm still adjusting, Sawyer. Just give me a little time."

"You've got it. Come over tonight for dinner. We've got news."

Her head jerked up and she stared into a set of blue eyes so much like her own. "Good news?" She asked because she couldn't take it if it was bad.

He nodded. "But you've got to wait until tonight."

"What time?"

"Is seven okay? Gina technically has the day off but knowing her, she'll want to make sure the dinner service at the restaurant goes off without a hitch. Then I thought we could go to the Coffeeshop, like old times."

That brought a smile to her face. When her grandfather was alive the Dry Creek restaurant was his home away from home. Growing up, she spent many meals at the little hole-in-the-wall, eating chicken and waffles and Laney's homemade chess pie.

"Jimmy Ray and Laney will go nuts when they see you." Sawyer laughed. "You ready for that?"

Surprisingly, she was not only ready but looking forward to it. "I can't wait to see them," she said wistfully. "Have they changed much?" Their sarsaparilla sure hadn't. It was every bit as good as Angie remembered.

Sawyer thought about it for a while. "I'm trying to remember the last time you saw them."

"Christmas seven years ago." It had been a few months before she left for Zaire. And the last time she saw her grandfather, Jace, and the boys. Cash and his parents had come to LA to see her off. Though by then, she'd been a world traveler and a joiner junkie, having volunteered for a gamut of international advocacy organizations.

So much had happened since then.

"Yeah, I guess that was the last time," Sawyer said, a hint of sadness in his voice. "I think they look the same. The thing about Jimmy Ray and Laney is they don't seem to age. They've definitely gotten ornerier, though. You should hear Laney and Gina go at it."

She had a sudden flash of Grandpa Dalton arguing with Jimmy Ray over a heated game of checkers. "It'll be good to see them." And despite her loss of appetite, she could almost taste their legendary fried chicken.

"We'll pick you up, then."

From the back of the store, Angie heard someone setting up for business. She'd already met Nina, the young woman hired to run the cash register.

"I think I'll hang around here for a while and lend a hand." Angie supposed it would help to know what kind of people shopped at Daltons. Besides, she had nothing else to do. "I'll take this home." She tapped the ledger. "And see if I can make any sense out of it."

"Thanks, Ange." He squeezed her shoulder. "It's good that you're part of this. Grandpa would be proud."

He put his hat on and started to leave, stopping just short of the alcove, where he gave her new belt another glance. "Hey, Angie, I'm glad you and Tuff have become friends. But...just be careful, okay?"

"Careful of what?"

He pinned her with a look. "He's not for you."

What was that supposed to mean? "Do you really think, after everything I've been through, I'm looking for a boyfriend?" She shook her head.

He shrugged. "Nothing wrong with it. Tuff's a great guy...But he's not looking for anything steady."

Nor was Sawyer until he found Gina. Angie nearly reminded him of that. But it would only help to convince him that she was putting the moves on Tuff. It showed how much he knew. She was no longer the trusting soul who fell at the feet of every likeminded man she met. After her last experience, it would be a long time before she got into another relationship again. Maybe never.

"Just some brotherly advice." He poked her in the arm the way he used to when they were kids. "See you tonight."

After Sawyer left, she went to the front of the store to assist with the setup. Nina put her in charge of a display of Gina DeRose pumpkin and spice cake mixes. Angie finished it off with some colored leaves she collected outside. The presentation didn't look half bad.

After that, Angie stocked a few shelves and inventoried a delivery of fresh pies from a local baker. There was a small rush of mostly locals around noon. They'd come for lunch at Gina's and browsed Daltons. A few bought cake mixes from Angie's new display, which gave her a little thrill, and other small ticket items.

"Is it better on weekends?" Angie asked Nina.

Nina waggled her hand from side to side. "It's mostly tourists on weekends. A lot of them are on their way up to Tahoe. So, you know, it's not like they're going to grocery shop."

Yes, Angie could see where that would be a problem.

"What about the locals? Do they come here to shop?"

Nina hitched her shoulders. "It's kind of expensive here. They just go to Raley's or Safeway."

Oh boy, she had her work cut out for her.

"You want to take your lunch break?" It was slow and Angie could probably muddle through figuring out the cash register if she had to.

"Sure." Nina went to the back to get her jacket.

"Where do you go around here?" Angie called to her, curious.

"I either bring a brown bag lunch or go to the Coffeeshop in town. I can't afford Gina's."

There wasn't even a microwave to nuke one of Angie's sister-in-law's frozen entrees.

"Take your time," Angie told Nina. Given the lack of crowds, it wasn't as if they needed both of them to man the store.

Angie busied herself flipping through the ledger, studying the numbers. The store was so quiet, she could hear the hum of the freezers. Then the door opened, sending in a rush of cold air, and she jerked up from staring at the books.

"Howdy." Tuff bobbed his head at her, then perused the pie display.

"Can I help you find anything?"

"Nah, I just got hungry and didn't want to run home. These any good?" He held up a package of cellophane wrapped cookies, also made by the pie lady.

"To tell you the truth I've never had one. But how bad can a cookie be?"

He smiled and she felt a little tug in her chest. It was just such a great grin. Kind of mischievous and sexy while making his brown eyes twinkle.

"You get my fish?"

"I did. Thank you."

He kept the cookies and grabbed an apple, which he polished on his jacket as he strolled to the cash register. "What do you got there?" He bent over the counter and nudged his head at her binder.

"It's the books for the store. I'm trying to get myself acquainted with the numbers." Because they suck. She didn't expand on the fact that she'd been tasked to fix them.

"Ah. How's that going?"

"Good, I guess. I'm not really a numbers person."

"No?" He held her gaze. "What kind of person are you?"

A dilettante. A thirty-four-year-old without a resume. "My background is in community organization."

"I didn't know that was a thing."

She studied him to see if he was ridiculing her, but he appeared genuinely interested. "Yep, serving as an advocate for communities in need or heading up social action committees is definitely a thing."

He nodded. "Fascinating work."

She had thought so when she'd gotten her degree, and had loved working with Greenpeace and the Water Project. But The Farm had been a culmination of all her dreams. And then, a nightmare.

"Different than retail." He gazed around the store.

"Yeah...well...family business. You know how that is?"

He nodded again, but she didn't get the sense that saddle making was his family's business.

"Look"—she came out from behind the counter—"I'm wearing your belt."

His eyes moved to her jeans and floated over her like heat. "You wear it well."

She could feel her face burn and couldn't remember the last time a man made her blush. Flustered, she tried to ring up his cookies and apple, but didn't get the buttons on the cash register right.

"I think you're supposed to total everything out first."

"I think you're right." Still, it took until the third try until she got it, relieved when the cash tray slid out.

By the time he left, she was a jumble of nerves. The cowboy had reduced her to a giddy teenager. Ridiculous, she told herself. She was a grown woman. A grown woman who had sworn off men.

Chapter 5

Tuff ate his cookies while flipping through his emails. Two new orders came in. At this rate, he'd have to hire help, maybe an apprentice. Every time his mind wandered to Angie—and to the exceptional way she filled out her jeans—he shut it down. She was a walking "No Trespassing" sign. The sooner he got that through his head the better off they'd both be.

He continued scrolling down his inbox, deleting junk mail and moving inquiries about custom jobs to another file to be answered later. If he was more organized, he'd address the questions as they came in, instead of putting it off until later. But he much preferred making saddles to answering inquiries about them.

The bell over his door chimed and he silently cursed the interruption. He put down his last cookie and wandered up front, expecting to see Ava. Not Ava but Jace, who today was in full uniform.

"Hey there." Tuff wiped a few stray crumbs from the side of his mouth. "You hiding from the wife and kids?" he joked. It wasn't unusual for Jace to pop into the shop on a slow day to shoot the breeze and check out Tuff's latest work. Tuff had always gotten the impression that it was Jace's way of escaping from the world for a few precious moments.

"Nope." He frowned. "I'm afraid I'm here on official business."

Something about the way Jace said it made Tuff freeze as if a pair of icy hands had him by the throat. "What's that?"

"It's your mom, Tuff." He motioned at the door. "Why don't I lock up?"

Tuff did it himself, keeping his hands steady as he turned the deadbolt and flipped the door sign to closed. "What's up?" He returned to the checkout counter, imploring Jace with a look to spit out whatever he'd come to say.

Jace gave an imperceptible nod. "I don't know any other way to tell you this. But the Missoula County Sheriff called. Two days ago, they found your ma in her trailer...dead." Stricken, he said, "I'm sorry, Tuff." He reached out and patted Tuff's shoulder.

Tuff griped the edge of the counter. He wasn't sure if he just needed something to hold onto or if the solid live edge piece of mesquite was holding him up. "Did they say how she died?" He assumed she either drank herself to death or it was the work of another abusive boyfriend.

"Yeah." Jace shoved his hands in his pockets. "Let's go in back."

Tuff nodded and dragged another chair to the studio. Jace followed him and signaled for Tuff to take a seat.

"They think it was suicide," he said after a long pause. "They found a revolver near the scene and a note."

"What did it say?" Tuff didn't know why he asked. Shock he supposed. Somehow, he couldn't fathom Mary Garrison taking her own life. Not when there were so many willing lovers to do it for her.

"I don't know." Jace put his hand on Tuff's shoulder again. "The coroner wants to talk to you."

"Why? We weren't close. I haven't been in touch with her in more than twenty years."

Jace got up and poured Tuff a cup of water from the bathroom sink. "They're still piecing things together and you're her closest next of kin."

Yep, and a whole lot of good that had done him.

"How'd they find me?" These days it wasn't hard. Between Facebook and cell phones no one believed in privacy anymore.

"Your website. They want to know what to do with her remains, her things, her trailer."

He wasn't going back there that was for sure. And he sure the hell wasn't talking to the sheriff.

"Tell 'em to donate it to charity." What a joke. Nothing Mary Garrison had was worth anything.

"What about her...burial? A funeral?"

"Yeah, I'll take care of it." What he meant was he'd pay someone in Missoula to make the arrangements, which is more than she would've done for him.

"I'm sorry, Tuff. Is there something we can do?"

"Thanks." Tuff got to his feet. "It just caught me off guard is all. I'm fine. I appreciate you coming and telling me in person. I'll handle all the necessary red tape."

"Okay. But please let us know if there is any way we can help. I'll leave the coroner's number on the counter up front."

He waited for the sound of the door to close, collapsed into Jace's chair, and buried his face in his arms.

* * * *

Two days later, he caught a flight to Montana and rented a car. He'd almost forgotten how to drive in the snow. November and already five goddamn inches. The roads outside Missoula could use a good plowing but he managed to get where he needed to go.

Nothing had changed. The same old signs and billboards. The same old shopfronts, including Mary's favorite liquor store. The highway was still as desolate as ever. Why the hell anyone would choose to live in Fontaine, Montana was beyond him. It's where broken-down old cowboys and the needy women who loved them went to die.

He hung a right onto Daven Road and followed the potholes to Fontaine Estates. *Estates*. He let out a mirthless laugh. Talk about lipstick on a pig. Like the rest of Fontaine, his mother's trailer park was still as rundown and depressing as he remembered it. An entire state of big skies and endless beauty and she chose to live here.

He swerved to miss a mangy dog and stopped short of hitting a mailbox. The dog halted in his tracks and stared at Tuff with sad eyes, almost as if to apologize.

Tuff swung open his door. "Come here, boy."

The hound inched closer with his tail tucked between his legs but timidly stood too far away for Tuff to touch him. He opened his palm and held it out to the dog in a sign of peace. The pup sniffed the air and hesitantly stretched his shaggy neck a little bit nearer.

He was pure mutt. Judging by his size and coat, a mixture of shepherd and lab. And smelly as hell. The animal hadn't had a bath in a while. If Tuff had to guess the dog was covered in fleas.

"Come on, buddy. I won't hurt you." Tuff turned his hand so the dog could sniff it.

He stuck out his snout until it was practically touching Tuff's skin.

"There you go. You hungry, boy?" He slowly reached into the passenger seat and found the beef jerky he'd bought at Sacramento International Airport but hadn't eaten.

The movement startled the dog and he cowered, slithering away from the car.

"Ah, we were doing so well there for a minute." Tuff unwrapped the jerky and held it out to the hound. "Don't be shy."

The dog once again moved closer, lured by the smell of the beef. "Go ahead, buddy. Eat it."

The guy must've been starved because he lurched forward, grabbed it out of Tuff's hand and backed up, scarfing the jerky down in big gulps.

"There's more where that came from." Tuff broke up a half-eaten muffin and spread it over a napkin on the snow. The dog ate that too, then rolled over to scratch himself. His skin looked like it had been attacked by red ants.

"Hey, buddy, that must hurt."

The dog gave Tuff another dose of sad eyes.

"Well, it's been good to know you, but I've got to get on down the road." The dog let out a low whine.

"You take care of yourself." Tuff opened his door and to his surprise his new friend hopped in. The dog did a full circle on the passenger seat, then laid down and stuck his snout between his paws. "Okay, I guess it's warmer in here." Tuff slid into the driver's seat and reached over to scratch the hound's head.

The dog gave a happy yelp and put his head in Tuff's lap.

Tuff sighed in resignation. "All right, you can stick around for a while. But we have to make a pitstop. After that, it's steak for both of us."

He pulled out onto the road and from memory found Mary's single-wide on a cul-de-sac next to an empty field. A trash can had been knocked over at the curb and garbage was strewn everywhere. There was a pile of empty wine and beer bottles on the front stoop. One of the windows had been boarded up, and the remnants of yellow police tape still covered the door.

"Home sweet home," he said to the dog. "You wait here. I won't be long."

He'd only come for one thing. The rest, the people he hired could haul away. They could burn the trailer to the ground for all he cared.

He got out of the car, stared at the single-wide where he'd grown up, and girded himself for what was to come next.

As he climbed the stairs, a woman in a housecoat with a cigarette dangling from her lips called, "Hey, you! That's private property."

He shot her a look, recognizing her instantly. "I'm a cop."

She came down her rickety wooden stairs in a pair of shower clogs. If she didn't go inside soon, she'd freeze to death. "You don't look like no cop."

He threw up his arms. "You caught me. I'm here to steal all of Mary's diamonds and gold."

"A real smart ass, aren't ya?" She let her gaze sweep over him. "I know who you are. That no-good son of hers. A felon." She took a pull of her cigarette and her scrawny body shuddered with a racking cough.

He ignored her and climbed the stairs of his mother's trailer, careful to avoid the bottles.

"I'm calling the police," she yelled in a hoarse voice.

"Knock yourself out."

The door was unlocked, so he let himself inside. There was a rust stain on the green carpet and blood splatter on the walls. Tuff took a deep breath, trying to calm himself. It felt like it was happening all over again. Trying not to look, he passed the old sofa bed he used to sleep on and made his way to his mother's bedroom.

The place reeked of cigarette smoke, perspiration, and death.

Not much had changed in here since he'd left. The old tube TV was still on top of the dresser. And the now threadbare curtains his mother had bought from Kmart when Tuff was just a boy still covered the windows. The tiger fleece blanket draped across the bed was new, or newer. Even so, the place was a freaking time warp.

He started in the closet, reaching around on the top shelf. There was no guarantee that his mother had kept it all these years. More than likely, she'd sold or hocked it for a bottle of rotgut. He pulled down her old hat box and sorted through the contents. A couple of keys, an old photograph, and five dollars in singles. Tuff stared at the picture, a million memories passing through his head. *This is how it could've been. Should've been.*

Next, he searched the closet floor, sifting through a couple of shoeboxes. Nothing but junk. He moved to the dresser and rooted through the drawers. A couple of pieces of trashy lingerie, a stack of concert T-shirts that were even too large for him, and a pile of assorted jeans and sweatshirts.

He looked under the bed. Other than a sea of dust bunnies, he came up empty. After combing the bedroom, he tried the bathroom and then the kitchen. There were empty bottles and half-eaten food containers everywhere but not what he'd come for.

She'd sold it. The only thing left of Tuff's father and she fucking sold it.

He was halfway out when he made a split-second decision to go back to the bedroom. He grabbed the photo off the bed and stashed it in his jacket pocket.

Outside, the cold was a welcome relief. He glanced over at Mrs. Lesher's trailer and saw her face pressed against the glass, watching him and the street. The old biddy. The dog was standing on the passenger seat, waiting for him. He was about to open the car door when he saw the flashing blue and red lights.

Well, that didn't take long.

His first instinct was to pull away, just drive off into the wild blue yonder, like he'd done twenty-five years ago. But he waited.

The sheriff's cruiser came to a screeching halt. Darrel Strong stepped out of the car, his uniform jacket gaping over his big belly. The sheriff had put on some weight since the last time Tuff had seen him. His hair was now a steely gray, but he had all of it. The same flinty blue eyes too.

"Why didn't you call?" The sheriff rested one arm on the top of his cruiser. "You shouldn't have gone in." He turned to the trailer, then cut back to Tuff. "A helluva thing for a son to see."

Tuff had seen worse.

"Someone will be here Monday to clean the place. The funeral's tomorrow." He didn't know why he'd shared that. It was none of Strong's goddamn business.

"I'm sorry for your loss, Ted."

"It's Tuff. No one calls me that."

Strong let out a bark of laughter. "I reckon it fits you. You always were a tough *hombre*. Even at fifteen."

The sheriff came around his car and gave Tuff a once over, eyeing his shearling jacket and Lucchese boots. "Looks like you turned out pretty well. According to your website, you've got a nice business going. Those are some real fine saddles in the pictures."

When Tuff didn't respond, Strong said, "Come down to the station, son."

"I'm not your son."

Strong let his gaze drop to the snowy dirt. "No, you're not. But I should've taken you in just the same. I was wrong, Ted. But I had four kids of my own. Four kids who needed food on the table, clothes on their backs, college educations. Still, I should've made room for one more. It wasn't Christian what I did."

Tuff snorted. Not Christian? It wasn't human.

Strong's breath turned white in the cold. He shoved his hands in his pockets "Come down to the station. I've got her note. It was addressed to you."

He didn't want her note or anything Mary Garrison had to give, which had been a whole lot of nothing. "Keep it. Throw it away. Burn it. I don't care."

"I can't force you to take it, but I think you should have it. She was doing better, Tuff. She sent the last guy packing and since then not one domestic call to the house."

Tuff intentionally stared at the pile of bottles on the trailer's landing. "She blew her fucking head off. Is that better to you?"

Strong flinched. "She was sick, son. She was never the same after your daddy died."

Tuff turned away. "Look, I've got to go."

"Where you staying?"

Tuff didn't answer. Darrell Strong had a hell of a nerve asking. "Nice catching up."

As Tuff walked to his car, he heard Strong curse under his breath.

* * * *

The next morning, Tuff put on a tie. He only had two and he'd brought them both. Buddy—the best name he could come up with on short notice— laid stretched out on the second bed in his room at the Doubletree.

He'd taken the poor critter for a flea dip after leaving Fontaine. And the two had dined off room service.

"What am going to do with you, boy?"

The dog let out a contented whine.

"Don't get too comfortable. This is a one-night stand. Tomorrow we go our separate ways." He swiped the leash he'd bought off the nightstand and clipped it onto Buddy's new collar. "Let's go for a walk."

He took the mutt out to do his stuff, wondering what kind of person left a dog out in the cold to starve to death. The same kind of person as Mary Garrison, he supposed. When Buddy was done, Tuff kept him in the motel room with the TV on.

"I'm not paying for any porn channels. Be a good boy," he told Buddy on his way out.

The cemetery parking lot was empty when he got there. He hadn't posted anything about Mary's funeral in the Fontaine rag or any of the Missoula papers, so he shouldn't have expected anyone to come. And even if he had, her drinking pals weren't all that reliable.

He straightened his tie in his rearview mirror and found his way to the plot the funeral director had picked out for him over the phone. It had a view of an old-growth Ponderosa Pine, the director had gushed. Mary would've preferred a neon bar sign but whatever. The way Tuff looked at it was the woman who gave him life—and nothing else—deserved more than a pauper's grave.

A rent-a-pastor was waiting when he got there and greeted him with condolences. "Would you like to say a few words?"

"Nope. Whatever you've got prepared will be fine." Tuff buttoned his jacket and blew on his hands. He should've worn gloves.

The pastor hesitated, clearly wanting to ask whether they should wait for the rest of the attendees to arrive but thought better of it. He cleared his throat. "Shall we get started?"

Tuff gave him an imperceptible nod, then only half-listened as he recited a few generic platitudes about Mary. None of them was remotely true. But they sounded nice.

The pastor eventually launched into, "Blessed be the God and Father of our Lord Jesus Christ, the Father of mercies and God of all comfort, who comforts us in all our affliction, so that we may be able to comfort those who are in any affliction, with the comfort with which we ourselves are comforted by God."

By the time he got to the "ashes to ashes" part of the sermon, Tuff felt someone behind him. He turned to find Strong, who gave him a cursory nod.

At the end of the service, they lowered Mary's casket into the ground. That's when it finally hit him. His mother was dead. The last vestige of his family, gone. He didn't even have grandparents, just an aunt who lived in a group home for people with severe cerebral palsy.

"It was a nice service." The sheriff held out his hand. "And good of you to pay for it."

Tuff wanted to be petty and tell the old man to go to hell. But what was the point? He had a good life now. A lucrative business. A nice cabin in the woods. Friends. He could afford to be magnanimous, so he shook the sheriff's hand.

"Thanks for coming. Mary would've been touched," Tuff said, sarcasm edging his voice. Ironically, Strong had been the one constant in Mary's life, there every time she got her head bashed in. She'd been as appreciative of Strong's interference as she'd been of Tuff's, which is to say she'd hated the sheriff as much as she'd despised her own son.

"I suppose you're going back to California now."

"Yep." Tuff had never been much good at small talk.

"Safe travels." Strong slipped an envelope into Tuff's hand. "Take it. You'll be glad you did. And, Ted, I really am sorry. For everything."

Tuff waited until the sheriff's back disappeared across the snow patched lawn of the cemetery before he looked at the envelope. Even after twenty-five years, he recognized his mother's handwriting. A loopy cursive that reminded him of a doodler's pad. Even as a drunk, she'd been creative.

On his way to the car, he dropped the envelope in a trash bin. He was just about to pull away from the curb when he went back, got it, and shoved it in his shearling jacket.

Chapter 6

Angie spent most of Saturday crying. She hadn't expected to be so overcome with emotion at finally seeing her parents after all these years that she turned into a soggy mess. They had that one, clandestine Skype meeting that Cash, bless his heart, had arranged last year. But seeing them in person…nothing had ever felt so good.

The day passed quickly without a lot of questions about The Farm, the investigation, or how she'd become mired in a militia group. Her sense was that Sawyer had filled them in on the gory details, and it had been decided that the reunion would be better spent not discussing them.

Nevertheless, her parents would need to know the full extent of Angie's harrowing six years eventually. A time she dreaded talking about.

"Let's go for a walk," her mother hooked her arm inside Angie's. "Dan come with us."

They followed the creek for a time, simply taking in the beauty of the brisk, clear day. Though the sun was shining, it was cold. They'd had early snow in the mountains, feeding the creek until it overflowed past its banks.

In her grandfather's last years, Dry Creek, and all of California, had suffered from drought. It had gotten so bad that he'd had to cull his cattle herd. As a result, the ranch had fallen into disrepair. But her family was doing everything they could to return it to its former glory.

"We wanted to take this time to talk to you," her father started. "We wanted you to know that we're always here for you, Angela. Always. It was true when you left to go to Zaire and it's true now. We may not have always agreed with your decisions or with the path you took, but you're our daughter. You're our heart." He started to choke up and waited to pull himself together before he continued. "You're our very soul and we hope that you know you can come to us with anything. You never have to be afraid to call us."

"Dad, I wasn't keeping anything from you. I called when I left Zaire to come back to the States. And then…things got out of control." Which wasn't exactly the truth. They didn't get out of control at first. She hadn't called because she didn't want them to know she was using her trust fund to buy the land. She'd wanted to wait until she could show them the fruits of her labor—or in this case the fruits of her money.

"All your father is trying to say is that if we'd known where you were, if we had been in touch, we could've come and gotten you."

"It wasn't like that Mom. There was nothing you could've done once I agreed to help the feds."

"We would've at least known—"

"Wendy." Angie's father put his hand up. "Angie, honey, we just want you to know how much we love you, how proud we are of the sacrifice you made to put these men away. And that we missed you every second of every minute of every day you were gone." There were tears in his eyes.

"I'm sorry." She choked on a sob. "I'm sorry I put you through so much."

Wendy pulled Angie into her arms. "We're together now and that's all that matters."

Despite what her mother said, guilt gnawed at her. She'd caused her family unbelievable anguish.

"Come on," her father said. "Let's walk around Dry Creek Village and look at the holiday lights."

* * * *

The following day, Angie ceded all the attention to Sawyer and Gina and their big pregnancy announcement.

They'd already told Angie the other day over chicken and waffles at the coffeeshop. She'd cried. It was just the best news. Her brother was going to be a great father and Angie couldn't think of anyone more loving than Gina.

Wendy and Dan of course went ape shit. And for a while they sat around the breakfast table, trying out names.

"We don't even know if it's a boy," Sawyer admonished when Angie suggested Jasper after their late grandfather.

"We might want the sex to be a surprise." Gina touched the slight swell of her stomach, which until now Angie hadn't noticed. "And even if we do find out, we're not having one of those stupid gender-reveal parties."

"Hear, hear!" Dan held up his mimosa in solidarity.

"They really are rather silly," Wendy agreed.

"I don't know, I think they're kind of sweet in moderation." Maybe not fireworks but a cute cake or confetti seemed reasonable to Angie.

The day passed so normally that it almost felt like the old days, before everything had gone to crap.

They took a walk around the adjacent property, which her parents had bought a year ago to increase grazing land for their cattle herd. Her family had leased some of the acreage to a grape grower.

"This is fantastic," her mother said as they strolled through a newly planted vineyard. "He should rent it out for parties."

Angie laughed. "Said a Hollywood publicist who lives in Beverly Hills. It's a working farm, Mom."

"I know. But I've been to some fabulous events in the Napa Valley."

Angie didn't have the heart to tell her mother that Dry Creek had a long way to go before it could compete with wine country.

"Sawyer says you're taking over Daltons." Dan draped his arm over her shoulder as they headed in the direction of her cabin.

"I don't know about taking it over. But I'm trying to help out where I can."

"So what are your plans, darling?"

Angie huffed out a breath. "I don't have any yet but I'm working on it. Unfortunately, sales haven't been that great. So far, it's mostly tourists coming through the store who are either on their way up to Tahoe or leaving Tahoe and are on their way home to the Bay Area. The drive is a little far for perishables."

"I can see the problem," Dan said. "So what's the solution?"

"Beats me. I think the guys should hire someone who specializes in grocery retail. What do I know?"

"You're a brilliant young woman. You'll figure it out."

"Spoken like a mother."

Her father took her hand. "You don't give yourself enough credit, sweetheart. We're very excited about you joining this enterprise. Your grandfather would've been so proud of all you kids. He left this ranch to you because he knew how much the four of you loved it. And now you're nurturing it back to life."

Sawyer, Cash, Jace, and their wives were the ones to nurture the ranch back to life. They'd been kind enough to take her into the fold. Angie had no delusions that she was anything other than a charity case. She might own a quarter of the land, but her brother and cousins were the heart and soul of the ranch. For her it was just a safe place to land.

"And what about the butcher shop? Will you be taking that over, too?"

"I'm happy to pitch in wherever I can. But I know this much about the meat business." She made an inch with her thumb and index finger. In fact, until not too long ago, she'd been a vegetarian. Had her grandfather known, he would've rolled over in his grave.

"You and Sawyer have always been good at research," Dan said. "This is the perfect opportunity to use those skills. Talk to some butcher shop owners in LA, San Francisco. Pick their brains. In no time, you'll be an expert."

She tried not to roll her eyes.

That evening, they had dinner at Gina's. Afterward, her parents came back to the cabin. They made hot cocoa and sat around the fire.

"I'd like to stay the rest of the month if it wouldn't cramp your style," Wendy said.

"Don't do that, Mom. You've got work and I'm fine. I'm better than fine. I'm really, really good."

"I know that. But I've missed my girl. What's wrong with us spending time together?"

Because it felt as if she was being coddled. "I just want everything to feel normal again. I've committed to the store and if you're here I'll want to play. I need the routine, Mom. I need to feel like I'm moving ahead with my life. Angela Dalton's life, not Katherine Moore's. It's not that I don't love you because you and Dad are the most important people in my life. But I've got so many things to figure out…and it's my journey. No one can help me make it. I have to do it on my own."

Wendy reached over and took Angie's hand. "We'll be together for Thanksgiving. Maybe then you'll consider coming to LA for a while or letting me stay here."

"Absolutely." She laid her head on her mother's shoulder. "I love you, Mom. Love you, Dad."

* * * *

Wendy and Dan left in the morning, leaving Angie a couple of hours to herself before she checked in at Daltons.

Over scrambled eggs and toast, she studied her ledger some more, hoping to pinpoint trends. She got up to pour herself a second cup of coffee and noticed Tuff's truck was parked in his driveway. The Ram had been missing for a few days and sometime in the night, she'd heard it come up Tuff's driveway. She assumed Tuff had been dealing with his mother's passing.

Tonight, she'd bring him something from the coffeeshop. Maybe one of Laney's legendary sweet potato casseroles. Or chicken fried steak. She knew Gina was bringing him a lasagna, Charlie enchiladas and Aubrey beef stew. Whatever he didn't eat he could freeze.

A dog she'd never seen before was rooting around his yard. She shrugged into her jacket and went outside.

"You lost, boy?" She crossed the footbridge, hoping the dog had a tag or a chip. Or that someone hadn't dumped him here. He appeared malnourished.

The dog backed away when she approached him, enforcing her fear that someone had abandoned him. The poor dog definitely looked as if he'd been on his own for a while.

"That's Buddy."

She spun around to find Tuff standing on his porch and walked to the foot of the staircase. "He's yours?"

Tuff chuckled. "I think I'm his, but yeah. I plan to talk to Cash today. We never discussed a pet policy for the cabin."

"I can't imagine Cash, or anyone else for that matter, having a problem with you keeping a dog. It's a working ranch for goodness sake."

"Buddy!" He whistled to the pup, who'd wandered to the creek bank. "Come here, boy." The dog trotted to the cabin, climbed the stairs, and plopped down at Tuff's feet.

"I'm really sorry about your mom, Tuff. We all are."

His gaze dropped to Buddy and he reached down to scratch the dog's head. "Thanks. I appreciate that."

"Was she very sick?"

He looked up and held eye contact with her as if he was assessing what to say. "Jace didn't tell you?"

"He just said she'd died. I assumed she was sick." Angie didn't know why. It could've been a car accident or countless other things.

"Yep, she was sick enough to swallow a revolver."

Angie jerked back.

"Ah shit." He rubbed his hand down his face. "I don't know why I told you that."

She climbed halfway up the stairs and took his hand, sandwiching it between both of hers. A look of surprise crossed his face. "I'm so sorry, Tuff. That's an awful thing. Just awful." Beyond that she didn't know what else to say to give comfort.

"Come over to my place for a cup of coffee. Bring Buddy." She tugged his hand afraid he wouldn't come otherwise. She didn't know Tuff well, but they didn't need to be lifelong friends for her to see that he was a solitary man.

She practically pulled him across the bridge, Buddy following at his heels. It wasn't until they got inside her cabin that she saw how tired he looked. How sad. There were dark circles under his eyes and the brackets around his mouth that usually looked like dimples now resembled deep grooves.

"Sit," she said and pointed to one of the barstools at the kitchen peninsula. "I'll put a fresh pot on." She emptied the dregs from her last pot and started over.

While the coffee brewed, she took a bowl from the cupboard, filled it with water, and put it down for Buddy, who had wrapped himself around Tuff's feet. His tail repeatedly thumped against the hardwood floor.

She got out the leftover banana bread from her parents' visit, put it on a plate, and slid it in front of him. "Eat."

"Yes, ma'am." His mouth slid up into a half grin.

"So you went for the funeral, huh?"

He nodded and popped a piece of the bread into his mouth. "This is good," he said over a mouthful. "You make it?"

"No, Gina did." She propped her elbows on the counter across from him. "Where did you get Buddy?" The dog was a bit of mystery.

"Montana."

"Was he your mom's?"

"Not that I'm aware of. Just an orphaned stray, I think. Or if someone owned him, he didn't deserve a dog. He was in pretty bad shape when I found him."

"You drove?"

"Nope, flew. Luckily, the flight home wasn't full." He reached down and gave Buddy another head scratch.

"That was nice that you adopted him."

He didn't say anything, just flipped his gaze to the now filled coffee pot. She poured them both a cup, got out the milk and sugar, and took the barstool next to his.

"So how are you doing, Tuff?"

He looked at her, his expression a giant question mark.

His stoicism was a bit exasperating. In a soft voice she said, "Your mother just died. Maybe you want to talk about it."

He fidgeted with the handle on his cup. "We were estranged for twenty-five years, so there isn't a whole lot to say. I went, took care of business, and buried her. That's all I've got."

"Are you sure? Because I'm a good ear."

She could tell her questions were annoying him, but he was too polite to tell her. "We don't have to talk about it if you don't want to. But if you ever do, I just want you to know that I'm a friend."

He started to say something, then stopped himself. "Thank you." He took a sip of his coffee and watched her over the rim of his cup. "What's going on with you?"

She wasn't sure how he meant that. Whether he wanted to know about her past or just in general. She opted for the easy way out. "My parents were here this weekend and we had a lovely visit. In fact, they left this morning but will be back for Thanksgiving."

Unlike him, she was rambling. Like him, she was being evasive. Apparently, they weren't so different.

"Sorry I missed them."

"Have you met?"

"A few times." He continued to watch her in a way that made her feel like she was under a microscope. "They visit the ranch about once a month."

It surprised but delighted her that they came so often. Her father and Cash's father had never taken to ranch life, and Jace's parents and baby brother had died in an automobile accident when he was just a kid. Grandma and Grandpa Dalton had raised Jace on the ranch. It was their wish that Jace and the rest of their grandkids take over when they died.

She supposed now that she was here, and with Sawyer and Gina's baby on the way, her parents' monthly visits would likely grow to more.

"Where'd you live before the ranch?" he asked.

She'd prepared for this question and was told to never tell anyone about Portland. "New Mexico. A little place outside Taos."

He raised a brow. "A lot of communities to organize there?"

"Mm-hmm. Native American communities." It was the truth, though she'd never actually worked with the Tiwa people, though it had been the plan up until Burt and his crew had shown up.

To stave off any more conversation about her time in Taos she changed the subject back to him. "I didn't know you were from Montana."

"Born there, left when I was fifteen."

"Where'd you go?"

"A little bit of everywhere."

"Was one of your parents in the military?" He was so damned reticent it was like pulling teeth.

He sat up straight. "My dad was a Marine."

"Oh, wow. Where's he now?"

"He was killed in a convenience store robbery." When he saw her recoil, he said, "We're a tragic family, huh?"

Not tragic, heartbreaking. "How old were you when it happened?"

Tuff jabbed his fork at his banana bread. "Eight."

"I'm terribly sorry."

"Not your fault." He gave a wistful smile. "He was trying to protect the cashier, a young woman, and one of the gunmen shot him. Police say he died on the spot."

"Did they ever arrest the guys who did it?"

"Yeah. The shooter's doing life without parole."

It was a horrible story and helped put her own ordeal into perspective. She was alive, living in a pretty creekside cabin, surrounded by her family.

She got up to top off his coffee because she needed something to do. Something physical.

"I'm just a ray of sunshine, aren't I?"

"I'm glad you told me." She filled his cup, put the pot back, and took her seat again. Their legs brushed and neither of them moved. The contact felt too good. "Are you going to take a few days off?"

"Because of my mom? Nah, I've got orders to fill, deadlines to make."

"I guess work is a good way to keep from thinking about it too much." She didn't know what she would do if one of her parents died. And by suicide no less. The thought of it was unfathomable.

"It's really not like that." He took a sip of the fresh coffee she'd just poured. "Like I said, we weren't close."

Still, it was his mother. He had to feel something. "Well if there's anything you need don't hesitate to ask."

He looked at her over the rim of his mug again, his brows halfcocked. Though she couldn't read what he was thinking, she got the distinct impression that he had something altogether different in mind than what she was offering. It should've offended her, instead a tingle danced up her spine.

He stood up. "Thanks for the coffee and banana bread. And the conversation." He reached out to brush a stray hair that had come loose from Angie's ponytail but seemed to think better of it and rested his hand at his side.

Buddy, who was startled awake, got up on shaky legs and stretched.

"Come on, boy. Time to go to work."

She saw them to the door and waved to him as he went inside his own cabin. He was an interesting man. Far from transparent, yet she felt like she knew him. Maybe because he was so much like herself.

Chapter 7

There was a bucket of flowers at Tuff's studio door when he got to work and a note of condolence from Ava and Winter. Jace had one hell of a big mouth. He meant well, Tuff knew. And at least he hadn't told everyone that his mother had shot herself. For some reason, he didn't think Angie would either.

The fact that he preferred people not know said more about him than it did suicide. Logically, he knew there was nothing he could've done to help her. Look where it had gotten him the last time he'd tried. But that didn't soothe the guilt.

He let himself in and watched Buddy sniff every corner of the room. Eventually, he found a spot underneath Tuff's cutting table, did a little spin, and lay down.

"We need to get you a bed, Buddy." Later, he'd make the drive into one of the neighboring towns and buy pet supplies.

As per his routine, he booted up his computer and flipped the closed sign on the door to open. Mondays were usually slow. But if they got snow up in Tahoe, there'd be a mad dash to the slopes. Dry Creek Ranch was a good stopping point, a place where folks could charge their Teslas, use the restrooms, and get a bite to eat. Inevitably, they stopped in at Tuff's studio for a look-see.

He checked his email, returned a few messages, and sifted through the snail mail. Nothing much to see. He'd lost a couple of days but could make it up if he stayed focused, which meant not thinking about the redhead.

He'd probably spoken more to her this morning than he had spoken to all his connections combined for the entire year. He hadn't intended telling Angie his whole life story. The stuff about his father...well, he usually kept that close to the vest. His memories were all he had left of his dad and he liked to hoard them for himself. His mother was another story. That was just bad road. No one liked talking about bad road.

It was colder today than it had been when he'd left for Montana. He built a fire in the stove, letting it warm his hands before he got started cutting leather. The door jangled. It was a little early for the snow crowd.

Just Ava.

"You forget your key again?"

She threw her arms around his neck. "Oh, Tuff, I'm so, so sorry."

He loosened her arms and managed to untangle himself from her embrace. "Thanks for the flowers. That was right kind of you and Winter."

Her gaze trailed to the bucket arrangement he'd left on the counter. "It was the least we could do. Hopefully, it'll help brighten your day."

"Already has." They were nice girls. "Where's your partner in crime?"

"She's got a bad cold. Carlos is taking care of her. Bryce won't get near me if I even show signs of a sniffle. Afraid he'll lose time studying for the bar." She rolled her eyes.

"How long you think she's down for?" Tuff was thinking about all those Thanksgiving floral orders they had.

Ava shrugged. "Probably just a day or two." She jumped up on his counter, swinging her legs.

He didn't want to be rude, but he had work to do and she clearly wanted to hang out.

Buddy snored and Ava peeked around the corner. "Who do you have back there?" She got down from the counter and strolled into Tuff's studio. "You got a dog," she squealed and knelt to pet Buddy.

"That's Buddy."

"He's so cute. A pound puppy?"

"Nah, just a stray."

She straightened and pressed her hand into the flat of her back. "Let me ask you something. Do you think I should break up with Bryce?"

Okay, that had come out of the blue. And he was the last one to ask. He was tempted to sic her on Sawyer but that would be shitty even for him.

"Ava, I'm not your guy for that kind of stuff. Why don't you bounce it off Winter?"

"Oh my God, she hates Bryce. She thinks he's cheating on me. You know what? I think you and I should have an affair."

He choked on his own saliva. "Yeah, that's not gonna happen."

"Why?" She got in his face. "You don't think I'm attractive?"

"Attractive has nothing to do with it." He backed up. "You're too young for me and I'm not looking for a girlfriend."

"Who said anything about me being your girlfriend? I just want revenge sex. How old are you, anyway?"

"Too old for you. And too old for revenge sex. Why don't you break up with Bryce and find a nice guy your age?" For chrissake he didn't need this right now.

"You're a nice guy."

He grasped both her arms. "That's where you're wrong, Ava."

The bells above his door rang and he'd never been happier to have a visitor in his life. He let go of Ava and went up front to see who it was.

Gina stood at the cash register counter with a big foil pan in her hands. "I come bearing comfort food." She leaned over and kissed him on the cheek. "Oh, hey, Ava."

"Hi, Gina."

Gina noted the floral arrangement on the counter. "Aren't these beautiful."

"Compliments of Ava and Winter," Tuff said. All the attention was getting out of control.

"I've got to boogie," Ava stepped closer to the door. "We've got a big order for a wedding this weekend. See you guys."

"Deep condolences from Sawyer and me." Gina put the pan down and gave him hug. "How are you holding up?"

"Good. And thanks for this." He fingered the edge of the dish.

"Lasagna. There's enough there for an army but it freezes well. I've got to go prepare a lunch and dinner service now. But I wanted you to know how sorry we are about your mom and that we're here for you. Anything you need, you just call us." She kissed him again and flew out the door.

Short and sweet, the way he liked it. The pan didn't fit in his studio's compact fridge and if he went home, he'd never get anything done.

"Stay here, boy. I'll be right back," he called to the dog.

He took the lasagna over to Daltons in hopes he could borrow some refrigerator space before he went home for the evening. Nina, the young woman who usually worked the cash register, was nowhere to be found.

"I'll be right with you," a voice came from the back. It was Angie's voice. "Hey." She smiled when she saw him and struggled to lug in a big fruit crate filled with mandarin oranges.

"Let me get that for you." He put down his pan and grabbed the box. "Where's Nina?"

"Sick. Apparently, there's a cold going around. I hope I don't get it."

"Yeah, Winter's got it too."

"Ah, that's too bad. How about Ava?"

"She's fine." Crazy but as far as Tuff knew not infectious. "Could I stick this in one of your refrigerators for the day? If not, I can run home."

"Of course." She glanced at the pan. "Gina's lasagna?"

"Yep. How'd you know?"

"She told me she was bringing it over."

He bounced the crate in his hands. "Where do you want this?"

"Oh, sorry. Over there." She pointed to an empty space on one of the farm table produce displays. "Let's put the lasagna back here." She led him to a refrigerator in the rear of the store. "We don't really use this one, so no one will mess with it."

"Perfect. I owe you one."

He grazed her breasts as he tucked the dish into the fridge. They both broke away. She with streaks of red riding her cheeks. Now why couldn't she throw herself at him like Ava had done? He had to remind himself that she wasn't much older than Ava and even more off limits. At least Ava's proposition was for revenge sex against her boyfriend. He didn't think Angie was the hook-up type. And even if she were, it wasn't smart to play where you worked. And lived. Especially with the lady of the manor so to speak.

He followed her to the cash register counter where she had her big ledger open. "You still figuring that out?" He bobbed his chin at the book.

"Trying to. Do you mind if I ask you something about your shop? If it violates anything proprietary just stop me."

"Go ahead."

"Do you make a lot of sales from the shop?"

"Not as many as I make from my website, which are the big-ticket items. But the small things, the belts, wallets, satchels, that I have on the shelves. Yeah. I'd say they do pretty well. Why?"

She deliberated, then said, "Between you and me, Daltons isn't doing as well as my family had hoped. I just wondered if it's only us or everyone in the center."

It wasn't for lack of foot traffic that was for sure. Summer had been crazy and it hadn't slowed down since, especially on weekends.

"There's always a crowd here."

"Except they're not buying anything. And when they do, it's small stuff to eat at one of the picnic tables. And the colder it gets the less they even do that."

"Maybe you need to market more to the locals." Tuff was no retail expert. He attributed his success to the fact that he served a niche market.

"I thought about that. But we're a gourmet specialty store—a little pricey for everyday groceries. And even if we wanted to change our model, which I don't think we do, there is no way we can compete with the big chains in Auburn and Grass Valley."

He cocked his hip against the counter. "What are you planning to do?"

"I don't know yet. I've been trying to see what people buy, what they don't buy, what they're looking for and maybe tweak things a bit. I don't know if it'll be enough but it's something. I have a meeting with Gina, Charlie, and Aubrey later this week to throw ideas around."

"This is Gina's wheelhouse. I bet she'll have some solutions."

Angie puffed out a breath. "I hope so. Because to tell you the truth I'm in over my head."

He peered into her big blue eyes. "I think you're on the right track by studying the shopping patterns of your customers. You've got this."

Her lips inched up into a spectacular smile. "I'm glad one of us thinks so."

"I'll come get my lasagna before you close."

The trip to Daltons had taken longer than he'd planned. But it was good time spent, he grinned to himself. For the rest of the day, Tuff tried to avoid Ava.

* * * *

Angie locked up at six. The entire center was dead, except for the restaurant. Past the parking lot lights, it was pitch dark outside. Tuff had gone home an hour ago. She kicked herself for not closing earlier and walking home with him.

She zipped her jacket and crossed the lot on the south side of the center. Even though Dry Creek was below the snow line, it felt like they might get some flurries. It was that cold. The wind howled through the trees and she hugged herself.

The center was closer to Jace's than it was to her cabin. Maybe she'd hike to his ranch house and get a ride home. Or not. What was wrong with her? The ranch was the safest place on earth. Even the bears were harmless. She'd walked these trails, climbed these trees, and played in the creek her whole life. And it was less than a mile home. Shorter, if she cut through the grove of trees that stood between the edge of the center and her cabin. Darker though. Much darker.

She chose the gravel road, which was the longer route. But it at least had a sliver of moonlight to guide her way.

All day she'd had the eerie sensation of being watched. First, when she took out the trash in the alleyway behind Daltons. And again, when she went to the storage room to find some Thanksgiving decorations Charlie had left for the store. She was positive it was just her imagination. The residual effect of constantly having to look over her shoulder at The Farm, and later, when she'd gone into the program.

Both times, no one had been there. Not even a shadow. The sad truth of the matter was she'd had only four customers all day. A local couple who'd come in to buy organic Gravenstein apples. A woman with a baby who was desperately in need of diapers, which Daltons didn't carry. An elderly pair, who purchased four of Gina's cake mixes. And a group of skiers that came in for a case of locally brewed ale and a bottle of Sierra Vodka. None of them seemed sinister.

She told herself she was being ridiculous but picked up the pace just the same. The last hundred yards or so home, she ran, careful not to trip and fall. At least she'd worn tennis shoes, part of the bounty from her Beverly Hills closet that Wendy had brought during her visit.

By the time she reached the porch, her sweater clung to her back like a wet towel. Before going inside, she did a quick sweep of her surroundings. Nothing looked remotely amiss. Again, she chided herself for being paranoid.

She unlocked the door and went straight for the thermostat. It was like an icebox in the cabin. She exchanged her sweaty sweater for a sweatshirt and searched for something to eat that wouldn't require much fuss. Tuff's kitchen lights were on and she wondered if he was eating his lasagna.

She grabbed one of Gina's entrees from the freezer and popped it in the microwave. While she waited for the bell to ding, she removed Deputy US Marshal Earl Ryan's card from her wallet and stared at it until the phone number blurred.

You're being crazy, she told herself. Zane and Burt and the others were locked up, awaiting trial. And she was safely tucked away at Dry Creek Ranch, which for all intents and purposes was in the middle of nowhere.

She took her dinner to the living room and ate it on the sofa, vacillating on whether to call.

Always go with your gut instinct. It had been Earl's mantra when she'd first gone into WITSEC. *If something doesn't feel right, assume it isn't. Better safe than sorry.*

She picked up her phone and dialed his number. After three rings she was about to hang up when her ex-handler's booming voice said, "Hello."

"It's me, Angela."

Silence.

"All right, Katherine." She'd broken the rules by going back to her real name. Then again, she'd blown up the rules by leaving the program in the first place.

"Are you okay?"

"I'm great...Everything is really good."

"And you called just to let me know how well you're doing?"

She hated when he took that tone. "No, I called to see if there was anything new on the case."

"Nothing new as far as I know. Are you being careful?"

"Yes, but why do I have to be if everyone is locked up?"

"Always safer to be careful. Doesn't mean you can't live your life. You just shouldn't flaunt it."

She kicked her feet up on the coffee table. "What do you mean by flaunt?"

"Stay away from social media and by all that is holy, don't get on one of those reality shows."

She laughed. It had taken her awhile to figure out that Earl Ryan had a sense of humor. He was often so dry she'd wondered if he had a pulse at all. They were polar opposites. He was a staunch conservative, and she was what he called a "lefty radical." He was from a black working-class family and she was from a white privileged one. He was a Baptist. She was an agnostic. He thought she should've stayed in WITSEC. She disagreed.

But for all their differences, she loved him like a father. During all those years she'd lived in fear, there was one constant: Deputy Marshal Ryan would've laid his life down for hers.

"I won't do any reality shows, I promise." And social media had never been her bag anyway.

"Are you milking cows these days?"

"They're beef cattle, not milk cows. But no, I'm working in my family's grocery store on the ranch."

"That's good. Stay close to home but change up your routine regularly. Always stay alert."

"You're scaring me. Should I be scared?"

There was a long pause, then, "I think it's over, Angie. Even so, keep on your toes."

"Better safe than sorry," they said in unison. He'd said it so many times it was inscribed on her brain.

"What about you? How are things going? Did your son get into LSU?"

"Yep. Kid wants to be a criminal defense lawyer. Kill me now."

"You're bad, Earl. He'll make you proud, just watch and see."

Ryan let out an exaggerated sigh. "It's raining in Portland. How 'bout there?"

"No rain. But it feels cold enough to snow."

"Cissy's calling me, so I've got to go. You take care now. And if you ever…well, you've got my number."

"I've got your number." She started to hang up, then blurted, "Earl?"

"Yeah?"

"Uh…Say hi to Cissy for me."

"You got it."

She hung up, deciding that it was best she hadn't told him. Really, there was nothing to tell. It had been a long, emotional weekend with her family and her mind was playing tricks on her was all. Tomorrow, she'd go back to feeling secure.

She took the rest of her dinner and dumped it in her compost bin. Tuff's kitchen light was off, but she could see the flickering of his TV in the living room through the window. She stood there for a while, staring across the creek as the trees blew. Maybe a part of her hoped he'd see her and come over. Not because she was afraid because she wasn't. Not anymore.

After a few minutes, she gave up and turned on her own television.

Chapter 8

The coffeeshop was crowded for a Friday morning. The Mill County Cattlemen Association was having its monthly meeting. At least ten tables had been pushed together and there were enough cowboy hats hanging on hooks and racks to open a Western wear store.

Angie waved to her brother, Cash and Jace across the dining room. It was comical to see them with the group of ornery old men. Grandpa Dalton used to be a permanent fixture in the crew.

The restaurant looked exactly the way it had when she first started coming here with him as a little girl. Same pictures of cattle on the wall. Same revolving glass cake case. Same eating counter. Same metal stools. Same antique cash register.

"We should've picked a different day." Aubrey reached across the table for the cream and poured some into her coffee. "It'll be hard to hear over those guys."

"Who's that?" A woman, dripping in gold jewelry in a pink jogging suit, appeared to be having an argument with Laney.

"Tiffany," Aubrey and Charlie said at the same time.

"She was Jace's campaign manager," Charlie added.

"Really? She lives here?" To Angie she looked more Beverly Hills than Mill County, where anything other than jeans and cowboy boots was for church.

"Yep. Up on Deer Lane." Aubrey took the cream from Charlie and added a few drops to her own coffee. "Her husband used to own an insurance agency in the city. Beaucoup bucks."

"What's her problem with Laney?"

Both Aubrey and Charlie followed Angie's gaze to where the two women were having a heated discussion.

"That's how they always are." Aubrey waved her hand in the air. "Secretly, I think they're BFFs."

"At first I wasn't too crazy about her," Charlie said. "Now, she's like part of the family. You'd never know it by the way they swipe at each other, but Jace is crazy about her."

Gina came in the door and Aubrey waved her over. She popped her head inside the order window and yelled hi to Jimmy Ray before making her way to their table. "Sorry I'm late. My chef de cuisine was having a meltdown. You'd think he'd be appreciative of the job after being fired from four restaurants, but the man is a complete diva." She shook her head.

She glanced at their coffees and let out a groan. "What I wouldn't do for a cup? I miss it more than wine and that's saying something."

"I thought you could have wine when you're pregnant." Aubrey looked so panicked that it made Angie wonder if she wasn't pregnant herself.

"My doctor told me everything in moderation." Gina unconsciously polished the top of the saltshaker with her napkin. "The problem is I don't do moderation. So I'm going cold turkey. Did Laney take your orders yet?"

"Not yet." Out of the side of her eye, Angie saw Tiffany coming their way.

"Hi girls." She scooted next to Charlie, sharing the same chair. "You've got a new addition I see." She looked directly at Angie.

"This is our cousin, Angela Dalton," Charlie said. "She's Sawyer's sister."

"I didn't even know Sawyer had a sister." She stuck out her manicured hand and gave Angie a limp shake that was more like a squeeze. "Are you single?"

"Uh...yes." Angie exchanged glances with Gina, who shrugged. "Why?"

"My husband's nephew is coming for a visit. Newly divorced." She said it like that explained everything.

Aubrey rolled her eyes. "Angie isn't interested in your nephew, Tiff."

"He's a radiation oncologist. Makes over four-hundred thousand dollars a year." Tiffany looked down at her nails and buffed them with her thumb. "Of course, he has to pay alimony now."

"Is this woman bothering you?" Laney pulled up a fifth chair and joined them.

"I was trying to set up Angela with my nephew, Lawrence."

"The bald one? Uh-uh. Hell no." Laney practically pulled Angie into her ample lap. "This is my baby. She's not dating your ugly-ass nephew."

"Hey, Laney, do you think we can order now." Gina looked at her watch. "I've got a chef de cuisine who's liable to quit on me any minute."

"Well that's what you get for hiring that fancy pants from Los Angeles when you could've just hired someone local."

"Yeah, yeah." Gina tapped her watch with her two fingers.

"What do y'all want?"

They went around the table. Angie got her favorite, chicken and waffles. Laney went to the window and yelled their orders to Jimmy Ray, then ran off to greet a couple and a baby who appeared to be local. The rest of Tiffany's party showed up and she excused herself to join them.

Charlie started laughing. "I can't believe she tried to set you up. But that's Tiffany for you."

Aubrey snorted. "The woman's lost her mind."

Gina pulled her chair closer to the table. "I hate to be rude, but can we talk shop before I have to skedaddle?"

Angie reached under the table for her purse and pulled out her notebook. "I made some notes."

Gina, Aubrey and Charlie waited for her to continue.

She braced herself. "I don't know any other way to say this but...the store isn't earning its keep." She turned the notebook so everyone could see the numbers. "That's what we're paying in expenses. I broke it down into categories. Between salaries, merchandise, and the electric bill, we're spending more than we're bringing in."

"Let me see that." Gina pulled the notebook closer and examined Angie's figures. "Shit."

Shit was right.

Charlie raised her hands to calm everyone. "We knew it would take a while. We're still getting the word out. In my opinion it's too early to panic."

"I'm with Charlie," Aubrey said. "I think the key is coming up with ways to bolster business, not freak out."

"Well I'm kind of freaking out," Gina said.

Angie bit the inside of her cheek. Gina really wasn't going to like Angie's next bit of news. She cleared her throat. "I looked at some of the other numbers too. Specifically, what seems to be selling and what isn't."

Three pairs of eyes looked at her expectantly.

"The produce, jams, and the other canned goods, especially the stuff in the pretty packaging is doing well. The baked goods also appear to be somewhat of a hit. Spirits aren't exactly flying off the shelf, but the profit margins are so good that it's where we make most of our money."

"And what isn't doing well?" Charlie asked.

She hesitated, then said, "Gina's frozen entrees and the meat from the butcher shop. In fact, I had to clear three shelves yesterday with stuff that was past its expiration dates."

"Oh boy, this isn't good." Gina reached for Aubrey's coffee. Aubrey slapped her hand away.

When their food came, they stopped talking just long enough for their server to move on.

"This is the thing," Angie continued. "Most of our shoppers are tourists either on their way to Tahoe, Sacramento, or the Bay Area. In some cases, even Los Angeles. They're not going to lug perishables halfway across California. Or Nevada for that matter."

"Then we should target locals." Aubrey took a bite of her Jasper, a steak sandwich named for Angie's grandfather.

"Some. Sure," Angie said around a bite of fried chicken. "But honestly, our business model is more Dean & DeLuca than Safeway. Folks around here just aren't willing to pay our prices. Most of them know our producers and can go straight to the source."

"I don't know. It seems like a lot of people like Tiffany, who have moved here from the city, would appreciate what we have to offer," Charlie said. "We just have to find them."

"No, Angie's right." Gina reached over and snagged a forkful of Angie's waffle. "We have to gear our merchandise toward tourists. My frozen entrees will survive with or without Daltons. What I'm concerned about is the butcher shop. It's a big part of the model and was designed to give us a more lucrative alternative to selling our beef wholesale. Direct to the consumer was where we were supposed to make our money from the cattle operation."

"What do we do?" Angie was out of ideas.

"We'll have to think about it and figure out a way to make it work. Failure isn't an option."

Okay, that certainly put the pressure on. "Maybe we go to mail order," Angie suggested.

"That's definitely part of the plan. But shipping meat ain't cheap. And why have brick and mortar if we're not selling that way?"

"We have to bring the guys into this conversation." Aubrey wiped the corner of her mouth with a napkin. "Maybe they have some ideas."

Jace had seen the numbers. Angie suspected if he had any suggestions, he would've told her already. She had hoped that Gina would know exactly what to do. But it appeared that she was just as flummoxed as Angie.

"What about the mixes? How are they doing?" Gina asked.

"They're doing fine." Not taking the world by storm but they were moving better than some of the other items. "Your housewares are the biggest hit. I propose that we dedicate more space to them and focus on showcasing the items better. Maybe Charlie and Aubrey could put their magic touch in that area. Even bring over one of those cute painted hoosier cabinets from Refind to display some of the dishes."

Charlie and Aubrey nodded with enthusiasm. "We could for sure do that," Charlie said. "We also have this great iron rack Aubrey designed that we could bring over for hanging some of the Gina DeRose pots and pans. We'll get right on it if you think it'll help."

"I do. And, Gina, if we could increase inventory, I think we could at least do well in that area."

"I'll have my shipping guy get on it. There's a good mark up on the kitchen stuff, so I'm in total favor of beefing up our stock. What about the booze? Should we work on that as well?"

"It couldn't hurt."

"But let's not turn Daltons into a liquor store," Charlie said. "It's one thing to carry local wine and craft beer, even spirits from that distillery in Truckee. But if we're talking about adding Coors and Bud Light, I think that's a bad idea and counter to what we're trying to create."

"Absolutely." Aubrey motioned to the server that she needed a coffee topper. "I'm in total agreement with Charlie on that front."

"Okay, nothing but locally made booze," Gina agreed. "But maybe you two could also wave some fairy dust on the liquor displays. I'm telling you guys, alcohol is where you make all your money. If we could sell it by the glass at the store I would."

They all laughed.

"I think the best thing is for me to continue watching shopping patterns and see where else we can make adjustments." According to Tuff, in the summer, shoppers had used the outdoor picnic tables. Perhaps she could gear some of their merchandise toward takeout.

"Absolutely." Gina reached for the pepper and sprinkled a good dose on what was left of her biscuits and gravy. "But if we wait too long, we'll go bankrupt. In other words, we've got to nip the bleeding in the bud. What do you say we meet again in a week and reassess?"

Angie didn't know if a week would make much difference, but it certainly didn't hurt to meet. "Should we bring in Sawyer, Jace, and Cash this time?"

"Yes," everyone answered.

"Let's do it at the restaurant early," Gina said. "That way Cash and Jace can get to work." She looked at both Charlie and Aubrey. "Will that work with getting the kids to school?"

"We'll make it happen," Charlie said, and Aubrey bobbed her head in agreement.

Gina flagged over Laney, who was gabbing at Tiffany's table with a few ladies Angie didn't recognize. Although the town still looked the same—the shops on Mother Lode Road and the post office and train station on Main Street hadn't changed one iota—the population had grown. It would take her a while to get to know all the new faces.

Then there was Laney and Jimmy Ray, who she'd known her entire life and had accepted her sudden reappearance without hesitation. Of course, Sawyer had given them a varnished story of why she'd been missing for the last six years. Though she suspected they knew more than they were letting on.

Laney hustled over. "What do you need, sugar?"

"Can I get the rest of this to go?" Gina nervously looked at her watch again.

Laney went behind the counter and came back with a cardboard container and started to take Gina's plate.

"I'll do it." Gina scraped the remains of her biscuits and gravy into the to-go box.

Laney watched the door as a second wave of diners filtered into the coffeeshop. "I'll see you girls later when I come by the center to drop off a new batch of sarsaparilla."

She started for the front of the restaurant when Gina grabbed her arm. "How's business at the kiosk?"

Laney let out a whistle. "Whoo-wee, Me and Jimmy Ray are finally getting a new car."

When she left to seat a family of five, Gina looked at the rest of them pointedly. "We've got to figure this out. For now, though, I've got a bitchy chef de cuisine to deal with. See you back at the ranch." She left a wad of cash on the table and made her way out the door.

Angie, Charlie, and Aubrey finished eating, steering the conversation away from any more shop talk. They paid their bill at the cash register and shared a ride to the ranch, squished in Aubrey's old Volvo station wagon.

If Angie didn't know better, she'd think the woman lived out of her car. There were fabric samples all over the back seat and a box of paint chips on the floor. The trunk was filled with so many catalogs and racks of various flooring and wood samples it was a wonder she could see out of her rearview mirror.

"I know, it's a mess." Aubrey glanced over her shoulder at the back seat. "It's the one area of my life where I allow myself to be disorganized. Sorry."

It was true. From all outward appearances Aubrey was organized. Angie had seen her office and conference room in the old barn that had been turned into Refind. Both were immaculate.

"No worries." Angie laughed. It was only a short drive from town to the ranch.

Charlie hung her head over the front passenger seat. "How's Tuff doing? I brought him enchiladas the other day, but he wasn't home. I haven't seen him since his mother passed."

"He seems to be okay." Angie emphasized the word "seems." With Tuff it was hard to tell. Though she felt like she'd made a breakthrough with him the other day, the man was far from an open book.

"I didn't even know he had family. He never talks about anyone."

"I don't think they were close." Angie didn't want to say too much, knowing that Tuff guarded his privacy.

"That's what Jace said. Sad."

Sad didn't even begin to describe it. Not only had he lost his mother to suicide. But his father had been taken from him violently at the tender age of eight. Angie hadn't stopped thinking about it since Tuff told her. But she kept the information to herself. She got the impression it wasn't something Tuff shared with others. Just her.

"Have you seen his dog, Buddy?" she asked, turning to a cheerier topic.

"He got a dog?" Aubrey sounded surprised.

"He said he was going to talk to Cash about whether it was okay." Shoot, maybe Angie shouldn't have said anything.

Aubrey laughed. "Cash loves dogs. Why would he care?"

"That's what I thought but he wasn't sure about the pet policy as far as the cabin."

"There is no pet policy. Except snakes. He can't have a snake." Aubrey turned onto the Daltons private road. "Who wants to get it?"

"I will." Charlie got out of the car and swung open the large iron gate.

"I keep trying to talk the guys into an electric one." Aubrey drove through and Charlie relocked the gate behind her.

It seemed gratuitous to Angie, given that there was a public road with a cattle guard that went through the ranch to the business center. She supposed her brother and cousins kept the gate, which had been erected by her late grandfather long before Angie was born, to pay homage to him.

"You want to be dropped home first or go straight to Daltons?" Aubrey waited for Charlie to get back in the car before pulling forward.

"Home. I left the ledger there."

Aubrey dropped her in front of her cabin and Charlie reminded her about dinner at the ranch house that evening.

She jogged up her porch stairs, opened the screen and looked for the tiny rolled up piece of paper she'd stuck in the stop of the door frame exactly two inches beneath the door's top hinge. It was a trick Earl had taught her.

The paper was gone. She froze, wondering whether she should open the door. The paper could've fallen on its own, she supposed. Or someone could've broken in. She backed down the stairs and stood there, paralyzed.

If she called Sawyer she'd sound like a lunatic. *Someone's watching me.* There was absolutely no evidence of anything sinister going on. It was simply PTSD and her overactive imagination.

Yet, the paper was gone.

"Everything okay?"

She jumped, nearly coming out of her skin.

A large hand pressed against her back. "Sorry," Tuff said. "Didn't mean to sneak up on you. But it looked like something spooked you."

She swallowed hard. "I thought I saw a mouse scurry under my door."

"Let's have a look." Before she could stop him, he climbed up her porch stairs and tried her door. "Throw me the keys."

"Don't go in."

He turned to where she was standing at the bottom of the steps, his brown eyes filled with laughter. "You think the mouse will get me?" He caught her gaze and the laughter was gone. "What's going on, Angie?"

"Nothing...nothing." She came up onto the porch and handed him the keys. "I just hate mice."

He unlocked the door and went inside. She followed behind him and did a quick visual turn around the front room. Nothing looked amiss. She spotted her rolled up paper on the floor, wedged between the corner of the door and the frame casing. It had probably slipped down on its own, she told herself. Next time, she would use a fatter roll of paper or Earl's fishing line trick.

Tuff searched the cabin. From the way he was looking behind doors and in closets, Angie got the impression he wasn't looking for her fictional mouse. He was kind enough, though, not to call her on her bluff.

"Does it look the way you left it?" His eyes drifted to the bra draped from her shower rod, she'd hung to dry.

"Mm-hmm." She followed him out of her bathroom to the kitchen.

"I've been home all morning. Haven't seen a soul." He looked at her for a long time, assessing. "Doesn't mean I couldn't have missed something."

"I'm just being ridiculous." She dropped her eyes from his penetrating stare.

"You think about getting an alarm?"

It wasn't a bad idea except for the fact that it would alert her family that she didn't feel as safe as she had let on. "It's nothing. I'm just used to living in the city where break-ins are rampant, I guess."

He gave her another look. "I thought you lived in a little place outside Taos."

"Yeah, but I grew up in LA."

He lifted a single brow. "What made you think someone broke in?" It was obvious he didn't believe a word she'd said.

"The door wasn't the way I left it." Truth. Just not the whole story.

"Look, Angie, whatever trouble you've got is none of my business. But you can drop the act. Even from my front room window I could see whatever happened here had you petrified. If you don't want to talk to me about it, I suggest you talk to your brother. Or if it's a police matter, Jace."

"I will," she promised but had no intention of telling anyone that she was turning into a bundle of paranoia.

Chapter 9

Tuff got in his truck and drove to his studio. He couldn't say for sure what had frightened Angie, but he had a few ideas. Someone was obviously hassling her. An abusive ex. Maybe a stalker. It fit in with why Gina would've asked him to look out for her. Well, he couldn't do that if he didn't know what she was up against. And Angie wasn't talking.

I don't need the headache, he told himself. The last time he tried to protect a woman…But he liked Angie—probably too much for his own good—and he hated to see her scared. And what he witnessed back at her cabin bordered on terrified.

There was a customer waiting at his door when he got to the shop. Buddy let out an uncustomary growl and bared his teeth at the man. It surprised Tuff. The dog usually shrank back when he met strangers. But he was never aggressive. It put Tuff on his guard.

"Can I help you?"

"This your shop?"

"Yep." Tuff held his key ring in his hand but didn't make a move to unlock the door.

While there was nothing threatening about the man, who was average in every way, including height, build and demeanor, animals had a keen sense of danger. Tuff was taking his cues from Buddy, who had stopped growling but was watching the man intently.

"Thought I'd poke around while my wife's at the florist. Peeked in your window. Man, you have some nice stuff."

"Thank you."

"Is it custom? Or imported?"

"Custom." Tuff played with his keys, pretending to find the right one while he assessed the guy. He was younger than Tuff, maybe in his mid-thirties, and was dressed like everyone else in the Sierra foothills. Jeans, flannel shirt, beanie hat, and steel-toed boots. The guy was probably in construction.

"You local?" Tuff did a quick scan of the parking lot. Ava's vintage Chevy pickup, Winter's 4Runner, and a number of other vehicles he recognized were scattered across the lot. There was a steel gray Ford F-150 parked in one of the spots closest to the shop. He memorized the plate.

"Yeah. We live in Colfax. My wife owns a hair salon and wanted fresh flowers for her shop." The man nudged his head at Tuff's plate glass door. "You have any holsters?"

Tuff unlocked the door. "Not at the moment." He occasionally made them for gun collectors out of state. But most of California didn't allow open carry. And in the sparsely populated counties that did, it was uncommon to find someone wearing a handgun in a fancy hand-tooled leather holster. Some might call it downright douchey.

He flicked on the lights and let the guy in. Instead of going straight to his dog bed, Buddy stood by Tuff's side.

"I didn't catch your name," Tuff said.

"John. John Black."

John Black wandered around the store, examining various items. "So you make this stuff yourself, huh?"

"Yep. I mostly do custom saddles."

John picked up a wallet, glanced at the price tag and let out a whistle. "A little rich for my blood."

"That's Italian leather. A little pricier than the wallets over there." He pointed to the shelf closer to the door.

John wandered over and sorted through the various billfolds. Buddy found a spot on the floor near the check-out counter but never took his eyes off the guy. A woman, carrying a bouquet of flowers, came inside and joined John.

They browsed a little longer, then John said, "Thanks. Really great stuff" and left with his wife.

Tuff watched them get in the Ford and drive away. Buddy got up, stretched, and went to his usual spot under Tuff's cutting table.

"Be right back, boy." Tuff locked the door and headed to the floral shop.

He'd seen Ava a couple times around the center since their weirdness the other day. Luckily, she'd dropped the whole sex revenge proposition and acted like it had never happened. Which suited him just fine.

Winter was at the front of the shop when he walked in. "Hi, Tuff."

Ava wandered out from the back when she heard his name.

"The woman who was just in here…you ever see her before?"

Winter glanced at Ava. "I don't know. Maybe. Why?"

"Her husband was over at my shop. I can't put my finger on it but something about him seemed off." Truly the only thing irregular was Buddy's reaction to the guy. For all Tuff knew, the dude reminded the dog of someone shitty from his past. Other than that, John Black seemed perfectly normal.

"I don't remember her coming in before," Ava said. "But I have a lousy memory."

"She seemed nice." Winter put down the tool she was using to remove thorns from a pile of long-stem roses. "She said something about having a salon and how she liked decorating with fresh flowers. She wanted something fallish, lots of oranges and reds."

Tuff was probably overreacting. The ranch seemed like a fairly unlikely place for a holdup, especially given that the county sheriff lived on the property. And there was only one way out and one way in. Not to mention that the main highway was miles away. He supposed he was being overly suspicious because of Angie and what had happened at her cabin that morning. "No worries. Just thought I'd check it out."

He returned to his own shop, jotted down John's license plate number on a post-it, and shoved it in a drawer. For the rest of the day, he didn't give it a second thought.

Around three, Sawyer strolled in. "I needed a walk and something other than my computer screen to look at it."

"What're you working on?" Tuff finished packaging his latest saddle, a special order from a saddle bronc rider who wanted something light with a cantle that would let him sit low in the seat.

"An article for *GQ* about the endangerment of the cowboy way of life." Sawyer let out a wry chuckle. "Not my idea but my editor thought I was the perfect guy to do it."

Tuff stopped what he was doing. "You think we're endangered?"

Sawyer huffed out a breath. "Let's put it this way, when my grandfather was alive, he would've laughed at the idea of turning part of the ranch into a shopping center. Hell, he would've downright forbidden it. But here we are because we didn't have a choice. It was either this or being forced to sell to developers. When my folks bought Beals Ranch next door, leasing some of the land to a grape grower paid off twenty times better than the cattle." He hitched his shoulders. "So yeah, I think the cowboy way of life is on its way to extinction. At least if we don't get more creative."

Tuff had never owned a ranch, though he'd worked on enough of them to see how the cost of land, hard-hitting drought, and the sheer amount of work involved was making it harder to stay afloat. It was sad. Being a cowboy had saved his life. Without it there was no telling where he'd be right now.

Sawyer took one of the stools and watched as Tuff finished taping up his package for shipping. "What do you have going today?"

"Just the usual. I've got to finish a big job for a rodeo queen who wants a lot of dazzle and a couple of boot bags for some Texas oil men."

"How's everything else going?" Sawyer looked at him pointedly the way men do when they didn't want to come right out and ask a personal question.

"My mother and I weren't close if that's what you're getting at." It was an understatement, and he was tired of saying it. But it was a cleaner version of the truth. "I hope she's finally found peace."

Sawyer reached over and patted Tuff's shoulder. "I know I already told you but I'm really sorry, man."

The Daltons were a good bunch. Tuff was lucky as hell to be associated with them. But he was ready to put the death of his mother behind him. He'd rather discuss Angie and what the hell was going on with her? He questioned whether to tell Sawyer what had happened that morning, ultimately deciding that it was up to Angie to tell her brother.

Still, he wished he knew more about her background. The story about Taos seemed fishy to him. There were rumors that she'd been estranged from her family for a while, that they hadn't been on speaking terms. But rumors were just rumors. There'd been plenty about him, too. Most of it bullshit.

He considered how to broach the subject without letting on too much. But Sawyer was an investigative reporter. He'd know in an instant that Tuff was digging for information.

"You and my sister seem to be friendly." Okay. It looked like Sawyer was going to start the conversation. His tone, however, sounded like a warning to Tuff.

"We're neighborly." Tuff had spent many a sleepless night wishing it was a neighbors-with-benefits situation. But he obviously kept that thought to himself.

"She's coming out of a bad few years. I'm trying to give her space but at the same time am pretty protective."

Again, Tuff detected a warning.

"I hear you loud and clear, Sawyer. It's not like that. Gina asked me to look out for Angie. That's all I'm doing."

"I appreciate that." Sawyer rubbed the back of his neck. "You're both grown-ass adults...I'm just being a big brother."

"That's your right. Not to step out of line here, but what happened? That is if you don't mind me asking." Tuff was surprised by his own audacity. It wasn't like him to ask questions, especially when he'd spent a lifetime avoiding having to answer them.

Sawyer seemed surprised as well. They'd never had a deeper conversation than the weather.

He seemed to ponder the prudence of discussing it, then finally said, "Man troubles."

It was what Tuff had suspected. Though unlike his mother, Angie struck him as a person who would stand up for herself. It certainly made sense why Sawyer didn't want him sniffing around his sister. He'd never hit a woman, but he wasn't exactly what you would call good boyfriend material.

"This dude pose any threat?" he asked as casually as possible.

"No." Sawyer paused, then in a steely voice said, "He's been dealt with."

"Good."

Chapter 10

Angie spent a week watching the buying patterns of Daltons' customers. The more snow they got in the mountains the bigger the crowds. Gina's steakhouse continued to be the draw. But word of Laney and Jimmy Ray's sarsaparilla had also spread, and skiers flocked to the kiosk in droves.

Inevitably, visitors came in the store, looking for something to eat with their sarsaparilla. Most often they settled on salty snacks or sweets, which Angie couldn't keep stocked fast enough. Liquor sales were also good. And adding more of Gina's kitchenware and gadgets, turned out to be a smart call. Fans of her FoodFlicks' show filled their baskets with them.

But the increase in revenue still wasn't enough to show a profit. The frozen entrees continued to sit in the cold case, taking up space. And no one was buying steaks or roasts or even ribs. Most of what sold were items people could eat immediately. It was too cold to sit outside, and some customers had taken to eating the snacks they'd purchased right inside the store.

"Nina, I'm taking a break." Angie took off her Daltons' apron and hung it on a hook in the back.

She shrugged into her jacket and circled the center until she got to Tuff's shop. In the last several days, she hadn't seen much of him. Occasionally, he'd come out onto his front porch to call Buddy in, then disappear inside. And he'd missed coming by Daltons for his late afternoon cookie fix. An insecure person might think he was avoiding her.

She opened the door and welcomed a blast of warm air. He had a fire lit in the wood-burning stove. "Anyone home?"

"Be right there."

She hopped up on a stool, not wanting to interrupt whatever he was working on. There were a few new pieces of merchandise on the shelves, including a pair of riding gloves that were perhaps the most beautiful she'd ever seen. She went over to have a closer look and tried them on. They were too big, but the leather was so buttery soft that she didn't want to take them off.

"When was the last time you went riding?"

She looked up from her hands and turned to face Tuff. "Oh it's been years."

He came up alongside her. "Why so long?"

Like always his nearness did something to her insides.

"I don't know." She pulled the gloves off and carefully laid them back on the shelf. "I just haven't had the chance I guess." The plan had been to eventually get horses on The Farm, which of course never happened. And in Portland it had been impossible.

"You have the chance now. The Dalton stable is filled with horses."

She'd avoided the barn. It reminded her too much of how she missed her grandfather.

"One of these days I'll get down there. Now, I've got my hands full with trying to save the store and butcher shop."

He moved away from her, putting the counter between them. She had the sudden urge to grab him back.

"How's that going?" he asked.

She waggled her hand from side to side, then sagged onto a stool. "I'm thinking of putting in a coffee station and clearing a space inside for some café tables."

"Sounds like a good idea."

"I'm worried I'll be competing with the restaurant and Laney and Jimmy Ray."

He contemplated that for a second, then said, "No one is going to the restaurant for coffee, and nothing can compete with Laney and Jimmy Ray's sarsaparilla. It's in a class of its own."

He was right about that. And it was just coffee for goodness sake.

"I'll talk to them about it," she said. "But honestly I doubt adding coffee will increase our sales that much."

"I don't know about that. Starbucks seems to be doing pretty well." He winked and her pulse did somersaults.

He looked especially good today. His green Henley picked up his deep brown eyes and showed off the width of his shoulders. And while she wouldn't call his jeans snug, they hugged him in all the right places. He'd traded in his square toed cowboy boots for a pair of pointed ones.

It suddenly hit her that he might be dressed for a date. The thought, though it shouldn't have, depressed her.

"You going somewhere after work? You look dressed up."

"Yeah?" He looked down at his shirt as if he'd forgotten what he had on. "No, not unless you count the coffeeshop. I was thinking of going for dinner. Between you and me, I'm a little tired of funeral food."

It took her a second in between silent cheers to remember all the casseroles and dishes everyone had brought him after his mother died. "I can see that. You want company?"

They both had to eat. Why do it alone?

He didn't answer at first. And she felt a combination of embarrassment and guilt. She'd sort of sprung that on him. And now his back was against the wall. How did he gracefully say no?

"I'm sorry, I forgot I have other plans." She tried to save him.

His mouth quirked. "Yeah, like what?" Clearly, he didn't believe her.

She searched for something that sounded plausible but wasn't that quick on her feet.

"Let's do it." He was laughing at her. "What time do you get off?"

"I should probably stick around until six." She locked eyes with him. "Are you sure? For a minute there you kind of looked like a deer caught in a really bright pair of headlights."

"No, I didn't."

"Yes, you did." She got down from the stool. "You want me to come over to your cabin when I'm ready?"

"Nah, I'll come and get you in my truck at the store. Unless you need to go home first."

She would've liked to have changed into something a little less boring than a pair of leggings and a sweater. A dress maybe. But now it would make her look like she thought it was a date, which she didn't.

"Nope. Pick me up after work. That sounds good."

She returned to Daltons and watched the clock. At six sharp, she peeked outside into the glow of the parking lot lights. There was Tuff, climbing down from his Ram pickup.

He opened the door to find her standing there. "You ready to go?"

"Ready." He put his hand at the small of her back and led her to the passenger seat door.

"Where's Buddy?" she asked as he got in beside her.

"I took him home, gave him his kibble, and set him up in front of the TV." He backed out and pulled onto the road. "What do you say we ditch the coffeeshop and try this Italian place in Nevada City I like?"

"Sounds great," though she wondered at the change of plans. Was he worried that folks in Dry Creek would see them together and assume they were more than friends?

Maybe he's just in the mood for Italian food, you ever think of that?

They caught Highway 49 and climbed steeper up the grade into the pine trees. Nevada City was only a quick car ride from Dry Creek, but it had more shops and restaurants. Like Dry Creek, it was a Gold Rush town but attracted ten times the tourists. With its quaint Victorian downtown and old Western charm, it frequently made the "best small-town" lists. In comparison, Dry Creek was just a barely discernable dot on the map.

"Do you go to this Italian place a lot?" The cab of Tuff's truck was so quiet that Angie felt like she had to carry the conversation.

"Not a lot but when I do it's always good." He slid her a sideways glance. "Are you hungry?"

"Starved." She hadn't eaten since breakfast.

"You think any more about that coffee bar?"

"I did. I'll probably call a meeting next week. If everyone is on board, I'll talk to Laney and Jimmy Ray about it. I don't want to step on anybody's toes."

"I hear ya."

Nevada City was lit up like a Christmas tree, reminding Angie just how romantic the little town was. The sidewalks down the main drag were jammed with people and it didn't look like there were any parking spaces along the street. Friday night.

Tuff found one at the top of the hill, though Angie didn't know how he'd fit his truck in the tiny space, which looked like it would only accommodate a Mini Cooper. But by some miracle he shoehorned his Ram in.

"Wow, you're a hell of a parallel parker."

He chuckled. "It's from years of running farm equipment. I know how to get in and out of tight corners." He came around to her side and opened the door.

Angie had never been into male gallantry. In fact, she thought it was a method to keep women in their place. But she had to admit that Tuff's manners were impeccable. And call her a hypocrite but she kind of liked the attention he showed her.

"It's hopping here tonight," she said as they walked down the hill, sharing the sidewalk with families and couples and teenagers milling in front of the shops and cafes.

"I hope there's not a long wait at the restaurant." He led her through an alleyway to a small cobble-stone street. There on the corner was Scola La Pasta.

The inside was cozy. The wood-fire pizza ovens threw off enough heat to keep the restaurant warm. On one wall was a mural of Venice. Above the fresco was a faux balcony and a trompe-l'oeil painting of a window with real shutters. Cute in a kitschy sort of way. Definitely old school.

The hostess was about Angie's age and couldn't take her eyes off Tuff. They waited less than ten minutes before she seated them in the corner, far from the door. She lit the votive in the center of their table, making sure to give Tuff an eyeful of her cleavage. Angie credited him for not noticing. Or at least, pretending to not notice.

"Your server will be right with you." The hostess sashayed off in a tight black skirt.

"What's good?" Angie studied the menu.

"I usually get the veal piccata." When Angie looked stricken, he said, "What?"

"Do you know how they raise veal? They lock them in tiny crates where the calves can't even turn around. It's torture."

"Okay, thanks for that image. I guess I'll just get the chicken piccata now."

She didn't have the heart to tell him how broiler chickens were raised in this country. "I think I'll get the eggplant parmesan."

He tilted his head and looked at her through the glow of the candle. "You sure the eggplant wasn't abused?"

"Ha, ha, very funny." She did wonder if it was organic, though.

The server came to take their drink orders.

"You want to get a bottle of wine?" Tuff asked Angie.

She'd gotten the impression the last time they'd had wine that he wasn't too crazy about it. "I'll just get a glass of the house chianti."

"Then I'll get a pint of whatever you have on tap," he told the server. "Is Peroni okay?"

He gave the server a thumbs up. She left and returned a few minutes later with their drinks and took their meal orders. Besides the chicken and eggplant, Tuff got an antipasto plate to share for a starter.

"Good choice." She glanced around the restaurant, which was starting to fill up. "And a nice break from the coffeeshop. But don't tell Laney."

"Nope. The woman scares me." He grinned and those legendary not-quite dimples came out to play.

"So what've you been up to all week? I haven't seen you around much."

He took a long pull on his beer. "Working mostly. Putting in some late hours to finish a few projects and get 'em out in the mail before the Christmas rush starts. You?" He put his beer down and held her gaze.

"Not much. I had dinner with my family at Jace's the other night. And dinner with Sawyer and Gina at the restaurant another. Other than that, I've been mostly focused on figuring out what to do about Daltons and the butcher shop."

"No more mice?" He watched her closely.

"Nope. No mice." That eerie sensation of being watched had disappeared. She chalked it up to feeling more settled and to having a routine. Still, she was careful to vary her hours at the store and take alternative routes to and from her cabin. As Earl had taught her it was never safe to be too predictable.

"Good." He toyed with his napkin before laying it in his lap. "Give me your phone."

"Huh? Why?

He made the give me sign with his hand. "I want to put my number in it and get yours."

She dug through her purse and handed him her phone. It was brand new. In WITSEC she had a cheap disposable that was only supposed to be used for work and to reach Earl and any of her other handlers.

He quickly found her contact icon, tapped on it, and plugged in his digits. "What's yours?"

She ticked off her number and he entered it into his own phone.

"Call me if you have any trouble...with mice."

"You think I'm a wackjob, don't you?"

"Not in the least." He took another slug of his Peroni. "I'm not kidding, Angie. Call me."

She wouldn't hesitate to call him if she thought she was in danger. But the other day she'd overreacted. Even Earl, who was the world's greatest worrywart, believed she was in the clear. Safe. And there had been no warning signs to indicate otherwise.

"It won't be necessary. But if it is, I'll call you," she said, wondering exactly what he knew. While her family would never get into the details of her past, she wouldn't put it past any one of them to ask Tuff to be her guardian angel.

Their antipasto came. She wasn't lying when she said she was starved and dived in. Their entrees followed. Scola La Pasta certainly didn't skimp on portion size.

Her eggplant was delicious. "Try this." She held a forkful of her dish to his mouth.

He took a bite. "Mmm. It's good. You want to try my chicken?" He started to cut her a piece.

"No thanks. I'll have enough trouble eating what I have." She stared down at her plate full of food.

"Yeah, they don't mess around here. Probably why I like the place so much." He took a bite of his spaghetti and pointed his fork at her. "Save room for dessert. Their tiramisu is off the hook."

"So how is it that you became a saddle maker?" It was an unusual profession and she'd been meaning to ask him how he came to it. He'd already told her it hadn't been his first choice as far as vocations.

"By accident. I've always been good with my hands." He bit back a grin, knowing exactly how that had sounded. Maybe he even intended it to be flirtatious. It was hard to tell with Tuff, who she was learning was rather wry.

"I think I told you that I started out riding the rodeo circuit. To save money I repaired all my own tack. I got proficient enough at it that I started doing it for other cowboys. Later, when I worked as a ranch hand, I became the go-to guy for any kind of leather repair. Slowly, I worked up to making small stuff. Belts, leads, boot bags, even a few bridles. I had a flair for it and moved on to bigger things and finally saddles. I took everything to the National Finals Rodeo, rented a booth, and sold out. I also got a couple of orders for custom saddles. The rest is history."

"Impressive. And totally self-taught, huh?"

"For the most part. I took a four-day hands-on seminar with a guy in Arizona. Learned a lot. But, yeah, mostly trial and error."

"What event did you ride in the rodeo?"

"Tie down roping and occasionally bull dogging."

It was an interesting trajectory. "Were you pro?" Angie didn't know all that much about the sport. But her grandfather had sure been a fan. He took his grandkids to all the local rodeos and he and Jace used to go every December to the finals in Vegas.

"Yes, ma'am. But it sure wasn't making me rich."

She nearly asked if his saddlery was, but it was a crass question. And what did it matter as long as he was happy?

"You know," he leaned across the table and stabbed a bocconcini with his fork and popped it into his mouth, "I never talked so much until I met you."

Her mouth curved up. "Is that a bad thing?"

"Nope. But it's your turn now, darlin'. Tell me about this fancy degree of yours and what you did in Taos."

She should've expected the question but was completely unprepared, so she went with the truth. "I founded a farm and food co-op. We'd planned to distribute the food we grew to needy communities, teach them how to grow their own in vacant lots, backyards, and anywhere there was a strip of empty land."

"But?"

"But what?"

"You said planned to like it didn't happen."

"No, it didn't." Her gaze dropped to the table. "Other people got involved and they had a different mission statement. I eventually left."

He leaned forward in his chair. "What was their mission statement?"

She raised her face and looked him in the eye. "I'm not at liberty to say." At some point, after the trial, she could probably talk about it. Until then, the feds had asked her not to discuss the case. She was hoping she'd never have to testify but if she did it was better if she saved the details for the jury. "And I would appreciate it if you didn't tell anyone about this conversation." She might be a poor judge of character, but she knew intrinsically that Tuff didn't gossip.

He studied her and she could tell he was trying to piece the little she'd divulged together. There had been no press about The Farm and no publicity about the arrests. Everything had been done under a shroud of secrecy. Not even someone with a good imagination could unravel the nightmare she'd lived through.

"You got it," he said. "Just tell me one thing. Is what happened in Taos have anything to do with whatever it was that you were afraid of that day at your cabin?"

She shook her head. "No, that was just me being ridiculous." She glanced around the restaurant. "Where do you think our server went? I'm ready for that tiramisu now."

He got the hint and flagged the waitress over. They shared a tiramisu and a panna cotta over coffee. By the time they left, her sweater felt two times tighter.

It was colder now than when they'd gotten here and she naturally gravitated closer to Tuff to gather warmth. For a second, she thought he might put his arm around her—she wanted him to—but he only adjusted his cowboy hat and let his hands fall to his sides. Despite the temperature drop, they took their time strolling back to his truck, looking in shop windows. It was such a pretty night.

"Thank you for dinner," she said. "It was supposed to be my treat. I'm the one who inserted myself into your plans. You should've let me pick up the check."

"Next time."

She hoped there was a next time but with Tuff she couldn't be sure. He was a tough nut to crack. Perhaps the reason for his name. "What's Tuff short for? Or is it a nickname?"

"Ted's my given name. Theodore actually." He rolled his eyes. "People have been calling me Tuff for so long I can't remember where it came from. But it's better than Theodore."

"I kind of like Theodore."

He pulled a face. "I guess it's better than Sue."

She didn't get the reference at first and then remembered the Johnny Cash song. Grandpa Dalton used to play it. "Sue definitely doesn't suit you."

Even though they'd ambled, they got to Tuff's truck sooner than Angie would've liked. The evening was coming to a close and she didn't want it to end. She considered suggesting that they go for a drink but didn't want to push her luck.

He opened the door for her, waited for her to get in, and got behind the wheel. The highway was pitch dark. Even with Tuff's high beams on it was difficult to see.

"Where's the moon tonight?" She looked out the windshield, tilting her head at an angle so she could see up.

"It's there. You just can't see it."

"I wonder if a storm's coming in."

"Nah, nothing in the forecast about it. You working at the store tomorrow?"

"Nope. I'm taking the weekend off. How about you?"

"I'll probably go in for a few hours. Get organized. Maybe go for a long ride. Muchacho could use some exercise."

Sawyer had mentioned that Tuff had a horse and that he stabled it on the ranch. "Was Muchacho your rodeo horse?"

"Yep. He and I go back a long way together." He paused. "Want to come?" He seemed as surprised by his spontaneous offer as she was.

"It's been a long time. I don't even know if my old saddle is still here."

"Use one of the others."

"They're Western. I ride English."

"What kind of ranch girl are you?" he teased.

"You sound like my grandfather. I suppose you can take the girl out of Beverly Hills, but you can't take Beverly Hills out of the girl." She shuddered at the thought. Perhaps that's why she'd tried so hard to break out of her little world.

"The saddles aren't all that different. You can make it work with a Western one."

"All right." She wanted to go and was thrilled he was asking. She just didn't want to make a fool of herself.

"Eight o'clock?"

"Eight o'clock? Are you out of your mind? That doesn't even leave time for coffee."

He slid her a sideways glance. "I thought you were a farmer."

"I'm an organizer, which means I get to sleep in on the weekends while someone else tends the crops."

"Okay, nine." Even in the dark she could see his lips curve up.

"Nine it is, then." It had been so long since she'd been on a horse's back that she hoped she still remembered how to ride.

He pulled off the highway onto the road to the ranch and took the private entrance. When they got to the gate it was open.

"That's odd." Tuff pulled through and stopped on the other side. "It's usually closed, especially at night."

"Someone probably forgot. It happens." They'd left via the public route so for all they knew the gate had been open all day. The cattle were in the south pasture, which was fully fenced. So it wasn't as if they could get loose. "I'll close it."

She was about to jump out when he put his hand over her leg. "I'll do it."

He shined a light from his keychain on the ground as he walked to the gate. He switched the light to some nearby bushes, making an arc, then closed and locked the gate.

"What was that about?" she asked when he returned to the truck.

"Just checking things out."

"Anyone can get in anyway." There were cameras in Dry Creek Village for security.

"Yeah, but not to the cattle unless they come this way."

She'd been thinking about personal safety. The cattle hadn't even entered her mind. "Has that been a problem? I mean cattle theft." Sawyer hadn't said anything about it being an issue on the ranch. And even though she knew Cash spent his days investigating livestock rustling, she never considered that it could happen to them.

"It's a problem everywhere. A ranch gets hit and it can set you back for years, especially if the thieves get your breeding stock."

Her grandfather had spent decades perfecting his herd. When he'd had to cull much of it for the drought it destroyed his operation. Her family was just starting to put it back together again. A theft would devastate them.

"Should we drive to the south pasture and make sure everything is okay?" They were probably overreacting, but it didn't hurt to check.

"It's more than likely nothing. But yeah, I'd feel better if we did."

He passed by their cabins and took a bumpy fire trail in the direction of Sawyer's house, then cut over and drove through an empty field. It was so dark she didn't know how he could see without a designated road. But he seemed to know what he was doing.

He stopped, jumped out of the truck, and held his penlight over the dirt. She unrolled her window. "What are doing?"

"Looking for tire tracks. Don't see any. This is the most direct way without passing the ranch house or Cash and Aubrey's spread. Not sure that thieves would know that, though." He got back in and cranked up the heat. Then he continued across the field to a barbed wire fence, where he stopped and got out of the truck again.

This time, Angie joined him. He put his finger to his lips and appeared to be listening. All she could hear was the wind. He flashed his light along the fence line. Everything appeared to be intact. He scanned the ground, presumably looking for tire tracks. Nothing as far as Angie could see.

"We're okay." He wrapped his arm around her waist and guided her to the truck with his penlight. "When we get home, I'll call Cash just to let him know."

"I'll call Jace," she said. "But I really do think someone just forgot and left the gate open."

"More than likely, yeah."

They sat in the cab for a few seconds. She rubbed her hands together.

"Cold?" He took her hands and sandwiched them between his larger ones, instantly warming them.

They locked eyes and he leaned across the center console, capturing her mouth with his. A shot of heat went through her. His lips were warm and pliable, and he tasted a little of beer. She twined her arms around his neck and closed her eyes, letting him take the kiss deeper. He cupped the back of her head and explored her mouth with his tongue.

Her tongue met his and the kiss became more fervent. More sensual. She couldn't remember a kiss that had roused her this much. He lowered her onto the seat and moved over her. She arched up, pressing against his chest, wanting the rest of him but the console was in the way.

A moan escaped her as his hands grazed her breasts over her sweater. He murmured something against her lips that was inaudible. And then, just like that, he stopped.

"What's wrong?" she tried to pull him back down, but he was already in a sitting position.

"It's time to go home."

She hoped he meant that they should resume what they were doing in the comfort and privacy of one of their cabins. He started the engine while she straightened up in her seat, then took the same rutted route back to the gravel road they'd come on.

The air in the cab suddenly shifted from hot and heavy to tense—and not the sexual kind of tension. They rode in awkward silence to her house while she searched for something to say. Something like *Are we doing this?*

It became abundantly clear that they weren't when he cut the engine, held out his hands for her keys and did a quick sweep of her cabin before leaving. On his way out, he muttered, "Goodnight" and then he was gone.

Chapter 11

Tuff paced the barn, wondering whether Angie was going to show. He'd found an English saddle in a storage room and had tacked up Muchacho and a gentle mare named Sugar, who was as old as Tuff. He thought about calling but didn't want to wake her if she'd slept in.

He glanced at his watch. Five more minutes, he told himself. But it was already closing in on nine-thirty. He thought they'd settled on nine. But maybe she'd stuck with the original eight and had shown up, believing that he'd stood her up.

Of course, there was a third possibility.

"You're here."

He turned around to find Angie, dressed to ride in jeans and a pair of cowboy boots. Her cheeks were filled with color, like maybe she'd jogged the mile to the stable.

"I thought we were walking over together."

He didn't remember that being part of the plan. "Sorry. I didn't realize you were waiting for me. I got here early, hoping to scout around for an English saddle." He nudged his head at Sugar.

She lit up when she saw what he'd found. "That's my old saddle. Where did you find it?"

"In one of the tack rooms. Ellie's got one too. I figured in a pinch we could make that work but then I found this."

She lifted one of the stirrups, admiring it with a smile as big as the ranch. "My whole family gave me crap for this saddle." She looked down at her shit kickers. "Had I known I would've worn my equestrian boots and my riding britches."

He was having enough trouble not ogling her in jeans. A pair of skin-tight riding britches would've done him in.

"You ready to go?"

"If I can remember how to do this." She mounted up as gracefully as any accomplished horsewoman.

"It's just like riding a bike."

"We'll see." She clicked her tongue. "Be kind to me, Sugar. It's been a while."

"You two are acquainted, huh?"

"Oh yeah. Sugar and I are like this." She held her two fingers together, then scratched the mare on her head. "Aren't we, girl?"

He took the lead, heading for a trail that wended gently through the hills but wasn't too grueling. Until Angie felt comfortable, they'd stick with mostly flat land.

It was sunny, not a cloud in the sky and less chilly than it had been the night before. But they both had jackets if the temperature dropped.

"I thought we'd ride to the south pasture, then into the foothills. Nothing too strenuous. That okay?"

"Sure." She reined her horse alongside his. "This must be Muchacho?" She leaned over to pet Tuff's gelding's muzzle.

"Yep."

"Hello, Muchacho. Pleased to meet you." Muchacho pushed his forehead into her hand. "You're a sweetheart, aren't you?"

Tuff turned in his saddle to take a look at Angie's seat. She might claim to be rusty, but the woman could ride. He didn't know why he was surprised. Her brother and cousins were as good horsemen as any he knew.

"You want to pick up the pace?"

"Sure."

Tuff loosened his reins, and gave Muchacho a slight tap with his heel, moving him into a trot. Angie did the same. From there they changed to a lope, or he supposed to a canter in Angie's case. They ran as far as the ridge, then slowed their horses to walk as they climbed the hill.

"That was fun," Angie said with the giddiness of a young girl.

Her mood was infectious because Tuff couldn't stop smiling. "Looks like you've still got it."

"I have to say you were right. It is like riding a bicycle. But I have a feeling I'm going to be sore tomorrow."

Where the trail narrowed, they rode single file. When it widened, they came up next to each other and took their time covering ground and taking in the sites.

"It's a great day. Not too cold and the wind has died down." Angie leaned forward over Sugar's neck to sniff the air, giving Tuff a nice look at her ass. "Can you smell the pine trees? It smells like Christmas."

He equated pine trees with nature, not Christmas. But he'd never been big on holidays.

"Should we go to the top or do you want to stay at this elevation for a while?" There was a switchback up the mountainside.

"I'm good with this."

They stayed on the trail they were on and maintained a leisurely pace, riding in companionable silence. Not a word was spoken about the kiss the previous night much to Tuff's relief. It had been a mistake, though he'd enjoyed it more than he wanted to admit. Hell, he'd laid awake most of the night reliving it, tempted to march across the creek and finish the job.

"We should've packed a picnic lunch." Angie pulled Sugar's head away from a patch of grass.

"You hungry?" He had a protein bar in his saddlebag.

"Not yet. But it's a perfect day for dining al fresco, don't you think?"

"Sure." He visualized the both of them laying on a blanket and his groin tightened. It was a better idea—and a safer one—to keep riding.

They circled the mountain and headed back across the field. There was a cluster of cows in the pasture, jostling for space under a shade tree.

Angie stared out over the field at a second group that had congregated at a water trough. "Did you call Cash last night?"

"Yeah. He drove out on one of the ATVs for a closer look but thinks one of the boys left the gate open."

"Makes sense. I know Travis was practicing his driving skills in Jace's pickup. He probably went through the gate and came around on the public road and forgot to come back and close it."

"According to Cash, the herd is all accounted for. So no harm, no foul."

"It was good of you to check last night."

He gave a slight bob of his head. The Daltons were his friends. Of course, he'd look out for their cattle and their property.

While they were on the topic of the previous night, he figured he say something about their kiss. Get it out in the open and put it to rest.

But before he could compose the exact words in his head, she spoke first. "What was your deal last night?"

"What do you mean?" He wanted to make sure they were talking about the same thing before he explained himself.

"We were kissing and then we weren't. And for whatever reason you seemed mad. Or at the very least upset."

COWBOY PROUD

He blew out a breath and reined Muchacho over to a tree, where he let the gelding munch on the tall grass. Angie followed him over, took her feet out of the stirrups and stretched her legs, while staring at him expectantly.

"I wasn't mad." Only at himself for his lack of willpower. "But I shouldn't have been kissing you."

"Why not?"

"A lot of reasons, starting with the fact that I'm not looking for anything complicated. And you living next door complicates things."

"It was just a kiss, Tuff."

He held her gaze. "You and I both know it wasn't going to end with just a kiss if one of us hadn't shut it down when we did."

Her cheeks turned red, but she didn't deny it because it was the damned truth. He'd been close to taking her on the front seat of his truck. He was forty damned years old and behaving like a besotted high school kid.

"I did exactly what I promised your brother I wouldn't do."

"My brother?" Her head jerked back. "What does he have to do with this?"

He looked away, realizing he'd stepped in it. The last thing he wanted to do was get in the middle of a family squabble. And it didn't take a genius to see that Angie was going to give Sawyer a rash of shit for messing around in her private life.

"Forget I said that. Can we get back to riding now?" He tugged Muchacho's head from the grass and nudged the gelding into a trot.

Angie followed behind him. He could feel her agitation burning through his back the whole way home.

* * * *

"The meddling has to stop now!" Angie pushed her way into Sawyer's house, brushed past him, and went straight to the kitchen.

"I don't know what you're talking about." He closed his laptop, which was sitting on the center island next to a reporter's notebook and a file of papers.

She got a bottle of water out of the fridge and spun around to face him. "Why would you tell Tuff to stay away from me?"

"I didn't tell him to stay away from you."

She knew he was obfuscating by being too literal. Maybe he didn't use those exact words with Tuff, but it was something close enough. "What did you tell him, then?"

"I've told him a lot of things. You'll have to be more specific." It was the kind of smart aleck answer he would've given when they were kids.

"If one of your sources said that to you, you'd laugh in his face."

His face softened and he gave her a hug. She knew from experience that he was getting ready to charm her—another childhood tactic he used as his "get out of jail" card. This time, she didn't plan to fall for it. She was a grown woman and didn't need him warning off her romantic prospects. Not that Tuff Garrison was a prospect or that she was looking for romance. She wasn't. But she still had to assert her independence.

"Ah, come on, Ange. I'm just looking out for you."

"So, you admit you said something?" She sat at the island and drank her water.

He shrugged. "I may have mentioned that you were coming out of a bad situation and didn't need any more upheaval."

"Why? Did he bring it up?"

He sat next to her. "I can't remember."

"Sure you don't." She poked him in the arm. "Sawyer, I know you mean well but please butt out. It's embarrassing." It was beyond embarrassing. It was mortifying at her age.

"Ange, Tuff's not for you."

"You already made your feelings clear on that. Not that it's any of your business, but there is nothing between us other than friendship. Though I don't know what your problem with him is." Tuff appeared to have it together a hell of a lot more than any of the other men she'd dated. Compared to Zane, Tuff was a veritable prince, starting with the fact that he wasn't about to become a felon.

"No problem. He's a stand-up guy all the way. But he's forty and still single. And I can tell you that it's not from a lack of female interest." He made that know-it-all face that used to drive her nuts.

"First of all, I'm not interested in him in that way. And second of all, I remember a time when you were single." She flashed a got-you smile.

"That was different," he protested.

"Yeah, like how?" She had him there.

He scrubbed his hand through his hair. "Did you come over just to harass me?"

"And to bum a water." She held up her bottle. "Where's Gina?"

"At the restaurant. The woman works too much."

"Kettle. Black."

"I'm not five months pregnant."

She loved how smitten her brother was with his wife. Before she'd left for Zaire, he'd been a confirmed bachelor. And now Sawyer was going to be a father.

"I'm sure she'll know when it's too much."

Angie spotted a nearly full pot of coffee on the counter and decided to switch beverages. She got up and helped herself to a cup. "You want a refill?" She spotted his empty mug on the center island.

"Nah, I'm good." He eyed her ancient cowboy boots. "What are you up to today?"

"No plans." She got the milk out of the refrigerator and fixed up her coffee the way she liked it. "I went riding with Tuff this morning." She tossed that out just to get under his skin.

"I guess that's when he told you that we had a conversation, huh?"

"He didn't tell me anything." As annoyed as she was that Sawyer and Tuff had conspired behind her back, she didn't want to sell out her neighbor. "It just kind of came out during our conversation."

"And what conversation was that?" Sawyer crossed his arms and pointedly stared at her.

"I don't remember. What are you doing today, besides working?" She nudged her head at his now closed laptop.

"I was thinking of going on a ride myself. Maybe checking some fences. Too bad you already went."

No way was she getting back on a horse today. Her muscles were still screaming from her ride with Tuff. She suspected she'd be even stiffer tomorrow. "Maybe Jace or Cash will go with you. I bet Ellie would be up for a ride. And if she goes, Travis and Grady could probably be talked into it."

"Not a bad idea."

The doorbell rang and Sawyer got up to look outside the window to see who it was. "Come on up," he yelled down.

A few seconds later, Cash bounded up the stairs. "Hey," he ruffled Angie's hair, "I hear you and Tuff had a bit of an adventure last night."

Sawyer shot her a look. "What's that about?"

"Someone left the gate open last night. Tuff and I drove over to the south pasture to make sure nothing was amiss." She didn't elaborate on how they happened to come across the open gate. But she was certain that Sawyer had already figured it out.

"He called me afterward and I went back out just in case." Cash grabbed a mug from the cupboard and poured himself some coffee. "Everything was fine. But we've got to remember to keep that gate closed at night."

"Have you talked to Jace about it?" Sawyer asked.

"I'm on my way over there next." Cash leaned against the counter, sipping from his cup. "What are you two up to?"

"Ange went riding this morning and I was putting the last touches on an article that's due on Monday. How 'bout you?"

"I promised to take the girls to Roseville. Ellie needs some things for winter. The girl is growing faster than a weed. You're welcome to come along, Angie. Aubrey and Ellie would love to have you."

"Thanks for the invite but I don't think I'm ready for a mall yet." In WITSEC, she'd been instructed to stay away from large gathering places or crowded areas where someone might recognize her.

"Everything going okay?" Cash tried to make it sound like a casual question but the three of them knew what he was really asking.

She shrugged. "I'm still constantly looking over my shoulder." She considered telling them that she had the sensation of being watched but knew it would sound crazy without any evidence to back it up. It was all in her head, she told herself. "Why, have you heard anything?" Just because Cash was no longer an FBI agent didn't mean he didn't keep his ear to the ground.

"Nothing that you don't already know." He rubbed his chin. "That doesn't mean we shouldn't all be on the alert."

Angie averted her eyes, not wanting him to see the fear there.

But Cash didn't miss much. "Ange, I'm just talking like a cop. I'll feel a lot better when these yahoos are convicted and locked up for a long time. But for all intents and purposes the case appears to be wrapped up, leaving you safe to live your life. I just think it's good to stay on your toes for the next several months, especially as we get closer to the trial."

She was. After the incident with the paper falling from the door, she'd taken to using one of Earl's other tricks. Whenever she left the house, she hid a fishing line over her door under a fall wreath she bought from Ava and Winter. She tied the line to a boot she placed on the inside of the house at the foot of the door. If the boot impeded her from coming inside, she knew it was safe. If the door swung in without interference from the boot, she knew someone had already opened the door before her. Low tech but it did the job.

"I am," she told Cash, leaving out the part about her booby trap. No need for her cousin and brother to think she was needlessly paranoid. "I've been keeping in touch with my handler from the marshal's office."

"Are you nervous, Ange?" Sawyer paced behind her. "Maybe we should get you some kind of a panic button that would alert all of us if anyone approached you. I don't know why I didn't think of it before. It would just be a little peace of mind before the trial. What do you say?"

"I don't think it's necessary." But a small part of her didn't think it was a bad idea.

"I like it." Cash told Sawyer, then turned to Angie. "Sawyer and I will look into it. It can't hurt. And if the feds decide to put you on their witness list…well, it doesn't hurt to amp up your security."

She couldn't argue with that, though she desperately hoped the authorities had enough evidence without her testimony to put the Liberty Fighters away for life.

Chapter 12

Tuff cast out his line in a smooth arc, letting it drop near an outcropping of rocks in the creek. He wasn't particularly trying to catch anything, just spending a peaceful Sunday afternoon, sitting on his porch. It was sixty-degrees out and he wanted to take advantage of the temperate weather while it lasted. November in the Sierra foothills could be fickle, cold one day and relatively balmy the next.

He popped a cap off his beer and took a slug, glancing across the creek at Angie's cabin. No sign of the redhead today. Around nine in the morning, he heard her drive off and hadn't seen hide nor hair of her since. They both needed a cooling off period, anyway.

They'd become just a little more neighborly than he wanted to be.

Whoo, that kiss. When he least expected it, the memory of her soft pliant lips came back to haunt him. The woman sure stirred something in him. Something hot and unpredictable.

He checked his line and took another drag of his beer. Buddy got up to stretch, walked in a tight circle and plopped back down on a sunny spot on the porch. Tuff wasn't the only one feeling lazy.

He checked his line and rested the end of the pole in a holder on the railing that he'd screwed in a week ago. Little by little, he was making the place a home. And his feet didn't feel itchy. He'd even bought a couple of outdoor Adirondack chairs at the nearby Tractor Supply and was considering upgrading the hand-me-down bed in the master to one of those memory foam mattresses.

It was as close as he'd ever come to a commitment in his adult life. It should've scared the shit out of him, but he was too damned comfortable at the moment to give it a second thought.

He considered what to have for dinner. There was a Dalton steak in the freezer or, if he wanted to treat himself, he could do takeout from Gina's. Or even eat at the bar while watching a game on the restaurant's oversized flatscreen. The world was just filled with possibilities, now wasn't it?

Angie's old Mercedes pulled into her driveway. Tuff watched her alight from her car in a fitted knit dress more Beverly Hills than Dry Creek Ranch that took his breath away. Her usual jeans and sweaters worked for him fine. But the dress skimmed over her body, reminding him of what he'd felt with his hands. For a petit woman, Angela Dalton had plenty of curves.

She caught a glimpse of him, shielded her eyes from the sun, and waved. "Catch anything?" she called across the creek.

"Not yet. You go to a party?"

She crossed the bridge in a pair of high-heeled shoes that would feed Tuff's fantasies for a good long time. "Sorry, I couldn't hear you over the water."

"I asked if you went to a party." He motioned at her dress.

"No, my grandfather's grave. The family decided to make a day of it."

Tuff cleaned the seat of the other chair with his arm and motioned for her to take it. "Where's he buried?" There were plenty of cemeteries in the region. Tuff had a somewhat morbid fascination with them.

"The Dry Creek Cemetery on River Road, next to my grandmother's and great grandparents' graves."

"Your grandfather sounded like a good guy." Everyone in town talked about Jasper Dalton with admiration. In Tuff's experience only an honorable man left a mark like that.

"The best. We all loved him and my grandmother to pieces," she said and waved her hand over his booted feet on the porch rail. "Looks like you're having a relaxing Sunday."

"Yup. My intentions were to put a little work in today, but I never made it to my studio." He leaned back and laced his hands behind his head.

"Good for you." She let out a contented sigh. "It's the first warm day we've had in a while." She tugged at her dress. "I need to get out of this thing."

You could do that, or you could just let me look at you in it for a little longer. Make a man happy.

A strange chirping sound interrupted his mental peep show. "What's that?"

She reached in her purse, pulled out her phone, and stared at the caller ID that flashed on the screen. Something close to fear flickered across her face and she stuffed the cell back in her purse.

"Something wrong?"

She shook her head. "Nothing, just one of those annoying robocalls."

He wasn't the most intuitive guy when it came to women, but even he could tell she was lying. "Angela?" He cocked his head to one side. "Who was it?"

She stalled, obviously trying to decide whether to come clean. "No one," she finally said and rose. "I've got to get home."

"Let me walk you over."

Angie gave an imperceptible nod, then seemed to think better of it. "That's okay. I'm fine." She went down the stairs and hurried across the foot bridge.

He'd been sitting on the porch for most of the afternoon and hadn't seen anything suspicious, so he let her go. But he watched her little cabin for the next hour, catching fleeting glimpses of her through the windows. All seemed normal but something was definitely off.

* * * *

Angie stared at the number on her phone screen. A New Mexico area code. Kari.

In WITSEC, she was forbidden from contacting her friend—or anyone from her old life for that matter. Anything concerning Kari was supposed to go through Earl. Angie wasn't sure whether the rule still applied now that she'd left the program. She could call Earl and ask him but didn't want to bother him on a Sunday. It was his time, which he had precious little of, to be with his family.

Tomorrow, she told herself. But the number beckoned. What if Kari knew something or was in trouble? Unable to stop herself, she hit redial. It rang three times and then a phone tone pierced Angie's ear and a recording came on. "We're sorry, the number you have reached has been disconnected or is no longer in service. If you feel you have reached this recording in error, please check the number and try your call again."

She hung up and tried again, getting the same results. It was odd and worrisome. Angie would've tried again if not for the knock at her door.

She checked through the peep hole to find Tuff standing there. It surprised her. Though he'd been friendly enough this afternoon, she'd gotten the distinct impression he'd been trying to avoid her ever since their horseback ride.

She opened the door and stood in the doorway. "Hi."

His eyes drifted over her dress and she remembered that she'd forgotten to change. He craned his neck around her and did a visual sweep of the cabin.

"You mind if I come in?"

"Not at all." She waved her hand over the threshold.

He walked into the front room and again did a quick assessment.

"What are you looking for?"

He shoved his hands in his pocket and rocked on his heels. "I've been watching you pace for the last hour. And although it's none of my business, I wanted to take a second stab at whatever that phone call was about and why it has you so worked up."

She exhaled. It was no use pretending she wasn't. The question was could she—should she—confide in him? It would be a relief to have a sounding board who wouldn't overreact, like her brother and cousins surely would. But how to tell Tuff without divulging too much would be nearly impossible. He was too inquisitive—and smart.

"It was an old friend. And for reasons that I don't want to get into we've been out of touch for a long time. I was surprised she called. I was even more flummoxed by the fact that when I tried to return her call, I got a message that her number had been disconnected."

"Just now?"

"Yes."

"Are you sure you called the right number?"

She had to summon all her willpower not to roll her eyes. "Yes. I hit redial. When that didn't work, I manually punched in the number. The results were the same."

"So in the hour between the time she called and you called her back, her phone was disconnected."

"More like forty-five minutes. But yeah, it would seem so."

"Maybe she didn't pay her bill and her provider chose now to shut her off." He watched her closely. "Seems to me that there is something else going on here. If you don't want to tell me maybe you should tell your brother or your sister-in-law, someone you trust. Because what I saw when you got that phone call was abject fear, not surprise."

She sank into the sofa. "It's not that I don't trust you. It's that it's complicated."

He sat across from her in one of the overstuffed chairs Aubrey had left behind and rested his elbows on his knees as he leaned forward. "Look, Angie, you're about as close to a friend as I have. If someone is threatening you or making you feel unsafe..." he trailed off.

It wasn't that she felt unsafe. There were a million reasons Kari could've called. For one, she might have wanted to let Angie know that her phone was getting turned off.

"So we're friends, huh?" She decided it was best to change the subject of her mysterious phone call. "I got the distinct impression yesterday that you were no longer interested in being my friend."

He leaned back and crossed his arms over his chest. "I never said anything about ending our friendship. What I remember saying, and I think you do too, is that there would be no more kissing. Now back to this call situation—or whatever it is." He looked at her pointedly. "At the very least talk to Jace about it."

"I will."

She went into the kitchen because it was easier than looking him in the eye while she was lying. There was nothing to tell Jace or anyone else for that matter. For all she knew the call was a butt dial, though it didn't explain the disconnected number. She chalked it up to an anomaly and told herself to move on.

"You hungry? I was thinking of throwing together some pasta and a salad."

"I was considering Gina's tonight, but if you're cooking I'm in."

She grabbed a bag of penne from her pantry and filled a pot with water to boil. "I can't promise it'll be as good as hers, but I make a mean tomato and herb sauce." She'd learned how from the chef at the restaurant where she'd worked in Portland. It wasn't anything complicated or fancy, but it was some of the best comfort food she'd ever had.

"Can I help?"

"You could set the table while I change. Plates are in the cupboard." She pointed to one next to the sink.

In her bedroom, she slipped into a pair of jeans, took one look in the mirror, and whipped them off. Too baggy. She found a second pair left over from her college days, doubtful that they'd still fit. Angie managed to shimmy into them and get them buttoned and zipped. Though they were snug, she liked her reflection in the mirror. They'll stretch, she told herself and found a cute blouse and Tuff's belt to finish off the outfit.

When she returned to the kitchen, she found him searching through her pantry. "What are you looking for?"

"Napkins."

"They're in here." She pulled out a drawer and removed two beautiful linen napkins, another Aubrey perk, and placed them on the table.

Angie dropped her pasta into the boiling water and got started on the sauce. "There's a bag of salad in the fridge if you want to grab it."

He got the salad and together they put together a simple dinner. Every time he brushed by her she felt a flutter in her chest. She'd been around a lot of fantastic looking men in her time. Her parents were publicists to some of the biggest Hollywood heartthrobs in the business. They were regular fixtures at her folks' house, routinely showing up for meetings or parties.

But with Tuff it wasn't so much about his looks as it was his sheer masculinity. Not that he flaunted it like a puffed-up rooster on steroids, which would've been a turn off to Angie. No, it was more an inner confidence than it was swagger. He was more protector than aggressor. He was more about kindness than physical strength. He was more willing to listen than to be heard.

And he'd made it perfectly clear that they were a non-starter.

Given the timing, it was for the best, she assured herself.

"I'll just heat the bread and we're good to go." She put the pasta in a serving bowl and placed it on the table. "Oh shoot, I don't have beer and I remember from our dinner that you prefer it over wine."

"No worries. I'm past my limit anyway. Water will be fine."

"What's your limit?" She laughed.

"No more than two a day." He was dead serious.

"Why's that?"

"My mother was an alcoholic. I don't want to wind up one myself."

"Is that why the two of you were estranged?"

"Partly," he said in a way that suggested the topic was off limits.

But it was no accident that Sawyer was a journalist. Nosiness ran in Angie's family, so she pressed forward, wildly curious about Tuff's life. "What about your father?"

"Nope. Straight as an arrow. Not a teetotaler but the most I ever saw him drink was a couple of beers with dinner. Occasionally, a shot of good whiskey."

"Was your mother an alcoholic while they were married?"

"I don't think so, but I was a kid. Sometimes you don't see things right in front of you."

"But you knew your dad wasn't."

He paused, considering his words. "Yeah, I'd bet my life on it. With her…" He shrugged. "I always got the impression that she held it together because of him. But after he died…" He gave another shrug. "Pass the salad, please."

She served him a healthy portion.

"What about your folks? You close with them?"

"Very," she said around a bite of pasta. "That doesn't mean we didn't have our problems."

"Yeah, what kind of problems?" He put his fork down and waited for her to answer.

"They haven't always approved of my decisions…my lifestyle."

"Like what in particular?"

"After college I wanted to save the world." She let out a wry chuckle. It all seemed like a big cliché now. Beverly Hills girl riding to the rescue on her white charger. "I spent a lot of years traveling the globe, joining up with various organizations and groups, volunteering."

"What's wrong with that? Seems like a worthy thing to do. Noble."

She rocked her hand back and forth. "My family thought I was flakey, jumping from cause to cause and keeping weird company."

"Weird? How so?" He served himself a second helping of pasta.

"Maybe weird was the wrong word." Criminal was a better descriptor. But not in the beginning. In the beginning, she'd cohabitated with some of the most spiritual people she'd ever met. "For starters, I spent six months in an ashram in India and another two months in a Buddhist monastery in Tibet."

She waited for the look, the derisive one that said how predictable. The little rich girl, trying to find herself. But all she got was a face wreathed in curiosity.

"I bounced around a lot," she continued. "Everything from Greenpeace to the Water Project. And lots of organizations in between."

"So, what's wrong with that?" He appeared genuinely puzzled.

"It wasn't the ashram or the monastery or even Greenpeace or the Water Project. It was the other stuff: me hitchhiking, couch surfing, taking up with strangers. It scared the hell out of them." And in the end, they'd been right to be scared. "I think they also worried that I was lost and would never find myself."

"Have you? Found yourself?" He held her gaze across the table.

It was a profound question. One she'd asked herself frequently. "I don't think so, no."

"Is that so terrible?"

Again, she was taken with his philosophical nature. In so many ways he reminded her of her grandfather. The quiet, unassuming cowboy. But as they said, still waters ran deep.

"At this point in my life, yes. I'd like to know who I am." She pushed her plate away. "What about you? Have you found yourself?"

He contemplated the question as she knew he would. "I know who I am. I also know what I am. The bigger question is whether I've found peace with who and what I am."

She watched him closely, waiting. And when he didn't finish the thought, she pressed. "Well, have you? Have you found peace with who and what you are?"

He paused, then simply said, "No, only torment."

Chapter 13

Tuff closed up shop early. He needed to take Buddy home before the party started and grab a quick shower. Holidays and gatherings…well, at least he was looking forward to Gina's cooking.

And to seeing the redhead if he wanted to be honest with himself. Angie hadn't been around the last few days. She'd been occupied with her folks and relatives. He should've welcomed the distance because nothing good could come of him chasing after Angela Dalton. She thought she knew him, but she didn't. She had no idea about his history.

No idea at all.

Buddy jumped out of the truck the minute Tuff opened the passenger door and the dog beat him to the front porch.

"You want to go inside, boy?" The temperature hovered somewhere in the thirties.

He unlocked the door to find it was even colder inside the cabin. "Let me get some heat on for you." Tuff flicked on the thermostat and filled the dog's dish with kibble.

He managed to get in and out of the shower in under ten minutes and dressed in something presentable, wondering if the Village's Thanksgiving party called for a tie. In the end, he went with a bolo, figuring it would pass a protocol test either way. He ran a comb through his wet hair and checked to make sure Buddy had fresh water.

"Hold down the fort while I'm gone," he called on his way out.

By the time he got to the restaurant, guests had already arrived. Ava, Winter, and their boyfriends sat at one of the tables, Bryce already double fisting a couple of drinks.

"I heard you been cheatin' on me." Laney's eyes slid up and down his torso.

"Never." He winked. "You're my one and only, Laney." He kissed her cheek, then whispered in her ear, "Don't tell Jimmy Ray."

She swatted his arm. "Don't you try to charm me, boy. Angie told me you've been stepping out at that Italian place in Nevada City."

"Ah, come on, Laney. It was only a couple of times. The coffeeshop is my main place. But every once in a while, a guy needs a little variety." She cast him with a gimlet eye.

"Am I forgiven?" he asked.

"I'll think about it." She bustled away to give someone else a hard time.

"Sorry." Angie appeared in a red dress that made his heart stop.

It took him a few seconds to find his tongue. "You sold me out." His lips tipped up.

"It was an accident. She was talking about a new shop in Nevada City that sells spices and I let it drop about us eating at Scola La Pasta. If it's any consolation she's mad at me too."

He wanted to say that she could make it up to him later, letting him do a number of wicked things to her in that dress, which was even better than the one she'd had on the other day. If that was even possible.

"Hey, Tuff. Good to see you." Charlie gave him a hug. "Happy Thanksgiving. Are you coming over tomorrow?"

"Uh...I didn't know I was supposed to."

"No one told you?" She looked at Angie, who shrugged. "You're invited for Thanksgiving up at the house. Darn it, Jace was supposed to tell you. I hope you don't already have plans."

The only thing on the agenda was to sleep in, take Muchacho for a ride, and hang out with Buddy. Maybe polish off the pecan pie he'd bought at Daltons the other day. "No plans."

"Great. Dinner is at six," Charlie said.

He guessed he was spending Thanksgiving with the Daltons. It would be rude to say no now that he'd disclosed that he didn't have any other plans. But the fact was large family dinners made him uncomfortable. "What can I bring?"

"Not a thing. We've got enough food to feed half of California. Just bring your appetite."

"Okay. Thank you for the invite. I appreciate it."

"Of course." Charlie reached in and gave him another hug, then went off to mingle, leaving Angie behind.

She held eye contact with him and he knew that she knew. Finally, she said, "It'll be my first holiday with my family in more than six years. It'll be fun. You'll see."

Six years. It appeared the rumors were true. Whoever the man was who'd had Angie under his thumb must've been a real son-of-a-bitch not to let her see her family. Unfortunately, Tuff was familiar with the type. Mary Garrison had had a string of son-of-a-bitches in her life. Each one worse than the next.

"I'm looking forward to it," he lied. "It's good of your family to include me," which was the truth. The Daltons were kind people. "Why six years?"

She took a sip of her wine, which seemed to Tuff like a stall tactic. "I had a lot going on."

He didn't press. It appeared that they both had pasts. Who was he to pry into hers?

Jace joined them and handed Tuff a beer. "I just got reamed by my wife for forgetting to invite you to Thanksgiving."

"No worries, man."

"I meant to do it, but the whole damn county is going crazy and it slipped my mind."

Tuff and Angie both looked at Jace quizzically. Mill County wasn't exactly a hotbed of crime. Tuff had only heard of one homicide since he moved here. A couple of bikers got into it at a bar alongside the highway. One pulled a knife and the other wound up in the morgue. Neither of them was from around here.

"A couple of high school kids have been spraying businesses in town with graffiti and I've got two idiots on the east side of the county warring over property lines. One of them is threatening to burn down the other one's barn if he doesn't move it. Three houses were burglarized up on Granite Hill. And if that wasn't enough, I've got three deputies out with the flu."

"I'm glad you're coming." Jace slapped Tuff on the back. "The women are handling the turkeys but I'm smoking two sixteen-pound briskets."

Jace was the official pit master of Dry Creek Ranch. During the summer, Tuff had been invited to a few family barbecues, where Jace had worked the grill like a boss. The ranch house had a great outdoor setup with everything from a gas grill to a wood one and a smoker that could accommodate half a steer.

"You sure there's nothing I can bring?"

"Just bring yourself. We've got the rest covered." He glanced around the restaurant. "I better go find my boys. By now, they're probably in a corner somewhere, killing each other."

Tuff chuckled. Jace's sons were a handful, especially Grady, the younger one. He was the most accident-prone kid Tuff had ever known. But he got a huge kick out of the boys. Cash's daughter, Ellie, too. All three of them were good kids. Respectful and hardworking.

"I should go and say hello to my parents and aunt and uncle," Angie said. "Where are you sitting?"

"Probably with Cash and Aubrey if there's room at their table. You sitting with your folks?"

"I'll sit with you guys."

He watched her cross the restaurant to the appetizer table where her parents stood with Cash's folks, filling their plates.

There was no sign of Gina, who was more than likely in the kitchen, overseeing the show. Tuff suspected that Sawyer was with her. He turned around only to bump into Ava.

"Sorry." He steadied her before she spilled her plate of food. "I should've watched where I was going."

"Come here." She took him by the elbow and dragged him into a corner. "I'm going to break up with Bryce tonight."

Here they went again.

"Or do you think it's cruel to do it right before Thanksgiving?"

Frankly, he thought she should've given Bryce the old heave ho months ago. But did he look like freaking Dear Abby?

"Whatever you want to do, Ava. Go with your gut." He tried to tactfully back away, but she had her hand stuck into him like a talon.

"Winter thinks I should do it tonight, after the party. But it seems rude. Like why did I make him come if I was just going to dump him?"

Yep, it did seem like a backwards way of doing things. But what the hell did he know about breakups? He'd never been with anyone long enough to make it necessary. Hell, his idea of a breakup was sneaking out a woman's bed in the middle of the night.

"Tell me what to do, Tuff."

He scrubbed his loose hand through his hair. "I'm not the right guy for this. Do what Winter says or ask Aubrey or Charlie."

"I want a man's perspective."

"Then ask Sawyer or Jace."

"No way. I barely know them. It would be weird."

"Okay, wait until Friday." It seemed like a reasonable thing to do. "Give the dude the holiday, then tell him it isn't working out."

"You think? Because I sort of want to get it over with."

"Then go for it. Do it tonight." *For Christ's sake, make up your mind, woman. But leave me out of it.*

"No, you're right. I should wait until Friday. First thing in the morning. Do you think it's wrong for me to sleep with him until Friday?"

How the hell should I know? "Do whatever you think is best. I've got to get another beer." He held up the nearly empty one in his hand and managed to pry loose of her.

Angie corralled him at the bar. "What was that about?"

"Boyfriend troubles," he said in a soft voice in case Bryce was around. "Don't ask me why she thinks I can help."

Angie laughed. "Because you're a nice guy."

Ava had said the same thing to him. It showed what a poor judge of character both women were.

He looked her in the eye. "That's the thing, Angie, I'm not."

* * * *

Angie was put on mashed potato patrol. She and Ellie stood at the sink peeling russets while Charlie's kitchen buzzed with activity.

"I'm still recovering from last night's party." Aubrey put the finishing touches on a cornbread dressing that smelled so good it made Angie's mouth water. "I ate too much."

"It was a lovely thing for Gina to do for the shopkeepers." Wendy popped two pumpkin pies into one of Charlie's ovens.

The big kitchen had been designed by Angie's grandmother. Though it had been more than a decade ago, the décor was timeless— marble countertops, industrial-sized appliances, a large center island—and matched the rustic vibe of the ranch house. Angie's favorite part was the enormous hand-crafted deer-antler chandeliers that hung from the iron trusses. Grandpa Dalton had collected the antlers right off the ranch.

What a lot of people didn't know was that bucks shed their antlers after breeding season every year and grew new ones. No animals were harmed in the making of the chandeliers, which made them even more special to Angie.

There were so many good memories in this kitchen that every time she was in the room, she felt embraced by love. And today was no different as her family jostled around, cooking together for their Thanksgiving feast.

"What time did you leave last night?" Charlie asked Angie.

"Mom, Dad, and I stayed late to help Gina put the restaurant back together." Though Sawyer had done the bulk of the work. "I think we got home at about midnight."

"That sounds about right." Wendy was on her second round of pies, this time pecan.

"You know you're welcome to stay here if you get tired of sharing a bathroom," Charlie told Wendy and wiped her forehead with the back of her arm. The kitchen was getting warm from all the activity.

"Thank you, dear. But I can't get enough of this one." Wendy joined Angie at the sink and pulled her into a hug. "Every second is precious."

Guilt jabbed Angie in the gut. And not for the first time she cursed Zane and wished Burt to hell and back.

"What time is everyone getting here?" she asked, trying to stay focused on the holiday and not the past.

"Laney and Jimmy Ray about four. Everyone else at five," Charlie said.

Besides Tuff, Charlie had invited Tiffany and her husband. With the magic of folding banquet tables and chairs, the dining room now spilled into the front room. Of course, Charlie and Aubrey had put their designer touches on everything from the linens to the centerpieces. The whole setup looked like a magazine centerfold.

"The briskets are halfway there." Jace came into the kitchen followed by Cash.

"I hope they're done in time for dinner." Charlie pointed to the dressed turkeys. "Those bad boys are ready for the fryers. I'm making a small one in the oven for the drippings to make gravy."

Cash and Jace each hefted a bird and headed to the outdoor kitchen. It reminded Angie of their big holiday dinners when her grandparents were alive. Last Thanksgiving, it had just been her in Portland, missing her family with a vengeance, feeling so alone that it physically hurt.

Angie thought about Tuff losing his mother. Although they'd been estranged, it had to be hard facing the holidays so close to her death. She was glad he wouldn't be alone, and that her large, extended family would make him feel at home.

"We're here." Sawyer wandered in, carrying two huge pans covered in foil. "Sorry we took so long." He kissed their mother's cheek and found an empty spot on the counter to set down his load.

"Where's Gina?"

"She's outside, bossing around the men, telling them how to fry the turkeys." He rolled his eyes. "You'd think the woman was a world-famous chef or something. I've got to go back to the car and get the vegetables and chaffing dishes."

"You want some help?" Angie followed Sawyer to his Range Rover.

"You have a good night with Mom and Dad?"

"Wonderful."

He cocked a brow. "They're not driving you nuts?"

"Nope, not yet." She grinned. "Mom wants me to come home with them, but I don't want to leave the store. I've got a few ideas I want to try out to bring up revenue."

He opened the trunk. "Ange, don't worry about the store. If you want to go to LA to spend time with them, go. Do whatever is good for you. We'll make it work until you get back."

"Can I be honest with you?"

"Always." He put his hands on top of her shoulders. "You know that. Or at least you used to know that."

It was a veiled way of him saying that she should've come to him when things began to disintegrate at The Farm. Couldn't he understand that she was trying to protect him and everyone else she loved? But today wasn't the day to get into the choices she'd made. Good or bad.

"At first, I didn't want to take over Daltons. What do I know about retail, Sawyer? Or the grocery business for that matter? I did it because I knew you all were trying to find a place for me here and I didn't want to seem ungrateful or entitled. Furthermore, I wanted to be of use. I wanted to make up for my absence while you, Cash, and Jace did the heavy lifting to save the ranch.

"But it turns out that I like it. No, it's not helping the needy, or saving the environment, or working for world peace." She let out a self-conscious laugh at her exalted dreams. "It's none of those things. But it's our family's legacy and it feels good knowing that I'm doing my part. And truth be told, I enjoy getting up every morning, coming to the market, and figuring out ways to make the store better. I've sort of begun to obsess over it. Not just because we need it to turn a profit but because I want to succeed at something. I want to leave my mark, even if it's a small one." She stopped, feeling foolish. She'd made a mess of everything, including spending her entire trust fund, which instead could've gone to the back taxes on the ranch. And here she was getting choked up about something she hadn't even accomplished yet. For all she knew Daltons was a lost cause. But it was important to her. It was important that she contribute, even in a minor way.

"What I'm trying to say is that I don't want to leave in the middle of the project." Just run off like the dilettante everyone no doubt thought she was. "I need to see it through." Then, maybe she could find her own way. Perhaps work at a non-profit or a charity, something where she could make a difference, even if it was just a small one.

"Then stay." Sawyer handed her a foil pan. "Mom and Dad will understand. And I don't have to tell you how much we appreciate the help. But, Ange, don't put too much pressure on yourself."

"Why not?" She stared him down, sick and tired of being handled as though she'd break. "Don't you put pressure on yourself to be the best journalist you can be? Doesn't Gina put pressure on herself to be a successful businesswoman? I'm fine, Sawyer. I'm not going to fall apart."

"I didn't mean to imply that you would. I'm just so freaking thankful to have you back, Angie. For all of us that's enough. Having you here... it's more than enough." He took a deep breath.

"Sawyer, don't you see, it's not enough for me."

He rubbed his chin and turned to the mountains, staring out over the horizon. "Yeah, I get it. I do. We better get inside before they send a search party."

"Give me another pan. I can carry two."

They went into the house and joined the rest of the chaos. Jimmy Ray and Laney arrived early. Between them and Gina working the kitchen like drill sergeants, everything got onto the table like clockwork. Tuff showed up just in time for the first course.

Angie could tell he'd dressed with care. A crisp white dress shirt, pressed jeans, and shiny black cowboy boots. Like at Gina's party, he wore a bolo tie. Every female in the house gave him an appreciative stare, including Angie's mother.

"Do you know how much work I could get that man if he'd only move to LA?" Wendy whispered in Angie's ear.

"Tuff doesn't strike me as a Hollywood type." About the farthest thing from it, Angie thought. "And when did you become an agent?"

"Oh, darling, I have all the top studios' ears. A good publicist is worth a dozen agents."

Angie shook her head. How different she was from her parents. Sawyer too. Both of them had eschewed the glitter of Tinseltown and its trappings. She'd gone into public service and Sawyer preferred to expose corruption and shine a light on the inequities of the world.

Charlie had made a seating chart to mix up the guests. Angie had slyly moved a few folks around to get herself a chair next to Tuff. She told herself it was to save him from Tiffany.

"Hey." She squeezed between him and Jimmy Ray into her chair. "You ready to do this again?"

"I'm always ready to eat," he said and gave her cream sweater dress a once over, his eyes lingering on her low-cut cowl. "You look pretty," he said in that deep drawl of his.

"Thank you. You look very nice too." More like sex on a stick. "My mother says she can get you work as a leading man on the silver screen if you're interested."

He choked on his water. "She didn't say that."

"Oh, she most certainly did. Want me to prove it?" She started to call across the table, but Tuff put a firm hand on her arm, his fingers splayed across her skin, leaving their warm imprint.

She felt as aroused as she did that first day in his studio. He slowly removed his hand and set it in his lap. She reached underneath the table and held it for a second, then let go.

"Tuff, can you pass the rolls?" Jace sat on the other side of Tuff, three seats away from Charlie, which he wasn't happy about.

"Sure thing." Tuff handed him the basket.

"Are you the one who brought the growler?"

Tuff nodded. "It's from that craft brewery in Auburn."

"Nice." Jace held out his glass. "I'll take a taste if you don't mind pouring."

Tuff filled his goblet and poured a splash in Angie's glass. "Give it a try and tell me what you think. Maybe you want to stock it in Daltons."

Their beer sales were good, so yeah. She took a sip. Though she was no expert, it tasted great. Not too hoppy but complex.

"Mmm." She wiped a dab of foam from her mouth with her napkin. "Let's see what Sawyer says. He's the beer connoisseur."

Sawyer was at the other end of the table. She got his attention and passed the growler down. Cash intercepted it and poured himself a glass. It made the rounds before it got to Sawyer. Everyone raved about it and Angie made a mental note to add it to her buying list.

"You'll have to hook me up with the brewery management," she told Tuff.

"I could do that. I know the owner. He had me customize a saddle for his kid, who has scoliosis."

"I never thought about saddles for people with disabilities. Do you do a lot of that?" She plucked a roll from the basket.

"Not a lot but a fair number. I like coming up with creative solutions for people who otherwise would have a problem riding."

"I imagine you would." He was deliberate that way. And caring. "I learn something new about you every day."

Something akin to dread flickered across his face. But it was gone so fast that Angie thought she might've imagined it.

"Could you please pass the brisket?" he said, avoiding eye contact.

Dinner was a buzz of activity with everyone talking at once and platters clattering as they were handed around the table. Angie sampled a little bit of everything, the tastes and smells eliciting so many happy memories of her childhood at the ranch.

Jimmy Ray talked Angie's ear off while Laney made a half dozen trips back and forth from the dining room to the kitchen for replenishments.

"It's your night off, Laney." Angie jumped up before Laney could fetch a second bowl of brussels sprouts, warming in the oven. "I'll get it."

She was dishing the sprouts into an ironstone serving bowl when Tuff came into the kitchen.

"Need any help?"

"Nope." She held up the bowl. "I've got it covered."

He took the bowl from her and cocked his hip against the counter. "Let me do something."

"There's nothing to do except put those on the table." She tried to move him along, but he wouldn't budge.

"Did I tell you how pretty you look?"

"You did. But you can tell me again if you want to."

A smile played on his lips. "Woman, what you do to a dress ought to be illegal."

"Are you flirting with me?" She put her hands on her hips. "Because I thought we weren't doing that."

"Doing what?"

"Flirting."

"I never said anything about flirting, just kissing." His brown eyes flashed with amusement.

"Well, as far as I'm concerned, they go hand in hand." She leaned into him until her breasts brushed against his chest. They were so close she could feel his breath on her face.

"You want to do this here?" There was a hint of challenge in his voice as he gazed at her lips.

Yes. No. Not when anyone could walk in. It was hard for her to think with him looking like he could devour her any second.

"You're a confounding man, Tuff Garrison."

"Yeah, why's that?"

"One minute you're saying we should just be friends and the next... this." She waved her hand between them.

He pushed himself away from the counter. "That's what happens when I'm over my two-beer limit. You ready to go back inside?" And just like that his flirting fell by the wayside and he went back to being all business.

The man really was mystifying.

Chapter 14

The call came in the middle of the night. Or was it the wee hours of the morning?

Angie rolled over and looked at her clock. Two a.m. What the hell? Her first inclination was to let it go to voicemail. It was probably a wrong number anyway.

Then she snapped fully awake. What if it was an emergency? Gina and the baby. Or one of the boys, who were no strangers to urgent care.

She searched for her phone on the nightstand but couldn't find it. Funny, she could've sworn she left it there. After all this time she still liked to have it close, especially at night. She padded to the chair in the corner of her bedroom and rifled through her purse. Just as she felt it in the palm of her hand the ringing stopped.

Angie tapped on her call log when the ringing started all over again. The screen lit up with a New Mexico area code.

"Kari?" she answered and cleared her throat. "Is that you?"

Silence.

"Hello. Is anyone there?"

More silence.

"Whoever this is, stop playing games." Her voice trembled. "Hello. Hello. Do you hear me?"

She hung up and hit redial. Perhaps it was a bad connection. Cell could be sketchy in the cabin, especially in bad weather. The first week of December had brought non-stop rain.

But she got the damned recording again. "We're sorry, the number you have reached has been disconnected or is no longer in service. If you feel you have reached this recording in error, please check the number and try your call again."

Sagging onto the edge of her bed, shaken, she wondered what to do next. It was too early to call anyone. And what would she say anyway? *The phone rang but no one was there.* Even though it was the second time it happened, it was probably a digital anomaly. A phone chip gone berserk, making random calls to anyone in Kari's contact list.

She considered calling Earl, who was used to his phone ringing at all hours of the night, but dismissed the idea. Again, she had nothing substantive to report and would sound like a wackjob.

Instead, she crawled under the covers and lay awake, trying to convince herself that there was nothing to worry about. No one from the US Attorney's Office or Marshals Service had contacted her since she'd been home. No news was good news, right? But the call continued to plague her and she couldn't fall back asleep.

Finally, she threw her blankets off, went into the kitchen, and made herself a cup of herbal tea. Maybe that would do the trick. She peered out the kitchen window and noticed that Tuff's own kitchen light was on. No telling, though, whether he was awake at this ungodly hour or if he'd merely gone to bed with the light on.

She stood at the window for a while, sipping her tea, looking for movement. And then she caught a glimpse of him at the refrigerator.

Angie went into the living room, wrapped herself in a throw blanket, and crossed the foot bridge that separated their two cabins. He opened the door before she could knock and stood in the entryway in a pair of unbuttoned Levi's and a bare chest.

"What's wrong?"

"I got another call from the same area code."

"Your friend?"

She shrugged. "I'm not sure. All I got was static. I thought it might be a bad connection. But when I tried to call the number back, I got that same recording as last time."

"Come in out of the cold." He looked down at her bare legs and silly fuzzy slippers.

She'd never been inside Tuff's cabin before. Though it was the same design as hers, it was pretty bare bones. No pictures on the wall, no color, no personality. Just a few pieces of plain, utilitarian furniture, including a leather sofa that she was fairly certain Tuff hadn't made. The cabin was tidy, she'd give it that.

"Let me turn on the heat."

It was freezing inside. Too cold to be walking around shirtless.

"Why are you up?" she asked.

"Couldn't sleep. Sometimes I get that way." He turned the dial on the thermostat. "This call…it got to you, didn't it?"

She didn't bother to lie. "Yes, though I hope you'll tell me all the reasons why I'm being ridiculous."

He motioned for her to take the couch, while he chose a dun-colored recliner. The whole house was awash in tan and beige. At least the log walls were charming.

"Clearly, you've got your reasons for being concerned. I wouldn't dismiss that."

It was difficult to concentrate on his words while he was half naked. Her eyes kept zoning in on his chest. Tuff was cut. Not like a body builder, which wasn't at all Angie's thing. But like a man who was used to physical labor. Add in the delicious sprinkling of dark hair that narrowed into a happy trail disappearing under the waistband of his jeans and she forgot about the disturbing phone call altogether.

"Can a phone just have a mind of its own, even if the number has been disconnected?"

"I don't think so. But it's out of my wheelhouse." He leaned closer to Angie. "What do you think is going on? Because you're obviously upset, or you wouldn't be here at two in the morning."

She sighed. "I think someone is intentionally trying to freak me out."

Tuff sat up straight and rubbed the bristle on his chin. She'd never seen him unshaven. Between the scruff and the bare chest, he reminded her of central casting's idea of a cowboy maverick. Rough and tumble and inordinately sexy.

"Who's this someone?"

"I don't know." Everyone with a motive was in jail. As far as she knew prisoners weren't allowed to have cell phones. Or else they'd terrorize everyone on their shit lists.

"Could it be this friend of yours?"

"Kari?" The name slipped out before Angie had had time to think. "No, though she may be trying to reach me."

"This seems like a weird way, don't you think?" He locked eyes with her and in a soft voice asked, "Could it be the guy you were seeing?"

She had no idea how Tuff would know about Zane unless Sawyer or one of her cousins had opened their big mouths. But they knew better than anyone not to give away the full story. "I highly doubt it."

"Why's that?" He continued to watch her.

"Because he's not in a position to make phone calls."

"Is he dead?"

She jerked her head back. "Why would you...think...or even say that? Of course he's not dead."

"Then he could be making the goddamn phone calls."

She had no intention of telling him that Zane was locked up in a federal holding facility. "Then how do you explain the recording?"

He got up, grabbed his phone off the kitchen counter, and fiddled with it for a few seconds. "Is this the message you got?"

"Yes."

"I got it straight off the Internet." He played the message again. "That's from my phone. I recorded it. Anyone with a cell phone and a little knowledge could make that their voicemail message."

"So, you're saying the number isn't really disconnected, it's just a ruse?" She didn't know why she hadn't thought of that.

"Ange, I have no way of knowing. But it's possible. I say we wait a day or so and call again. This time from a different number, something unrecognizable to your caller, and see if he picks up."

It was a clever idea. "Or am I making too much of this? Maybe it was an accidental dial." Kari might have put the message on her phone in an abundance of caution. Unlike Angie, she'd rejected the protection of the federal government and was going it alone. Faking that her phone was disconnected might help throw unwanted callers off her trail.

He hitched a brow. "Twice? I'm not a big believer in coincidences."

"Okay, now you're kind of freaking me out." What if someone had gotten to Kari and now had her phone? But who?

"Do you have reason to be afraid of this guy? Or could he just be messing with you?"

She was definitely afraid of Zane. If he were free, instead of behind bars, she'd be terrified. In Zaire he'd been the gentlest of souls and kind beyond belief. Not until they moved to Taos did she realize he had a mean streak a mile long.

But it was Burt and his men who she feared the most. Besides having a total disdain for the law, they believed women were for sex and little more. Their contempt for any woman who dared to defy them was swift and brutal. She'd experienced it firsthand, though not as badly as some of the others.

She had Jet Ackerson, an undercover ATF agent, to thank for that. If he hadn't infiltrated the group, she'd likely be dead right now.

"I don't have any reason to be afraid of him," she said but even she could hear the hesitancy in her voice.

Tuff didn't say anything for a long time. He got up, went to his room, and returned with a sweatshirt on. Unlike before, he took the seat next to her on the sofa. "I know you're not being straight with me, Angie, which is your prerogative. But it's clear to me that there's more going on here then you're letting on. The bottom line is if you don't go to Jace I will."

* * * *

The last time Tuff kept a woman's secrets, it had ended in bloodshed. He wasn't doing it again. Whatever Angie was dealing with—and he had no doubts left that whatever it was it was scaring the shit out of her—was for the police to decipher. Not him.

He'd built a life here. A good life. He wasn't going to let his infatuation with Angie screw with his judgment. And everything about this situation screamed police matter.

Sure, on the face of it, it was nothing more than a couple of prank calls. But her reaction to them told him she was hiding something. Sawyer all but confided that she'd been in a bad relationship. In Tuff's experience that meant abuse. He'd seen it up close and personal. And the phone calls and the day Angie stood petrified in front of her door, afraid that someone had broken in…well, they all held the hallmarks of a woman afraid of being stalked.

Unfortunately, he knew the psyche of an abuser all too well. His mother's lovers weren't happy unless they were controlling every second of her day. The last one, Floyd, got himself worked up if Mary paid too much attention to Tuff. Her own goddamn kid. God forbid she should give Tuff a couple of bucks to get a hamburger. Or help him with his homework without Floyd going berserk and cracking them both across the face.

Yeah, Tuff knew the type all right.

"Did you hear me, Angie?"

"There's no need to get Jace involved. I'm just being paranoid. That's all."

"Paranoid will save your life." He took her hand in his and held it. "You know what else can save your life? Going to the police. You're lucky enough to have a cop in your family. Whatever this is," he pointed to Angie's lap where her phone sat in the folds of her throw blanket, "Jace will figure it out. And if it turns out to be nothing you'll sleep at night."

She gave an imperceptible nod. "Can we at least try tomorrow to call from a different phone before I go to Jace?"

He thought about it. "We probably only have one shot at it before the jig is up. Jace should be involved in the call, Angie. What's your problem with going to him?"

"I sound hysterical. Nothing has happened except for a couple of phone calls."

"And the other day when you thought someone had broken into your house." He jutted his chin at her to make his point.

"That's the thing, no one did. I'm letting my imagination run away with me."

"Maybe. Maybe not. Nothing wrong with alerting the sheriff."

She rolled her eyes. "My brother wants to get me a panic button."

That told Tuff all he needed to know. Sawyer wasn't the type to overreact. In fact, he was one of the most level-headed guys Tuff had ever met. And as a journalist he'd seen some things. Some really bad things.

"Why not? It certainly can't hurt."

"Thank you." She reached up and touched his face. "I bet you wish I never moved in across the creek. Before me it was probably nice and quiet. Drama free."

He wished she'd never moved in across the creek. But it had nothing to do with preserving the quiet and everything to do with his attraction to her. "Nah, drama free is highly overrated."

Damn, he wanted to kiss her. She looked so beautiful cuddled up in her blanket on his couch. Her hair mussed from her bed and her eyes blue as topaz, looking at him like he had all the answers.

Only by dint of will did he keep himself from pressing his lips against hers.

Instead, she did it for him, catching his mouth with hers. The kiss started slow, hesitant at first as if she was testing the waters. She pressed her body against him and he rested his hand on her bare leg. Her skin was warm and soft. He let his fingers creep under her nightgown. Not the flannel one she wore that morning on the porch. This one was silky to the touch and floated over his fingers like feathers. He wanted to see her in it, but the blanket was in the way.

She must've read his mind because she moved it, giving him an unobstructed view. The whole number was held up by two thin straps and clung to her breasts like a second skin. Tuff grew harder, his erection straining against the fly of his jeans.

He went in for another kiss, plunging his tongue inside her mouth. She tasted like chamomile. Her hands slid under his sweatshirt, touching his stomach, and he held his breath. Tuff moved over her, but the sofa was too small for the both of them.

Without saying a word, he lifted her into his arms and carried her into his room. The blankets were shoved to the foot of the bed, evidence of his fitful night. He brushed them out of the way and laid her down.

She stared up at him with her big blue eyes and his pulse quickened. He wanted her. Despite all the reasons it was a terrible idea, he couldn't seem to stop himself.

She reached up and pulled him down on top of her. Afraid he'd crush her, he went up on both elbows and gazed down at her. She was so beautiful she took his breath away. He couldn't remember a woman who'd ever made him this willing to break his own self-imposed rules. He'd always been a rigid man when it came to his romantic entanglements. Either this new stable life of his had him he slipping, or she'd casted a spell over him.

Don't over think it, he told himself. Take what she's offering.

He rolled them both to their sides and touched her breasts, watching her nipples pebble through the silky fabric. He licked them, leaving wet spots on her nightgown. She shivered and he immediately reached for one of the blankets.

"No," she murmured and rolled onto her back, stretching her arms over her head.

"You're not cold?"

"Uh-uh. Hot." She caught his mouth with hers and arched up to kiss him.

He tugged her straps down her shoulders, exposing her breasts. They were small and pert and fit perfectly in his hands. As he fondled them, she moaned and threw her head back. His hands were rough from working with leather and he feared he'd scrape her soft skin. But the more he touched her the more turned on she got.

He dragged the hem of her nightgown over her head, leaving her in nothing but a pair of white panties. His eyes heated at the sight of her.

"Your turn." She rucked up his sweatshirt, pulled it off, and tossed it on the floor. Her hands roamed his chest and his arms, making him suck in a breath. Then she went for his jeans, undoing each button one at a time.

Impatient, he lifted up and shucked them off in one fluid motion.

"These, too." She tugged at his shorts, dragging them down his legs.

In return, he slid her panties off and arched a brow at the sight of her. The carpet didn't match the drapes. "And here I thought you were a real redhead."

She erupted into a fit of giggles.

"Shush." He rolled her on top of him and ran his fingers through her hair. "Disappointed?"

"Nope. Never." He reached down and caressed her curvy backside. "You're about as perfect as it gets."

She propped herself up and stared down at him. "Do you mean that?"

"I never say anything I don't mean." She was a knockout. There wasn't a man alive who wouldn't tell her that. "Come 'ere."

He cupped the back of her head and kissed her deeply as he rolled her under him. "We doing this?"

"I hope so." She reached between his legs and stroked him and he nearly lost his mind.

"Take it easy there. I don't want reach the finish line even before we get started." He trailed kisses down her throat, in the valley between her breasts, over her taut belly until he hit the promised land.

"Ooh." She grabbed his shoulders. "Oh, Tuff."

He took her to the brink, then kissed his way down the inside of her thigh and back up again. This time, he planned to take her all the way. But she tugged his head up.

"I want you," she whispered. "Please."

He leaned over her, pulled open the door of his nightstand, and found a condom. She grabbed it away from him, ripped it open, and rolled it down his length. He was inside of her so fast, he'd probably beaten his all-time record.

"This okay?" It was a tight fit. He stopped moving to give her time to adjust to him. "God, you feel so good."

"Mmm." She tilted her head back on his pillow and ground into him, begging for more.

"You sure?"

She cupped his ass and pushed him deeper, thrusting upward. He moved again, pumping in and out at a steady pace. She whimpered and wrapped her legs around his waist so he could go even deeper. Then she met him stroke for stroke.

They were perfectly in sync and he couldn't remember ever being this turned on. Her body, her scent, the sexy noises she made was like a wild aphrodisiac. He moved faster. Harder. She moved with him as they took each other higher.

He touched and kissed her everywhere, consumed with giving her pleasure. She was close, he could feel her body pulsating, ready to take its release. He worked her with his finger and watched her come apart as she called out his name.

"Tuff? Tuff?"

"I'm right with you, baby."

A few minutes later, he collapsed on top of her, sated, covered in a sheen of sweat. He waited for his breathing to even out and pulled her on top of him.

"Wow."

"Yeah," he said, "I wasn't expecting that."

"What do you mean?" She rolled off him, turned on her side, and propped up on one elbow.

For it to be so intense. "I don't know. You coming over. Us winding up in bed."

"Oh." She sounded disappointed. "I didn't plan it if that's what you think."

He sifted a strand of her hair between his fingers. "That's not what I was saying."

Tuff swung his legs over the side of the bed. "Be right back."

By the time he returned from the bathroom, Angie was curled up like a cat, sound asleep. He stood back, watching her for a few minutes, trying to will away the tiny ache in his heart. This is a one off, he told himself. *Never get too attached.*

Chapter 15

Angie woke up to find dawn's early light seeping through the window shades. She reached for Tuff, but he was gone.

She got out of bed, found a flannel shirt in the closet and slipped it on before going in search of him. He was nowhere to be found. The only hint that he'd been there at all was a half pot of freshly brewed coffee. She went outside to check the porch only to find that his truck was also gone.

She knew he liked to ride Muchacho in the morning. Maybe he was at the barn.

Angie returned to the kitchen and rummaged through Tuff's refrigerator. There was a carton of milk hiding behind a six-pack of beer. She fixed her coffee the way she liked it and drank it at the sink. Buddy trotted in from the living room and demanded a pat on his head.

"You want to go outside, Buddy boy?" She walked him to the door and waited on the porch for him to conduct his business. He halfheartedly peed on a tree and came running back inside.

Angie gathered up her stuff and went home. She stood in the shower until the water turned cold and quickly dressed. It was too early to call Earl. She charged her phone and flicked on the TV. Nothing on but those morning shows.

For the sake of something to do, Angie made another pot of coffee. She peered out the window at Tuff's cabin while she waited for it to brew. He'd probably go straight to his studio. For all Angie knew he was there now. Maybe he'd had an early morning appointment. But even as she thought it, she knew it wasn't true.

At seven she called Nina and told her she'd be late to the store. At eight she dialed Earl's number, dreading the conversation she needed to have with him. But if anyone would know what to do it was Earl.

"Hi."

"This is early for you. Everything okay?" His voice said he knew it wasn't.

"Yes, but I've gotten two calls from Kari's number. The first one was a couple of weeks ago. I missed her call and when I tried to call her back, I got a message that the number had been disconnected. I dismissed it as an unexplained weirdness. Then I got another call last night. When I answered there was static. I thought it was a bad connection, so again I tried to call her back and got the same message."

There was a long silence on the other end of the line. Either Earl was pissed or he was trying to parse what Angie had just told him.

She waited patiently until Earl said, "I'll look into it. In the meantime, don't call Kari again and change your number."

"Why? Zane or Burt, or any of the others…they can't call me from jail, can they? They're not even allowed phones."

"Jails…prisons… are full of contraband. Drugs, weapons, phones, you name it, they can get it. Change your number, Angie."

"Okay. But how would they have co-opted Kari's number?"

"I'm not saying they're responsible. I'm going to do some nosing around. But I don't like it. I don't like it at all."

"What do you think it is? What do you think is going on? I'm worried about Kari. Is there a way we can do a welfare check on her?"

"There's no we, Angie. Leave that to me. I don't know what's going on. It's more than likely nothing. But I still don't like it. Anything else you'd like to tell me?"

She vacillated on whether to divulge the day she'd come home to find the rolled-up paper dislodged from her door and decided it was silly. No one had broken into her cabin. "That's it. Other than the phone calls, everything is fine."

"Don't wait weeks before you call me again, Angie. This is how people mess up. They ignore the signs."

"Now you're scaring me."

"Good," he said. "That's how you stay alive."

She was used to his unvarnished and sometimes harsh advice. Yet, a shiver went through her. "When will this end, Earl? I just want to feel safe again."

"I know you do." His voice softened. "It's what we all want. But I don't need to tell you what kind of people these are. Until the case is fully resolved you need to stay on your toes. The last thing they want is you testifying against them. And I wouldn't put it past them to try to intimidate you. Even from behind bars."

"But all they can do is try to scare me, right? It's not like they can actually get to me?"

There was a long pause. "Just stay on your toes and loop your cousins in on what's going on. Let 'em know I'm looking into these phone calls."

"I will." And she'd remind Sawyer about getting that panic button for her. "You'll call me as soon as you check on Kari, right?"

"Yep. I'll be in touch." He signed off.

Angie hurried off to work, desperately needing the distraction. Nina had dragged their holiday specials out onto the curb. It was something new Angie was trying in the hopes of luring more people into the store.

"It looks great. Sorry you had to do it yourself."

"No problem," Nina said from the top of a stepladder as she cleaned the front windows.

Angie wished she could give her a raise. But until the store was in the black, there wasn't money.

"Your brother was in looking for you."

Angie went to the little alcove she called her office, took off her jacket, and called Sawyer. She got his voicemail and left a message.

A few customers wandered in and Angie drifted up front. From the familiar way they chatted with Nina it was clear they were locals. Two of the women wandered over to the kitchenware department and picked up a set of Gina's jadeite measuring cups. Angie heard one of them say, "These are the ones she uses on her show." They both added a set to their baskets.

"Do you ladies need any help? We have a special today on Dalton ribeye steaks."

The women followed Angie to the butcher shop in the corner of the store, took one look at the price, and made their excuses.

"I still have a quarter of a 4-H steer we bought last spring in the deep freezer," one of them said.

No question it was the price tags scaring off the locals. Angie had already discussed lowering the prices with the others. But after doing the math it didn't pay. They just couldn't compete with the chain and big-box stores. Plus, as Jace said, their product was far superior. Too good to give away. Their target market had to be foodies, who were more concerned about knowing the producer's story than they were about price.

She met the two women at the cash register and rung up their measuring cups, two Gina DeRose cake mixes, two jars of Gina's famous spaghetti sauce and two bottles of wine from a local vineyard.

Angie could see a trend emerging. The locals only came to buy Gina DeRose merchandise or specialty items only found at Daltons. They bypassed staples that were cheaper at the local supermarket and balked at products that were too high-end, like Dalton steaks.

Maybe it was time to cut back on the number of staples they carried. It wasn't as if tourists were flocking to Daltons to buy rice and flour. Once again, she found herself facing the same conundrum with no solutions.

Sawyer entered the store at the same time the local ladies walked out.

"I heard you were looking for me," Angie said.

"Yep. Let's take a walk."

Angie gave him a quizzical look, which he greeted with "You have a jacket? It's cold outside."

For a flash she thought he might've found out about her and Tuff and was here to give her another lecture. But it was highly unlikely he knew where she'd been at two in the morning.

She grabbed her coat and together they followed the creek, which meandered through the center. One of her favorite things about Dry Creek Village were the trails and picnic tables Sawyer and her cousins had installed. It was so picturesque and inviting, like a sweet country square. And with all the Christmas decorations it was magical.

"What's going on?"

"I got your panic button." He reached in his jacket pocket and pulled out a small carton. "There's an app that all of us will have to download on our phones. You can either use your phone to alert us or this." He shook the package.

After the previous night's bizarre phone call, Sawyer's timing was impeccable. "How does it work?"

"It's a simple panic button you wear around your wrist like a watch. The minute you fall and can't get up, you press the button and we come running." He smirked and she socked him in the arm. "It's not a hundred-percent waterproof, so take it off before you shower. Other than that, you wear it wherever you go. It has a built-in tracker so we can see your location on the app."

They stopped strolling and sat at one of the picnic tables. Angie was glad she had on her warmest jacket but wished she'd worn gloves. She stuck her hands in her pockets while Sawyer removed the plastic wrapping and opened the box.

The creek was heavy from a recent snowfall in the mountains. She watched the water crash over a rock formation and wondered if the waterfall would still be there come summer. Either way, it was a great spot for picnickers.

He fidgeted with the watch for a while, then handed it to her. "It's all programmed. Just wear it and you're good to go." He pointed to the side where there was a small, discreet button. "Give me your phone."

"It's in my purse at the store." He gave her an impatient look. "What? You rushed me off. How was I supposed to know that you'd need it?"

"I'll download the app when we go back." He reached into his pocket and took out his own phone and spent a few minutes on it, presumably adding the panic tracker.

She watched over his shoulder as he went through the setup. "Where did you find out about this?" It was so basic, yet brilliant for their purposes.

He laughed. "Did you think I was kidding about the 'I've fallen and I can't get up?' It was invented for elderly people so their kids and caretakers can monitor them when they're alone. It got great reviews but was on backorder. I finally got it yesterday."

She should've known Sawyer wouldn't have forgotten.

"Thank you." She weighed it in her hand. It looked like a smartwatch or one of those exercise monitors that measured your walking steps.

"Put it on. It's no good if you don't wear it all the time."

"Okay, Mr. Bossy Pants." She poked him in the arm. He was a good big brother. The best anyone could ask for.

"I'll make sure everyone downloads the app." He paused, then said, "I know it's just a precaution and we'll never need it but it's peace of mind."

She nodded, wondering whether she should tell him about the phone calls. Angie had promised Tuff that she'd go to Jace. And if she did that, Sawyer would find out any way. Her family had never been good at keeping secrets. But now that she'd told Earl maybe she didn't have to fill Jace in. Or at least not until Earl learned what was going on. If it was nothing, why get her whole family upset and involved?

"It's good," she agreed. "Just until the trial."

He pulled on her ponytail like he used to do when they were kids. "It's good having you on the ranch, Ange." There was a world of meaning in those simple words. *Thank God you're alive. I've missed you, Angie. I love you.*

"I love you too, Sawyer." Her eyes misted and she swiped at them with the back of her hand. "Do you know how happy I am that I'll be here for the birth of your child? It means the world to me."

"Me too." He slung his arm around her neck. "Shall we go back? It's freezing out here."

"Yep." She rose. And despite the cold, they took their time returning.

"I think we should cut back on staples at the store," she said.

"Why?"

"They're not selling. Locals don't come to Daltons for sugar or boxed cereal. And tourists are definitely not interested. For the Walberg's honey, yes. For the Bake Shop's legendary Sierra Foothills Granola, yes. But not for C&H and Cheerios. It's just not happening. And it's taking up valuable shelf space, though I don't have a clue yet what to replace those products with. Nothing we're selling, even the reasonably priced local stuff, is flying out of the store."

"If it'll save us money, I'm all for it. What about more of Gina's products?"

"That's what I'm thinking. But non-perishable ones. And I want to put in a coffee bar. I've put it off because of concerns over competing with the restaurant and Laney and Jimmy Ray's sarsaparilla stand but I know it would make money."

"How so?"

"Because travelers come in, looking for it. They'll buy something from the bakery and ask for coffee. Before it got too cold, they'd sit outside at one of the picnic tables and eat their slice of pie, banana bread, or cupcake. Sans the coffee. I was thinking that if I added a few bistro tables in the store and a serve-yourself coffee setup it would be profitable. And who knows, while they're sitting there sipping their coffee, eating one of the Bake Shop's monster cookies, they might glance over at the kitchen display and discover they can't live without a cast iron pan from Gina's collection. From everything I've read, coffee is good business. The markup is fantastic, and it'll be a good way for us to showcase some of the local roasters we sell."

Sawyer rubbed his jaw. "I see what you're saying. But yeah, I would hate to piss off Laney or interfere with the restaurant's profits. Right now, they're our bread and butter. Let's talk to them. If they're good with it, I say full speed ahead." He put his arm around Angie's neck and gave her a noogie on the head. "Wow, you're into this, aren't you?"

She laughed. "You sound surprised. See, I'm not the flake you always thought I was."

He didn't argue, which reaffirmed it.

"I'll talk to Aubrey and Charlie about bistro tables. Maybe we can do something fun, not just your run-of-the-mill restaurant supply furniture."

"And something cheap." Sawyer punctuated the word "cheap." "This can't be a big investment. We're already bleeding money where Daltons and the butcher shop is concerned."

"Gotcha. There's another issue I wanted to raise."

"Shoot."

"We're wasting a lot of food. Every day, Nina and I go through expiration dates and are chucking stuff left and right. I'd like to find an organization we can donate the food to. A soup kitchen, a homeless shelter, something."

"Absolutely. I say you spearhead that. No one is going to argue that it's not a good idea. And that kind of thing is your specialty."

Either Angie had missed the sarcasm or there wasn't any. She took a good look at Sawyer just to make sure she hadn't missed it. But there was no smirk playing on his lips or condescending twinkle in his eyes.

"Then I'll take the reins on that and find a good group we can give to." Since she'd been tossing out perfectly good food it had been weighing on her. Her life's mission had been to feed the hungry and here she was worrying about profit margins and the great markup on coffee.

"Thank you," Sawyer said. "I don't think any of us thought about the waste or how it could help someone. We should've."

After Sawyer programmed her phone with the new app, she spent the rest of the morning looking for a worthy organization. Around lunchtime, she wandered over to Tuff's shop. It was time to take the bull by the horns.

He was on the phone when she got there. It sounded like a client wanted a show saddle. He was sketching an elaborate drawing of it on a pad as he talked. When he saw her, he gave her the five-minute sign. She spent the time strolling around the store, looking for any new items.

Angie peeked in his studio and spied a new shipment of leather in a rich burgundy. She moved closer and touched the edge. It was buttery soft and smelled like Tuff. She stood there for a moment, just letting the aroma surround her.

Tuff finished his call and found her sitting at his worktable. "Sorry about that."

"No worries. It sounded like a customer with an interesting assignment."

"Yep, but a tight deadline."

"They want it for Christmas?"

"Nah, February. But it's intricate and there are others ahead of her."

"It's good to have the work."

"I'm not arguing with you. I'm damned happy to have it."

She hadn't meant to come off as chiding. The whole conversation felt forced. And the air between them crackled with awkwardness.

Angie pasted on a smile. "Where's Buddy?" She'd noted that he wasn't in his usual spot under the table.

"Home. I left him with you."

She started to ask him why he'd left so early and stopped herself. He didn't owe her an explanation. And it would only make her sound like she had expectations from their night together. She didn't. It was just something that happened.

"I've got to get back to the store. I just wanted to make sure you and I are okay."

Tuff used a box cutter to finish tearing open the carton with the new leather and hefted the bolt onto an empty holder. "Yep, we're good."

Then why did he sound as if he regretted sleeping with her?

"Did you talk to Jace?"

"Not yet. But Sawyer gave me this." She held up her wrist to show him the panic watch.

He stopped what he was doing and took a closer look. "How does it work?"

Angie showed him the app on her phone. "Everyone in my family will be notified if I push the button." She motioned to the pin on the watch. "It's that simple."

"It's good but it's not a substitute for telling Jace about the phone calls." He shot her a look that said he'd go through with telling Jace himself if Angie didn't.

"I'll tell him, Tuff. As soon as he gets off work."

"Good." He reached out and stroked her arm, then immediately pulled his hand back as if she might get the wrong idea.

Did she come off that needy? She had a mind to tell him that their night together meant nothing to her, that it was just sex. But it would be a lie. So she mustered all her pride and left the store with a happy, superficial we're-just-friends wave in the air.

Chapter 16

Tuff watched Angie walk out the door.

He should've offered to be on her panic list, but he needed to pull back. It wasn't right to lead her on or get involved with something he couldn't finish. He'd learned from the first time how much standing up could ruin a man's life.

He tried to work but he couldn't concentrate. The day dragged. He never finished the final touches on a bridle that had been commissioned by a rider for the Rose Parade. It was supposed to go out in the mail in two days. But he'd idled away the day, thinking about his night with Angie. He tried to tell himself that it had been a mistake. However, he knew he'd do it again given the opportunity. Not just because the sex had been fantastic but because he was drawn to Angie in a way he'd never been drawn to anyone else. That was the part he didn't quite understand. She was beautiful, smart, caring. But there had been plenty of beautiful, smart and caring women in his past.

Maybe it was his own stupid savior complex. Nah, not it, he told himself. Her troubles might add another dimension to the complexity that was Angela Dalton, but it had nothing to do with his attraction to her. The fact that she was from money and a good family should've put him on the wrong side of those proverbial tracks. Yet, she never came off as being too good for him. She was as down to earth as her brother and cousins.

He'd like to chalk up his inexplicable desire for her to chemistry, pure and simple. But that seemed like a cop out. All he knew was that every time he was with her, he felt like he was home. Even more startling about that revelation was that before Angie he hadn't even known what home felt like.

By the time he locked up for the evening, he was exhausted from doing nothing. He swung by Gina's and got a burger and fries to take home and drove the short distance to his cabin.

Angie's old Mercedes was gone. He figured she'd driven to work so she wouldn't have to walk home in the dark. Tuff had only taken his truck because he'd gone to the feedstore in the morning. And if he was being honest, he'd been intent on making a quick getaway before the vision of Angie curled up in his bed convinced him to stay.

He grabbed his food from Gina's and got out of his truck. The hairs on his arms went up before he even got to the door. The front window of his cabin was smashed.

He took the driveway at a jog when Buddy came bounding towards him from the footbridge just as Angie pulled up on her side of the creek. The dog barked like he had the devil on his heels and ran around Tuff in circles.

"What's wrong, boy?" He dropped his carry-out bag on the ground and caught Buddy by the collar. The dog had chips of glass in his fur and one of his paws was bleeding.

"Is everything okay?" Angie crossed over the bridge and did a double take at the broken window. "What happened?"

"I don't know. Just got here." He inspected Buddy closer to make sure he wasn't bleeding anywhere else. "You didn't leave him out, did you?"

"No." She came closer. "Do you think he did that?" She looked over at the window again.

"He's never done anything like that when I've left him home alone before." Tuff supposed there was a first time for everything. Thank God his windows were safety glass, or the dang dog could've killed himself.

"Is he hurt?" Angie crouched down and Buddy stuck his head under her arm and whimpered.

"It looks like his paw might've been cut by a piece of glass. I want to take him inside and get some light on him." The glow from the porch lamp wasn't bright enough. He swooped the dog up, unlocked the door and carried Buddy to the dining table.

Angie followed him in with the takeout bag he'd left on the ground.

"Could you grab me a bath towel from the linen closet?"

"On it." She put the bag down on the counter and raced into the hallway, returning a few seconds later with a towel, which she spread over the top of the table.

Tuff laid the dog down. "You mind getting the lights?"

First, she flicked on the fixture over the table, then got the ones in the kitchen and living room. He ran his hand gently over Buddy's back and sides, searching for injuries. The dog licked his hand while his eyes followed Angie around the room as she headed for Tuff's floor lamp.

"Better?"

"It's good. Thanks." Tuff examined Buddy's belly, then moved to his legs. "He seems okay. No cuts other than the one on his paw." Tuff cleaned the small wound and applied pressure with a kitchen towel to stop the bleeding.

Angie went over to the broken window. "I'm no expert but it looks like it was busted from the inside."

It was consistent with Buddy hurling himself at the glass. Tuff couldn't imagine the hound doing it, though. Buddy wasn't what you would call high strung. Hell, he spent most of the time sleeping in the pet beds Tuff had bought him. Other than chasing an occasional rabbit or squirrel, he was a well-behaved dog.

"I let him out this morning before I went home," Angie said. "Do you think he needed to go out again?"

The dog was house broken, but it seemed extreme that he would jump through a closed window to prevent having an accident in the house. "I don't think so but it's probably the longest I've ever left him in the house alone. Guess I better put in a dog door."

He carried Buddy to his dog bed and joined Angie at the window for a closer inspection. Yep, it had definitely been smashed from the inside, given that most of the glass was on the outside.

"Are you going to take him to the vet?"

"I'll wait and see how he feels. But I think he's fine." Just crazy.

Tuff went into the kitchen and filled Buddy's bowl. The dog jogged over and wasted no time scarfing down his kibble. "Doesn't look like he lost his appetite, which is a good sign."

Angie came into the kitchen, rubbing her arms. It was cold but there was no sense turning on the heat with half his living room exposed to the elements.

"I'll have to board up the window until I can get a replacement." He probably had some plywood at the shop that would work temporarily.

"Sorry." She frowned. "I'm guessing it was the last thing you wanted to do tonight."

"It'll only take me a few minutes. I just can't imagine Buddy doing something like this." It meant he couldn't leave the dog home alone for any extended period of time.

"He must've really had a running start for it to break that way."

Tuff wondered if maybe the glass had been defective and all it had taken was for Buddy to jump up on the window for it to smash. "It's times like these when one of those dog cameras would've come in handy."

"You can still get one. Well, I'll leave you to your dinner." She waved her hand at the takeout bag sitting on the counter. "If you need anything let me know."

He followed her outside to clean up the broken glass. Between their two porch lights, the footbridge was illuminated well enough for her to see her way across. He waited for her to get to her porch stairs before he went in search of a rake and a shovel. That's when she let out a blood-curdling scream.

* * * *

A rat was hanging from a noose, strung from the light above Angie's front door. There was nothing subtle about the message. Whoever left it was calling Angie a rat.

She backed off the porch, doubled over, holding her knees and tried to calm herself. Two strong arms slipped around her waist. Buddy ran up and down the stairs, growling and barking.

"Jesus Christ," Tuff muttered under his breath, staring at the rat. "Go to my cabin. I'll clean up and check the house." He whistled for the dog. "Go with Angie, boy."

"No, you shouldn't go in there alone. They're dangerous."

"Who are *they*?"

It was then that she realized her mistake. "Whoever did this." She couldn't look at the door, so she pointed.

"There's more than one of them?" His voice was steely.

"I don't know." It was the truth. The only men who could've been culpable were behind bars. "We should call Jace."

"Go to my place and call him." He held up a shovel. "I'll take care of that."

"Don't go inside until Jace gets here." She didn't think anyone would leave a package like that at the door and still think they could take her by surprise inside the cabin. But like Earl always said, it was better to be safe than sorry.

Buddy appeared torn over whether to go with Angie or to stay with Tuff. He followed her to the bridge, made a few circles, then trotted back to Tuff. Tuff yelled at him to go with her and the dog ran back. Together, they crossed the creek.

Angie phoned Jace as soon as she got inside. Within ten minutes, headlights flooded the yard. Angie counted three trucks, including Sawyer's Range Rover. Jace alighted from a Mill County Sheriff SUV. Buddy got excited, raced toward the broken window and jumped out.

Angie called to him, but it was of no use. She met Jace, Cash, and Sawyer on the porch. Buddy sat between them, thumping his tail on the wood deck.

"What happened here?" Cash pointed at the broken window.

"We think Buddy broke it, trying to get out. Tuff found him outside when he got home."

Tuff met them on the porch. "Your door is still locked and it doesn't look like anyone got inside."

"Let's have a look." Jace led the way. He wasn't in uniform, but he was wearing his badge and service weapon. Angie suspected he'd just gotten home from work when she'd called him.

"You okay?" Sawyer wrapped his arm around her shoulders as the five of them headed to her cabin.

"Yeah," though she wasn't sure how true that was. It had only taken a month for someone to pop her safety bubble. She had no illusions that it was anyone other than the Liberty Fighters.

"We'll take care of this." He gave her a hug in an effort to be reassuring.

But she'd been up close and personal with these people. They were more than her brother, the Mill County Sheriff, and the California Department of Agriculture could handle. Just ask Jet Ackerson. The ATF agent was lucky to have left The Farm alive. Angie wouldn't expose her family to that kind of danger. That's why she'd gone into WITSEC in the first place.

"I started to remove the rat," Tuff told Jace. "Then I thought better of it, figuring you might need it for evidence. I took a few pictures, though."

Tuff led them to Angie's doorstep. She held back, her heart still pounding. Even from a distance, she could see that Tuff had taken down the noose from the porch light. From the way the men were crouched down, she assumed Tuff had left the package intact on the deck floor.

"Ange, throw me your key," Sawyer called to her.

She moved a little closer, trying to avert her eyes, and tossed them up to him. "Are you going in?" Tuff couldn't be completely sure that someone hadn't broken in through one of the back windows. "Be careful."

Buddy stood guard over her as she watched Jace unlock her front door and go inside. After a few minutes, he called that it was clear. Relief poured through her. At least no one had breached her sanctity. The rat was more than enough.

Jace came out of the cabin and brushed by her.

"Where are you going?"

"To get an evidence bag."

She followed him across the bridge. While Jace sorted through his trunk, she sat in his front seat with the door open and Buddy on the ground at her feet.

"What's Cash doing?" She'd seen him go inside her cabin after Jace had come out.

"Giving everything a second look. He used to work counterterrorism when he was in the bureau." *Counterterrorism*. The Liberty Fighters had been classified as a domestic terrorist group. The special designation could put them away for life.

Jace came around to the door of his SUV. "You okay, Angela?"

"Of course." She swatted away a tear, hoping Jace didn't see it. But it was too late.

He pulled her into a hug. "Hey, Ange, we've got this. No one is going to let anything happen to you. Not on my watch."

"It's not me I'm worried about." She wiped her nose with the back of her hand.

"You're worried about us? Ah come on. That's insulting." He pulled her in for another embrace. "Love you, Ange. Have a little faith." Jace let her go and held up his evidence bag. "As soon as we clean up, come inside."

When he walked away, Angie spotted Tuff standing a few feet from the SUV.

"I came to check on you."

"I'm fine." She took a glance around Jace's cab, looking for tissues and wound up wiping her nose with the back of her hand again.

"Here." Tuff reached in his back pocket and handed her a handkerchief. It reminded her so much of her grandfather that she teared up again and quickly blotted her eyes.

"Thank you for dealing with this. You should go home with Buddy and eat your dinner. Fix your window."

"I'm thinking Buddy saw whoever did this." He nudged his head at her porch. "He must've gone wild and threw himself out the window to go after him…them." He held her gaze.

"Yeah, I guess I owe you an explanation. But I can't do it right now." She rubbed her temple where her head was starting to ache. "It's long and complicated and I don't have the bandwidth tonight."

"I'm going to hang around for the sitrep."

She didn't know what a sitrep was but assumed he meant the family meeting Jace had alluded they were having. "Okay," she said, even though she realized Tuff hadn't asked for permission. She didn't want him involved but he was part of this now. Those assholes had made him part of this.

Suddenly her fear gave way to fury. How dare these people bring this to the ranch? How dare they bring it upon her family and friends?

Buddy got up and stretched, then inserted himself between them, thumping his tail. Angie could've sworn the dog was smiling as if he'd brought his two favorite people together, safe and sound.

Sawyer whistled and waved his arm in the air for them to come inside the cabin. She and Tuff walked across the creek together. Jace was taking pictures of the driveway and it dawned on her that Jace, Cash, and Sawyer hadn't parked on her side of the creek in order to preserve any possible evidence, like tire tracks.

"Did you find anything?" Tuff asked Jace.

"Nah, just the Mercedes tire treads. In the morning, I'll check around the back to see if anyone hiked in. But without good lighting it's too hard to see."

They all went inside the house.

"Should I make coffee?"

There was a round of nods. Angie went in the kitchen and started a pot. While it was brewing, she got down five cups. In the refrigerator was a pound cake she'd brought home from the store. She put it on a plate and took it to the coffee table with napkins. It was dinnertime and everyone had to be starved.

"It's the best I can do on short notice." She found a package of nut mix in the pantry and poured everyone a cup of coffee.

"Did you find anything inside the cabin?" She directed the question to Cash.

"Nope. Whoever did this, stuck to the outside. Maybe Superdog here scared them off." Cash reached down where Buddy had lodged himself between the sofa and coffee table and scratched the dog's head.

"What time did you leave the house this morning?" Jace asked her.

She caught Tuff's gaze and quickly turned away, hoping he didn't give anything away about how they'd spent those early hours. Everything about her life—her habits, her acquaintances, her comings and goings—was about to become an open book. She wanted those few precious hours with Tuff for herself.

"A little before nine. I was running late for the store." She paused and decided she needed to tell them everything. "At eight I called Deputy Marshal Earl Ryan about two suspicious phone calls I'd received from a friend's number." She didn't dare look at Tuff, who had to be wondering why she had a US deputy marshal on speed dial. "The first call came a couple of weeks ago," she continued. "I missed the call and when I tried to ring back only seconds later, I got a message that the number was no longer in service. A similar situation happened last night."

"And you didn't feel the need to tell any of us about these calls?" There was no mistaking the anger in Sawyer's voice.

Jace held up his hand. "We'll get to the phone calls. First things first. So when you left a little before nine you didn't see anything suspicious?"

"No."

Jace jotted something down in a notepad and turned to Tuff. "How about you? What time did you leave?"

"Around six, maybe earlier." Tuff scratched his chin, which had veered past five o'clock shadow territory. "I went to the feedstore in Dry Creek, then to the barn. On my way out I didn't see anything suspicious."

"What time did you get home?" Jace was back to Angie.

"Uh." She turned to Tuff because she hadn't been paying attention to the time. Nina was in charge of locking up Daltons tonight. "Do you remember?"

"She got here a little after I did, sometime after six."

"Any chance you can be more specific?"

"I stopped off at Gina's for takeout. The receipt probably has a time stamp. Then add on however long it takes to drive from the center to here. What, five minutes, max?"

"Would you mind getting the receipt? I'd like to tighten the timeline as close as we can get it."

"Sure." Tuff put his coffee down and told Buddy to stay.

Angie watched through the window as Tuff jogged to his cabin.

"How much does he know?" Sawyer asked. They all knew he was talking about Tuff.

"Just about the phone calls and whatever you told him." She glared at her brother.

Both Jace and Cash turned to Sawyer and said in unison, "You told him?"

"No, not the whole thing. I made it sound like a relationship gone bad."

Cash took a sip of coffee. "It doesn't really matter. As long as Angie is out of WITSEC, she's free to tell anyone she wants." He cut his attention to Angie. "But with the case pending trial, I'd be careful who I confided in."

"He's trustworthy," she said, and Sawyer rolled his eyes. She'd hate to see how her brother would behave with a man he didn't approve of. Because she knew Sawyer liked and respected Tuff. Even admired what he'd done with his business.

Before they could continue the conversation, Tuff returned with the receipt and everyone clammed up.

"Twenty after six is when I got the food." Tuff handed the receipt to Jace. "I was probably home no later than six thirty. First, I noticed my broken window. Then I discovered Buddy roaming loose. I was examining him for injuries when Angie drove up to her driveway. I'd guess it was no more than five to ten minutes after I got here."

"Okay." Jace nodded. "That helps tighten the timeline. I'd like to take a look at your window after we're through here."

"No problem. It was broken from the inside. I've gotta think Buddy became agitated when he saw someone across the creek and jumped out the window."

"He ever do anything like that before?" Jace seemed skeptical.

Angie assumed it was because the dog was usually so serene. He barely lifted his head when a customer strolled into Tuff's shop.

"I've only had him a short time. But I've seen him go on alert and growl at people before. I don't know if in his zeal to protect the cabins he hurled himself out of the window or if it shattered under the pressure of him jumping against the glass. But when I found him, he was coming across the bridge, as if he'd been at Angie's."

"And that was about six thirty." Jace made a note in his book.

"Give or take a minute or two. There was glass in his fur and his paw was bleeding. Seems to me that everything was pretty fresh."

"Like he'd gone through the window shortly before you arrived?" Cash subconsciously reached for the dog and gave him another head scratch.

"I can't be sure, but yeah. Which says to me that whoever did this waited for the cover of darkness."

"Kind of risky, knowing that one of you might show up at any minute," Jace said.

"I was earlier than usual. Typically, I don't get home until closer to seven."

"And I usually stay to close the store and sweep up," Angie said. "I'm rarely home before eight." Half the time, she went to Gina's for dinner or stopped off to visit with Charlie or Aubrey.

"Do you think whoever did this has been casing your movements?" Jace got up, topped off his coffee with a warmer, and motioned with the pot to see if anyone else wanted a refill. They all shook their heads.

Tuff shrugged. "I'd like to think I would've noticed someone lurking around. But…who knows?"

Jace cut a look to Angie. There was that time weeks ago where she'd had the creepy sensation of being watched in the center. It was nothing concrete, just a sixth sense that someone was following her movements. But like

Tuff, she hadn't noticed anyone prowling around the cabins. And paying hyper attention to her surroundings had become second nature to Angie.

"I haven't seen anyone either."

Cash jumped up. "You got a good flashlight?"

"I don't know how good it is." She rifled through a junk drawer and found a light she'd inherited with the cabin.

Cash laughed. "I think that used to be mine. Let me see it." He went outside and the rest of them followed.

"What's he doing?" Angie asked as Cash swept the light through the thickets near the creek.

"Looking for a camera," Jace and Sawyer said at the same time.

Angie gasped. "You don't think? Oh my God." The idea that someone had been recording her and Tuff's movements made her want to puke. Half the time, she didn't even close the blinds on her windows.

"I doubt it." Jace threw his arm around Angie's shoulder. "But we want to check it off the list."

Cash returned and motioned for them to go inside. When they were all seated again, he said. "It was too dark. I'll come first thing in the morning and go over that underbrush with a fine tooth comb."

"If there is a camera, haven't we now sort of tipped our hats to whoever is monitoring it?" Tuff asked.

"Probably." Cash nodded. "Or they just think I was looking for footprints. I think it's pretty unlikely that a camera is out there, though. They'd have to use cellular technology or somehow tap into one of your Wi-Fi passwords. Seems like too big of a hassle." He looked at Jace, who acknowledged his assessment with a nod of his own. "But it's worth looking into."

Angie, who until this point had managed to refrain from asking the obvious, felt it was finally time to address the elephant in the room. "This has to be them, right?"

"That's the direction I'm going." Jace blew out a breath.

Cash was more circumspect. "Tell us about the phone calls, Angie."

"Yeah, Angie, tell us about the phone calls." Sawyer glowered.

She knew she was going to get an earful from her brother when everyone left. That's what she got for holding out on him. But it wasn't as if she hadn't gone to Earl. Or Tuff.

She recounted both incidents, including her gravest concern that something had happened to Kari.

"The woman in Santa Fe."

She shot Sawyer a look. "As I said before I won't get into that."

"Send me the phone number." Cash held up his phone.

"I don't know if I should." She chewed her bottom lip. "But I gave it to Earl and he's looking into it."

"From the Marshals Service?"

"He was my handler."

"Whoa," said Tuff, who until this point had been sitting quietly, taking it all in. "You lost me on US Marshals and handler." He looked from Angie to Cash, then to Jace. "What am I missing here?"

Silence filled the room.

"You think we can finish this tomorrow morning?" She wanted to be alone with Tuff when she explained everything to him.

"Yeah," Jace said. "Come stay with Charlie and me and the boys. There's a nice guest suite with your name on it."

"Nah"—Sawyer stood up—"Angie will come home with me."

"On your fold-out couch?" Cash pulled a face. "I've slept on that thing. There's room with us, Ange. You'll thank your back for it."

Angie shook her head. "I want to stay here."

"That's not happening." When had Sawyer gotten so bossy?

"I'll stay with her."

Four pairs of eyes turned to Tuff.

"I don't have a window and the house is as cold as Antarctica in winter. I need somewhere to stay, and this couch looks more comfortable than yours, Sawyer. I think Buddy will feel better about it too."

Sawyer started to protest but Angie stopped him. "I'm staying here. And Tuff, you and Buddy are welcome to stay as long as it takes to get your window fixed." She linked her arm in Sawyer's and the other one in Jace's and walked them to the door. "I love you all. Thank you for coming…for everything. I'll have coffee and breakfast waiting in the morning."

"Ange—"

"Sawyer, I'll be fine. No one's going to come back tonight, not after the stir they caused with their rodent gift."

Sawyer glanced over Angie's shoulder at Tuff. Something seemed to pass between the two men because Tuff gave a slight bob of his head and Sawyer stopped pressing.

"Tomorrow morning," Sawyer said.

When everyone one was gone, she asked Tuff, "You want to get your dinner and I'll reheat it for you?"

"I'd rather hear what the hell is going on."

She sighed. "I'll tell you. But first you should eat. You've got to be starved." Though the rest of her story wasn't something anyone should hear on a full stomach.

Chapter 17

Tuff reluctantly went to fetch his food, returning with Buddy's bed and bowls. "I've got to do something about that window. Otherwise, critters are going to get in."

"I'll help you."

"Don't worry about it. Stay here with Buddy. It'll only take me a few minutes."

While he messed with the window, Angie tried to salvage his cold burger and fries. Everything was soggy and as far as she was concerned inedible. She searched her freezer for a package of Dalton ground beef and defrosted it in the microwave. By the time Tuff returned, she had a meatloaf in the oven and was tossing a salad.

"Your burger is toast. I'm making meatloaf."

He sniffed the air. "Smells good."

She put the salad on the table and got out two placemats and a couple of plates. "What did you do about the window?"

"For now, I covered it with a plastic bag. Tomorrow, I'll call a glass company in Auburn or Grass Valley."

"What a hassle. I'm sorry, Tuff."

"What do you have to be sorry about?"

"I don't think Buddy would've done that if he hadn't felt threatened. He felt threatened because of me."

"No, he felt threatened because some assholes trespassed and vandalized Dry Creek Ranch. He was doing what dogs do, protecting his turf."

"I'm just grateful nothing happened to him."

Tuff looked over at Buddy, whose ears had pitched forward as if he was listening to the conversation. "I have a feeling Buddy can handle himself."

He pulled out a chair at the table and straddled it. "Why are you involved with the US Marshals Service?"

She'd dreaded this moment. But he was enmeshed in this now and deserved answers. "Because I'm a material witness in a federal case, involving a group of survivalists and arms dealers."

He seemed to be absorbing that information, silently mulling it in his head. Then, "Were you a member of this group?"

She let out a weary breath. "No, but I unwittingly financed it." Angie joined him at the table and served them both some of the salad. "The meatloaf has a while left in the oven."

"How? How did you finance it?"

"I bought land near Taos for a farm. It was supposed to be a co-op. Everyone who lived there was supposed to take part in working the fields and growing the food, which would later be distributed to the poor. We were creating a model for something bigger, a way to feed the hungry in poor neighborhoods. Or food deserts, where access to healthful and nutritious food is restricted or nonexistent. But The Farm ultimately got taken over by the Liberty Fighters."

Tuff shook his head. "I've never heard of them."

"That's good because they're bad people."

"And that's who you think was behind this?" He bobbed his chin at the door.

"I can't imagine anyone else having a motive to do that. And I think the threat, while cliched—these folks aren't particularly clever—was crystal clear. I'm the rat and they plan to hang me."

"Ah, Jesus." Tuff rubbed his hand down his face. "If you know who they are why don't you send the FBI after them?"

"Because they are already in jail. The trial is scheduled for next summer."

"Then who did this?"

"I don't know." She shook her head. "The Liberty Fighters were just a rag-tag group that used to meet on the Internet." That's where Zane met them. "According to the authorities, they arrested the last member two months ago. That's when I left the program."

"What program?"

"I was in witness protection." She waited for that to register, then continued. "I had to cut ties with everyone I knew and basically go into hiding. I hadn't seen my family in six years. Part of that time I was at The Farm, working with federal authorities to get enough evidence for an arrest warrant."

"Holy shit."

She could see him trying to wrap his head around everything she'd told him.

"So you were like a plant?"

"Not exactly because I was already there. I was what you would call a snitch. But not really a snitch because I was never part of the Liberty Fighters. They came and commandeered what we were doing and for all intents and purposes held us hostage."

"And your family knew about it?"

She got up to check on the meatloaf. "Not at the time. For years, I couldn't talk to them because the Liberty Fighters restricted our outside communications. And when I went into the program contact was forbidden."

"Years? How long were you in this place?"

"Two, and then four in WITSEC. Last year, Cash, through his sources in the FBI, found out I was in the program. Before that, my family didn't know if I was dead or alive. They'd hired private investigators to find me, but the trail ended in Zaire."

"Zaire?"

"I was there volunteering with the Water Project before I went to Taos. While in Africa, I communicated with my family regularly. They weren't aware that I'd come back to the States. But a couple of years ago, Sawyer hired a new PI, who traced me to Taos. By then, though, I was living as Katherine Moore in another state under the watchful eye of the US Marshals. Cash ultimately put the pieces together and pulled some strings so that I was able to have a short video call with my family. That was the first time I'd seen them in five years." Warm tears trickled down her face.

"I'll get that," Tuff said in a soft voice. He took the meatloaf from her, put it down on the stovetop, and wrapped her in his arms. "Shh, it's okay. It's over now."

"I don't think it'll ever be over." She buried her face in his shoulder and let herself have a good cry. "I hate them, Tuff. I've never hated anyone in my life, but I hate them."

"It's okay to hate 'em. I hate 'em too."

For some reason that made her laugh. She clung to Tuff, laugh-crying until she could pull herself together.

"Let's eat," she finally said and pulled the dish towel from a hook and wiped her nose with it, which was gross but the only thing she had on hand. "Come on."

He took the meatloaf to the table and they ate in silence until Tuff said, "I've got more questions."

"Ask away." She supposed it would be cathartic to let it all out. And there were things she'd never be able to tell her family that she could confide in Tuff.

"How did you wind up working with the police?"

"It's a long story. But the short version is that my friend, the one who I thought called me, got out. I was hurt and she escaped in the middle of the night to get me help. It turned out that The Farm had been under surveillance by the ATF. They didn't want my friend to screw up the case they were trying to build. So instead of sending the cavalry, they sent a lone undercover agent, who pretended to be one of them. I worked with him as much as I could to gather information and eventually he got me out."

"Why were you hurt? Did they do something to you?"

"I challenged them at every turn. They didn't like that, but it was my money that paid the bills. It's probably what kept me alive. There were two others who went up against them and I don't think they fared as well as I did. They both magically disappeared, never to be heard from again. Fortunately for me, they needed me too much. But when I got out of line"—she made air quotes around "out of line"—"they had their ways of punishing me."

Tuff made a noise deep in his throat. He wasn't an easy man to read but tonight he had murder in his eyes.

"It was better when Jet got there. He made sure to keep me out of harm's way most of the time. But he had to walk a thin line. Zane didn't trust him and didn't like the fact that he'd claimed me."

"Jet was the undercover agent?"

"Yes. Not his real name. I suspect I won't find out what it is until the trial."

"Who's Zane?"

She didn't want to talk about Zane. The way he'd betrayed her, the way he'd betrayed all of them…it was something she wound never understand. If Rich and Diana were dead, Zane had their blood on his hands.

"He was a man I met while volunteering for the Water Project. He was one of the founders of The Farm. I thought he was a good man. I was wrong."

"Is he one of the people the cops arrested?"

"Yes." It happened while she was in a safehouse in Portland. The relief that Zane was locked up had been overwhelming. But it was Burt the feds wanted the most. It had taken them six months to the day of Zane's arrest to finally nab Burt.

"Does he know that you're a witness for the government?"

"Judging by the gift that was left on my door today, I'd say he does. But I can't know for sure. It could've been one of the others who orchestrated it. According to my former handler, it's not uncommon for inmates to smuggle phones inside. For all I know one of them called a friend."

"How did Jet get you out of there?"

"He convinced them to let him take me to the bank, where I was supposed to withdraw a large sum of money for the purchase of guns. Then, he promised them that he would coerce me into leading him to the friend I told you escaped. They were worried she was working with the feds. Little did they know Jet was a fed." She gave a half-hearted laugh, though nothing about it was funny. Sometimes, she wondered how she'd managed to get through the years. It was amazing what the mind and body could tolerate, that the will to live was that strong.

Tuff poured himself a glass of the red wine Angie had put on the table but hadn't touched. She'd barely eaten any of her meatloaf.

"And what happened after your supposed bank run?" he asked.

"Jet had promised the others that after he cleaned out the rest of my trust fund and found my friend, he'd eliminate me. Eliminate being a euphemism of course."

Tuff sighed. "This just keeps getting better." He looked a little green. "So initially the group thought you were dead."

She shook her head. "We were on our way to meet a team of deputy marshals in Santa Fe who were supposed to whisk me away when Jet got a call from his supervisor that his cover had been blown. Zane, who'd always been leery of Jet, did some digging while we were gone and found a seven-year-old newspaper clip from the *Albuquerque Journal* with a picture of Jet and a dozen other agents doing a raid at the home of an arms dealer. The ATF picked up chatter about it on one of the bugs Jet had planted inside the compound. Needless to say, he didn't go back."

"How do you think they found you here after all this time?"

"Zane knew I grew up in LA, who my parents are, and that my grandfather owned a ranch in Northern California. I presume he told the others, since I was their golden goose and all. It wouldn't have been difficult for any of them to find me."

"Why didn't you stay under protection?"

Because being away from her family and everything she loved wasn't a life. "Everyone had been arrested. I thought it was safe to leave."

Tuff got to his feet, took his plate to the sink, and started clearing the table. Angie got the impression that he needed something to keep busy.

"The Marshals office thought it was safe too," she added, trying to justify her decision because now she was questioning herself. The thought of putting her family or the ranch in danger sickened her.

She got up to help him with the cleanup and for a while they worked in silence, washing and drying the dishes. Even from across the room, Angie could feel his tension while he worked out her story in his head. One thing she'd learned about Tuff was that he was deliberate. She had seen him hunkered over a piece of leather like it was an intricate puzzle, mapping out each step before ever making a cut. It was something she admired about him. He took his time to get it right.

"What was the gun deal about?" he asked as she stowed the last of the meatloaf in the fridge.

"They were planning an Oklahoma City–style bombing and were eyeing either the Texas Capitol in Austin or the California Capitol. Their scheme involved being armed to the hilt, so they'd be prepared for a standoff at The Farm when the law came to get them."

"Nut jobs," Tuff muttered under his breath.

"That's the understatement of the century." They were crazy to be sure but if they hadn't been stopped, Angie believed they would've pulled it off, killing thousands of government workers and civilians.

"And this guy Zane…he's the one who brought these people to your door?"

She nodded. "I thought he was someone else. I thought we both wanted the same things: to help people. But somewhere along the way he became radicalized and turned into a different person entirely. For him, the ends justify the means."

They moved into the living room. It wasn't even nine yet, but it felt later, like an eternity had gone by. It was hard to believe that just the night before she'd felt safe wrapped in Tuff's arms.

"Would you like dessert? I've been known to stash a little chocolate in the pantry for times like this." Judging by his afternoon visits to Daltons for a cookie fix, she knew he had a sweet tooth.

"No thanks."

She feigned shock. "You don't know what you're missing."

He apparently wasn't interested in her attempts at levity because he scowled. "When's that guy from the Marshals Service calling you back?"

"When he has news." Though given the events of today, she needed to fill Earl in on what had happened.

Tuff exhaled. "You think the phone calls are tied to what happened today?"

"I don't know. But probably."

"Me too." He took her hand and held it.

It was such a small thing and yet it made her feel better. Safer. Tuff Garrison had made it clear he wasn't a man she could rely on. But here he was. Solid as Dry Creek Ranch's foundation.

"Let's make a fire." She wanted to exorcise those horrible people from her home. If she had a big bundle of sage, she'd burn it too for good measure.

In no time, Tuff built a nice blaze. Buddy got up from his dog bed and laid in front of the hearth.

"I was thinking of getting a tree," she said happy to be talking about anything other than The Farm and the Liberty Fighters. "Do you get one?"

"A Christmas tree? Nah. The truth is most of my life I've lived in a bunkhouse with half a dozen other men. I wouldn't know what to do with one."

"Well, you can help decorate mine." She instantly felt him tense. He was more than willing to rush to her side in a crisis. But an invitation to hang a few stinking ornaments on a tree? He reacted as if it was a marriage proposal. "Or not."

He gave a wan smile. "Holidays aren't really my thing."

"Why?" When his response was a nonchalant hitch of his shoulders, she pressed. "I just told you my whole ugly story about living with a militia group. I think you can tell me why you're the Grinch who stole Christmas."

His mouth curved up, showing off those not-quite dimples. And once again Angie marveled at what a looker he was. Not in a Ken doll generic way. Tuff Garrison had definitely seen some miles, but he wore them well.

"Nothing dramatic. I just moved around a lot. Christmas was no different than any other day for me."

"But you're not moving around now. So why not enjoy it?"

"I will," he said but she got the impression he was blowing her off.

He got up and added another log to the fire. Buddy raised his head to see what was going on, licked Tuff's leg, and went back to sleep. Tuff wandered over to the window and gazed outside. Angie couldn't tell whether he was keeping watch or if she'd stumbled into tricky territory with the whole *why don't you like Christmas?* He was the son of an alcoholic. That couldn't have been easy during the holidays.

"You sure you don't want dessert or a snack? I have some of Gina's frozen cookie dough. I could pop a sheet in the oven."

"I'm good. The meatloaf filled me."

She wondered if she should go to bed so he could have the living room to himself. But she wasn't sleepy. And the idea of being alone in her room, knowing that there may be a camera outside with someone watching the cabin made her less inclined to leave Tuff and Buddy's sight. So, she pulled the throw blanket from the back of the couch, wrapped herself up in it and stared into the fire.

Under different circumstances it would have been a perfect night. Good dinner. Warm fire. Sweet dog. And a gorgeous man to spend it with.

Tuff came back to the sofa, took the other side, and stretched his long legs across the ottoman.

"You want a blanket?"

He eyed hers. "Nah, I'm good." What he was was low maintenance.

She grabbed the remote and turned on the TV. "Anything you want to watch?"

"You pick. I'm not a big television watcher."

She turned the set off. "Checkers?" She was kidding. She didn't even own the game.

So of course, he said, "Sure" and even perked up.

"You're out of luck, pal. I don't have a board."

He lifted his arms. "Then why did you suggest it?"

"I was just testing to see if there was anything you actually liked."

He was quiet for a long time, then out of nowhere said, "I like you. That's the goddamn problem."

Before she could respond, he kissed her.

"What's wrong with liking me?" she murmured against his lips. Part of her didn't care what the answer was as long as he didn't stop.

"I'm not what you need."

How the hell did he know what she needed? But the truth was it was just the opposite. Angie wasn't what he needed. She was the target of criminals and her life was a mess. But none of that mattered while he had his arms around her.

She snuggled closer and he took the kiss deeper, winding his hands through her hair. He tasted of the wine they'd had at dinner, a combination of tart and sweet.

Her hands drifted under his shirt and she felt him shudder in a breath. His torso was rock solid. She loved gliding her hands over his abs and the way his chest hair sprang back as she touched him.

He pulled off his shirt, giving her untethered access. His skin was bronze, even in winter, and his arms were ropey with muscle.

She touched and kissed him to her heart's delight. He wrestled with the buttons on her blouse and finally, desperately, yanked it over her head. Reverently, he traced the lace on her bra with his finger, kissing the tops of her breasts. His eyes roved over her and brimmed with appreciation. She'd never felt sexier or more beautiful than in that moment.

"Let's take this to the other room," he said in a hoarse whisper.

She took his hand and walked him to her bedroom, where she drew the curtains. He lost his jeans and stood there only in a pair of boxer briefs. From the evidence of his arousal, she thought he might be done with foreplay.

But he was only beginning.

He wrapped his arms around her waist and pulled her into his lap on the bed. Then he kissed the back of her neck. His warm lips sent shivers down her spine. Tuff unfastened her bra and cupped her breasts, feeling the weight of each one in his hands. She liked the way his rough, calloused fingers felt against her skin.

"Damn, you're beautiful."

He skimmed her belly, making her shudder and dipped one hand down her skirt. Soon, she was so wet she could hear his fingers playing inside her. She moaned, signaling that she wanted more.

He lifted her just enough to drag her skirt off. "These are nice." He ran his finger around the elastic waste of her panties.

They were nothing special. Just black cotton bikinis.

But he looked at her with such heat in his eyes that it made her even more desperate for him. She'd never wanted a man as much as she wanted Tuff Garrison. Angie straddled his lap and kissed him. She felt his arousal grow harder and she rubbed herself against him. The friction felt so good, it almost brought her to orgasm.

She tried to push him down on the bed, but he was in no hurry. His hands slid down the back of her panties and he cupped her butt as he ground into her. She moaned with a combination of frustration and pleasure.

"Tuff, please. Please."

He left a trail of kisses along her collarbone and fondled her breasts.

"Tuff," she pleaded a second time.

He flipped her onto her back and slowly drew her panties down, letting the soft cotton brush against her legs. When they were off, he got rid of his briefs. She reached up and stroked him, then crawled over him.

He grunted something unintelligible, threw his head back, and closed his eyes while she pleasured him with her mouth. Tuff gently pulled her head up and rolled on top of her until she felt him between her legs.

"Please." She didn't know how much more she could take.

"Soon." He worked her with his fingers until she was panting. Begging.

He hung over the bed, grabbed his pants, then his wallet and rolled a condom down his length. No one could say he didn't come prepared. Thank goodness one of them was taking precautions. She was too far gone to even think.

In one powerful thrust he was inside her, moving. Unlike the first time they'd come together, she immediately stretched to accommodate his size. She wrapped her legs around his hips. And Tuff reached under her so he could go deeper.

He moved faster. Harder. His muscles bunched with every stroke. She clutched his shoulders, trying to hang on for a wild ride, meeting him thrust for thrust.

His hands and lips were everywhere, fondling, touching, kissing. Her body purred with sensation, every stroke bringing her closer to the edge. She'd never been with a lover like him, so intent on giving her pleasure. Angie felt worshipped and her body tingled from head to toe.

She clenched and everything inside her burned. Then she dropped like she was on the highest point of a roller coaster, racing down.

He followed, crying out her name, his head thrown back and his eyes closed. She liked looking at him that way. As if he was completely sated.

Tuff lay there for a few minutes, then rolled off her, and headed for the bathroom. She wondered if he would leave like he did last time. But a few seconds later, he returned, got under the covers, and took her in his arms. He didn't speak. There was no praise, no flowery words, not even a whisper of goodnight. But he held her until the wee hours of the morning and was still there when she woke up.

Chapter 18

Tuff called a window repair company while Angie made breakfast.

Sawyer, Jace, and Cash showed up at about eight. The four of them fanned out around the grounds, looking for a hidden camera or any sign that someone had been there, spying. They searched for about an hour but found nothing.

The cabins were tucked away in a corner of the ranch, far enough from the public road that a trespasser would have to hike in under the cover of night to go unnoticed.

"The store," Jace said. "It was probably a two-person operation. Someone watched Angie at Daltons—probably Tuff too—while the other was here."

"Makes sense." Cash filled his plate with the eggs Angie had made. "Did either of you notice anyone who seemed out of place?"

"How do you define out of place?" Angie huffed out a breath. "I mean all day long strangers come into the store. Ninety-nine percent of the time I've never seen them before."

"Someone who seemed like he was paying too much attention." Jace looked from Angie to Tuff.

"Not that I can remember." Angie refilled everyone's cups with coffee. They'd gone through the first pot and were now working through the second.

Tuff shook his head. The truth was Friday had been slow. He didn't remember even one person coming in the shop. Only Ava, who'd misplaced her key to the storage room again.

"Think about it for a while." Jace buttered his toast, took a bite and with his mouth full said, "Sometimes things don't register right away. In the meantime, I'll check the security cameras in the parking lot."

"For what?" Angie asked. "We're a shopping center. There were all kinds of people here on Friday. How do you distinguish between a normal customer and a nut job?"

Tuff could see that Angie was getting frustrated. Without thinking about it, he leaned over and took her hand. Everyone at the table noticed and pretended not to. Tuff was sure he'd hear from Sawyer later.

"I have a pretty good antenna for nut jobs." Jace took another slice of toast and passed the plate around the table. "I looked closer for tire tracks when we were out there and didn't see any. Whoever left the surprise, walked here, which is pretty damn brazen if you ask me."

Sawyer sighed. "I don't like it. Ange, I think you should go to Mom and Dad's for a while."

"Why would I be any safer there?"

"Because they have state of the art security. They live behind a locked gate."

"So do we," she fired back, challenging Sawyer.

"Which is a joke." Sawyer threw his hands up. "Come on, Ange."

"I went into hiding once. I don't want to do it again."

Sawyer snorted. "I wouldn't exactly call Beverly Hills going into hiding. Mom and Dad would be thrilled, and you'd be safer there than here."

"Why? They know who my parents are and where they live. Why would it be any different?"

It felt like a vice was tightening around Tuff's chest. He wanted Angie to be safe, but his gut told him if she left, she wouldn't be coming back. It would be for the best, he told himself. They shouldn't keep sleeping with each other. She deserved more than he could give, which was nothing.

"At least here I have trained law enforcement at my beck and call." She tried to smile but failed miserably.

Jace didn't say anything but it was clear he was itching to talk.

"What?" Angie poked Jace on the arm. "Just say it."

"I think if we want this to go away, we lure them in and cast our net."

"With Angie as the bait." Sawyer slammed his fist down on the table. "What the hell is wrong with you, Jace?"

"Jace is right, Sawyer." Cash gave Angie an encouraging rub on the back. "If these guys want to scare Angie out of testifying, it won't make a difference whether it's here or LA. Our best bet is to catch them. The feds will help us. Intimidating a witness carries a stiff penalty."

"I lost my sister once; I won't lose her again."

"None of us is going to let that happen," Tuff blurted, knowing he was an interloper in the tightknit Dalton clan, but couldn't help himself. "I think what Jace said has some merit."

Jace threw his hands up. "Yeah, 'cause I'm only the freaking sheriff."

"Then Angie moves in with us. One of us will escort her to and from the store every day." He looked from Jace to Cash, avoiding eye contact with Tuff. Sawyer was clearly pissed at him.

"Nope." Angie wasn't having it. "I won't put Gina and the baby in danger like that. I'll stay right here. Or I'll go back to Portland."

It was a threat. Tuff could hear it in her voice. He suspected Portland was where the US Marshals had stashed her, though she'd never specifically said so.

"I'll call Earl right now and tell him I want back in." She squinted her eyes at Sawyer. "He'll take me in a heartbeat. This time, I won't come out until every one of the idiots is convicted and has exhausted all his appeals. There's no telling how long that'll take. Maybe never."

Tuff realized it wasn't just a threat. She was dead serious.

"She can stay with me," he said before he could stop himself. If he'd wanted to provoke Sawyer, he might as well have poked him with a sharp stick.

"As much as I appreciate all your concern, I'm not staying with anyone. For six years I took care of myself and managed to survive, thank you very much." She cut to Jace. "How do we lure them in? I want to take down whoever did this."

Sawyer banged his head on the table. "This is insane. We don't know who or what we're dealing with. And I'm supposed to leave you in a cabin in the forest all by yourself. Not happening."

"I have this." Angie held up her wrist where she wore the panic watch. She slipped her hand back into Tuff's. "And I have Tuff and Buddy next door."

"And all of us," Cash said. "We'll put in some cameras and have eyes on this place 24/7."

"Don't forget my department," Jace added. "Angie's a citizen of this county and we don't tolerate the threatening of a federal witness in our jurisdiction. I'll put a deputy on the case full time."

"I say we bring in the US Attorney's Office. I can make a few calls, though it would probably go over better if Jace was the one to ask, since as a cow cop I don't have any skin in the game."

"Yep, though I'd rather not have a bunch of fan belt inspectors crawling up my ass."

Cash snorted. "I used to be one of those fan belt inspectors, asshole."

Tuff knew it was just good-natured ribbing, but he'd prefer if they stayed focused on Angie. "So how do we do this? How do we bring these yahoos into the open?"

The oven dinged and Angie brought a coffee cake to the table. "Compliments of one of Gina's mixes."

Jace cut into it before it even had time to cool. "I'm pretty sure they'll show themselves all on their own. With good surveillance we'll be ready to pounce when they do."

"How do we keep Angie safe in the meantime?" Tuff didn't care if he was being presumptuous. He wanted this shit over. Then he'd go back to minding his own business and keeping to himself.

"One of us will stay here with her at all times," Sawyer said.

"If they've got eyes on the place that's not going to work," Cash said. "I think there's pretty good evidence that they know Angie and Tuff's comings and goings. Either they're watching them at Dry Creek Village or they're conducting their own surveillance and we just didn't find it."

"I'm not leaving her here alone."

"No, one of us will have to sneak in." Cash cut himself a piece of the cake. "It would sure help to know how they're keeping tabs on these two."

"What makes you think anyone is watching me?" Tuff asked.

"The fact that they were here when you weren't." Cash got up and looked outside the window at Tuff's cabin. "I lived across the creek when Aubrey lived here. Take it from me, I could see everything on this side. Whoever did this knows that and wouldn't want to risk you catching them."

It made sense. But the vandal had misjudged Buddy. "What about tracking devices on our vehicles?"

Jace got to his feet. "I'll check but sometimes you guys walk, right?"

"I hardly ever do anymore," Angie said. "Not now, when it gets dark so early."

Tuff still did occasionally but most of the time he drove. "Like Angie, I rarely walk in the winter."

Jace went outside and the rest of them followed him out. Jace took Angie's Mercedes, while Cash crossed the bridge to Tuff's Ram. It took them less than ten minutes to give each vehicle a thorough inspection.

"Anything?" Jace called.

"Nope," Cash hollered back.

"Nothing here either. But it was worth a shot."

They returned to the kitchen. It was closing in on ten o'clock and the window repair people were due soon. But Tuff wanted a plan that didn't solely rely on one of them sneaking into Angie's cabin at night. He wanted these people and he wanted them yesterday.

Angie checked the clock on the stove. "I've got to get to the store. I promised Aubrey I'd help change out some of the displays. Make them look more Christmassy."

"I'll run over to Best Buy and install the security cameras on the cabins." Sawyer looked from Cash to Jace. "Which one of you is going to check the history on the cameras we have at Dry Creek Village?"

"I'll do that," Jace said. "Cash?"

"Yup. If it wasn't Saturday, I'd call the US Attorney in New Mexico. But I've got a buddy who's a supervisory agent in the Bureau in Albuquerque. I'll give him a call." Cash turned to Angie, who had started clearing the table. "You want to give me the number of your handler at the Marshals?"

Angie shook her head. "I'll call him and explain everything."

"Damn right you will." Sawyer took his plate to the sink. "As soon as you're ready I'll take you to work."

Angie didn't put up an argument. Everyone helped with the rest of the KP, which didn't take long.

Tuff kept one eye on the window. When the glass folks arrived, he went to meet them, leaving Buddy at Angie's. He planned to lend his new best friend to the cause.

* * * *

Sawyer drove up later in the day with the cameras. Tuff, who'd been fishing from his porch in the cold, trying to work out everything that had happened in his head, strolled over to Angie's cabin to offer Sawyer help with the installation.

He wasn't sure what kind of reception he'd get. Tuff had never dealt with the brothers of the women he'd slept with before. Probably because he'd never hung around long enough for him to feel their wrath.

He found Sawyer installing the first camera on a tree facing Angie's cabin. "You need a hand?"

"Sure." Sawyer sounded cordial enough. "If it's okay with you I'd like to put one on your cabin that'll face this side."

"Absolutely. I'll start on that one."

"Let me show you where I'm thinking."

Sawyer finished with the one he was installing and together they walked over to Tuff's place.

"I'd like to capture the front of Angie's cabin from here." Sawyer pointed to a section of Tuff's roofline where the camera could be angled down to view most of Angie's porch and all of her front door.

"I'll get this one." He dragged one of the Adirondack chairs over. "Just need to get my drill."

"What's going on with you and my sister?"

Tuff stopped at the door. "With all due respect, that's between Angie and me."

"With all due respect, she's my sister and I'm sure it hasn't escaped your notice that she's got enough shit going on in her life. So please don't complicate it anymore."

Tuff nodded, though he wasn't sure whether he was complicating Angie's life more than she was complicating his. Before she'd come along, he knew what he wanted and where he stood on relationships. Now...

"Know this," he said. "I'll look out for her."

"I appreciate that. We all do. But I don't think you know what you're getting yourself into. These people are crazy. For God's sake, their plan was to blow up a state capitol building in the middle of the day. You don't have any idea what these lunatics are capable of."

Tuff turned slowly to Sawyer and looked him directly in the eye. "You have no idea what I'm capable of."

Chapter 19

Angie couldn't get excited about changing out the kitchen display. Her heart just wasn't in it. Aubrey and Charlie buzzed around Daltons, doing most of the work. It was their area of expertise anyway. Both her cousins' wives had a talent for creating eye-catching window displays. And today's was gorgeous. Even in Angie's funk she could see that.

They'd brought an old wooden hutch that Charlie had painted a fire-engine red and dragged it to one of the end windows at the front of the store. That way passersby would immediately be drawn in. Then they filled the hutch with Gina's earthenware and boughs of fresh holly and winter greens they'd gotten from Ava and Winter.

In another window, they displayed an antique farm wagon loaded with old wooden produce crates embellished with vintage Christmas postcards. The fruit and vegetables were plastic, but Angie couldn't tell. They looked that real. In between the crates were pots of poinsettias.

"Ready to do the last one?" Charlie sized up the corner window. "I think one of the farm tables will fit."

The three of them cleared merchandise off the smallest of three tables in the kitchenware department and carried it to the window.

A couple of customers came through the door after standing outside on the sidewalk, gawking at the hutch. Angie left Aubrey and Charlie to work on the display and headed to the cash register.

"Let me know if I can help you find anything," she told the customers, two women dressed for snow.

"That ironstone pitcher you have in the window is darling. Do you have any more?"

"That's our only one." Angie made a mental note to order more from Gina. "But you can have that one if you like."

"Really? I hate to ruin your beautiful display."

"No worries. We have lots of other pretty things we can put there." Angie went to the window and grabbed the pitcher. "You want me to keep it at the register while you look around?"

"Yes, please."

Judging from their designer ski jackets and boots, money wasn't an issue. The pitcher was less than thirty dollars anyway. That was the beauty of Gina's kitchenware. It looked like a million bucks but was affordable.

"Were you all eating at Gina's?" Angie asked just to be conversational.

"We were," said the pitcher woman's friend. "It was fantastic. I've never had a better steak."

"They're amazing, aren't they? You know we sell the steaks here. Of course, you must prepare them yourselves. But you won't find better beef anywhere, though I'm a little biased. My family raises the cattle."

"Really?" The pitcher woman stopped browsing through Gina's jadeite kitchen accessories and came over to the cash register. "Is Dry Creek your ranch?"

Angie wished she'd kept her mouth shut. With everything going on, she probably shouldn't have advertised who she was. Though these women appeared harmless. They were more than likely on their way to Tahoe to ski for the weekend or returning to the Bay Area after a few days on the slopes.

"Uh-huh." Too late to pretend she wasn't a Dalton now.

"It's gorgeous. We live in Danville but have a timeshare at Northstar. This is the first time we've stopped in here. But it won't be the last. A friend told me about the furniture store...Refind...and I've been wanting to eat at Gina's for forever. We're both huge fans of her show."

Angie glanced over at Charlie and Aubrey, who were eavesdropping. "Those two ladies over there—my cousins—own Refind."

"We just came from there," said pitcher woman's friend. "I bought the deer antler lamp for our place at Sea Ranch."

"You have great stuff," pitcher woman chimed in.

"Thank you," Charlie said. "Sorry we missed you. I hope Taylor was helpful." Taylor was a local teenager Charlie and Aubrey had hired to help on weekends.

"She was terrific. We'll be back. I saw so many great things, but I only have the Prius."

"Come by anytime. We also do private appointments if you need help with design work," Aubrey added.

"Ooh, I might just do that. Nice meeting you both." Pitcher woman turned back to Angie. "Tell me more about the steaks. I'd love to bring some home for my husband."

Angie led the two women over to the meat counter, where their butcher, Mark, was stocking the cold case. Jace had stolen Mark away from Safeway. But at the rate Daltons' sales were going, he would have to beg for his supermarket job back.

"These ladies are interested in some Dalton steaks." Angie turned to pitcher woman, "What kind did you have at Gina's?"

"The filet mignon. It was fabulous. Could I get four packed up with dry ice?"

Dry ice. Wow, why hadn't Angie thought of that?

"Unfortunately, we don't have dry ice." Or any ice for that matter.

"I have a cooler in the car, but we've got a three-hour drive. I wouldn't want the steaks to spoil."

Charlie overheard the conversation and came rushing to Angie's aid. "I have a few ice packs at the house. Why don't I run and get them? They should work fine in a cooler."

Both women seemed pleased with the solution because the second one also ordered four steaks. By the time Angie packed the meat and rang them up, her head was swimming with possibilities. And keeping her mind on work was a handy diversion from the uncomfortable phone call she still had to make to Earl.

She further procrastinated by joining Aubrey and Charlie as they finished the farm table display. Together, they loaded the table with goodies wrapped in ribbons and bows. Then they went outside to view their handiwork through the window.

"Looks so good." Aubrey snapped a couple of pictures with her phone. She backed up to get a different angle and bumped into a couple who were also enjoying the displays.

The center was crowded today. Angie supposed it was the snow in the Sierra that had brought so many people out. She couldn't help scanning faces, wondering if any of them were spying while some budding Liberty Fighter further defaced her cabin.

And just like that her short-lived cheer faded away. All she could think about was someone out there wanted to do her harm.

Suddenly, she couldn't breathe.

"Are you okay?" Charlie looked at her oddly.

"Yes, of course. Why wouldn't I be?" But Angie's chest felt tight, like someone tied a rope around it and pulled it with all their might.

"Let's go inside." Charlie put her hand at the small of Angie's back and guided her into the market.

Aubrey went to the rear of the store and returned with a glass of water. "Drink this."

Angie dutifully took the glass and tried to gulp down the water, but her hands were shaking. "I was doing so well."

"Too well if you ask me." Charlie ushered Angie to the back alcove. "Sit down and try to relax. For a second it looked as if you were having a panic attack. I've been there myself, so I know what one looks like."

Before Charlie moved to the ranch and fell in love with Jace, she had been in an abusive relationship. According to Sawyer, who'd told Angie the entire story, Charlie's ex had nearly killed her. Luckily, Jace had arrested the awful man.

"Take some deep breaths." Aubrey craned her neck around the corner to make sure no one had come into the store.

"When I saw all the people walking around outside, I panicked."

"Cash and Jace are adding more security cameras. And we're all here. Safety in numbers." Charlie rubbed Angie's back. "Aubrey's right. Just breathe."

The worst part about all of it was that Angie's family was getting dragged into it. Part of the reason she'd gone into WITSEC in the first place was to protect them. To keep them safe.

"I'm okay." She tried to stand but feeling wobbly, immediately sat down again. "It just came on so suddenly."

"With all that has happened I'm surprised you're even here today," Aubrey said. "Don't rush getting up. We're here for you."

"Hey, where is everyone?"

"We're in back," Aubrey called.

Gina appeared with three big white to-go bags. "What's going on?" Concern etched her face.

"Nothing."

"She had a bit of a panic attack," Aubrey said. "We were outside, looking at the displays and Angie freaked a little because of the crowds."

Gina put the bags on the desk and crouched down until she was eye level with Angie.

"Did you see someone you recognized?"

"No, it was nothing like that." Angie felt foolish. If anything, it was safer here in the center with all the people strolling around than it was at the cabin. "I think the events of last evening suddenly hit me is all." Tuff and their night in bed together had managed to distract her. But today... everything had sort of hit a crescendo.

"I know Sawyer's at the cabin putting up cameras. And I brought food." Gina held up one of the sacks. "If you want, we can close the store and you can come over to the restaurant and eat this."

"No." Angie shook her head. "We actually sold eight Dalton steaks today. I'm not going to interrupt that momentum." She tried to laugh but it came out rusty.

"You sure? No one expects you to work today."

"I could take over," Aubrey volunteered. "Madison has Refind covered. And I have the day free."

"Me too," Charlie chimed in. "Aubrey and I can split shifts, or we can do it together."

"I'm fine. I really am. It's good for me to be here. It feels safe and it keeps my mind occupied."

"I get it. But at least eat. I brought enough for an army." Gina looked around the small space. "Should we take the food out there? Too bad you don't have the café tables yet. But we can move a display and spread out on one of the farm tables in the kitchen section."

"That's a great idea." Charlie got started moving things around.

Aubrey gathered up four chairs. It probably wasn't the most professional look for the store. But screw it. Angie needed her family. And the smell of Gina's delicious food was a balm to her anxiety.

Gina helped set up their picnic while Angie rang up a cupcake and a bag of mandarin oranges for a man and his little girl.

A couple came in and spotted their impromptu lunch setup. "Oh, isn't that lovely," the woman said and glanced around the store, her eyes stopping at the butcher counter, then veering back to Gina's picnic. "Do you serve deli food? It's so inviting in here."

It was as if a lightning bolt hit Angie right between the eyes. She ignored her earlier panic attack and became laser focused on the woman's deli suggestion. Angie caught Gina's gaze and could tell she and her sister-in-law were having the same epiphany.

"We're working on it," Angie told the couple. "We're still fairly new and the deli counter isn't up yet. But it will be soon. So don't forget about us."

"We won't," the woman said. "We own a cabin in Cascade Shores and pass this way every weekend. The restaurant is a great addition but a little heavy for lunch." She shifted her gaze to the butcher counter. "We stopped by for a chuck roast. We got one a few weeks ago and Charles is still raving about the pot roast I made." The man—presumably Charles—nodded.

The second the couple left with their roast, Gina squealed, "How did we not think of a deli counter before? You're a genius, Angie."

"You can thank that couple and this lunch." Angie eyed the offerings. Gina hadn't been kidding. There was more food than the four of them could eat at one sitting. Tri-tip, mashed potatoes, beans, garlic bread and a big salad. She'd also brought paper plates, napkins, and utensils. "But will it cut into your business too much?"

"It's our business, all of ours, not mine. We need the entire center to do well to keep this ranch going. And if we can sell Dalton beef on sandwiches and in salads for people to eat here or take to go, I'm all for it."

"I don't think it'll compete." Aubrey took some of the steak and passed it around the table. "Gina's is a destination. People who eat there either made reservations or have planned their visit days in advance. Grabbing a sandwich from a deli counter is more impulse. It's like 'I'm here, charging my car and am hungry.' Or someone sits down with me for a design consultation and two hours later, they realize they're starved. Or they come to buy groceries and while they're here, order a wrap to go. It's really smart."

"I agree," Charlie added. "A high-end steakhouse owned by a celebrity chef is not competing with the deli counter at a gourmet grocery store. It's brilliant, actually. And could be what saves the butcher shop."

"About that," Angie said around a mouthful of garlic bread. "Those earlier women who bought the steaks gave me another idea. Why don't we sell Dalton beef in cooler bags with dry ice? That way customers can schlep it up to Tahoe, especially during grilling season, or take it on the drive home without having to worry about the meat spoiling. We can even do some kind of cute packaging with our logo."

"I love it!" Gina pumped her fist in the air. "This is exactly the kind of strategy I'm talking about. We can include a couple of recipe cards, some complimentary seasoning, a pamphlet about the history of the ranch and how we raise our beef with a link to our website for re-orders. Boom!" She held up her hand and pretended to drop a microphone. "I could even put a brochure on every table at Gina's, saying don't forget to buy your Dalton beef care package at the butcher shop with a picture of our adorable cooler bags or however we decide to do it."

"It's a fantastic idea." Charlie clapped her hands.

"But will the guys go for the added expense?" Angie knew her family had already spent buckets of cash building Dry Creek Village and Daltons.

"If they want to save the butcher shop, they'll have to." Gina served everyone salad.

"We'll need to hire more people."

"The restaurant can do a lot of the prep work. But yeah, we'll need someone to work the counter."

"We'll need a counter with a refrigerated case, which probably isn't cheap," Aubrey added. "We'll also have to reorganize the store, which isn't a big deal, but it will cut into our shelf space."

Shelf space for items that weren't selling.

"That's where we do our thing." Charlie waved her hand between her and Aubrey. "I'm pretty used to shoving a lot of stuff into a small space without it looking crowded and messy."

"If it looks anything like your and Aubrey's windows"—Angie nudged her head at the displays they'd completed—"we'll kill it."

Charlie reached over and gave Angie a hug. "I'm so glad you're here. And the thing that happened yesterday…it will pass."

"Yep." She put on a good face. But she knew the Liberty Fighters. They wouldn't leave her alone until blood was spilled.

"Okay, enough bad shit. Let's talk about something uplifting, like say, Tuff Garrison." Gina poked Angie in the arm. "According to Sawyer, he's been sticking to you like a guard dog. If I wasn't married to your brother and having his baby, I could get used to having a guard dog like Tuff around." She waggled her brows. "Sounds like you've been holding out on us."

"There's nothing to tell. He's a good friend." Angie didn't know what else to call him and there was no way in hell she was confiding in her sister-in-law and cousins that she was sleeping with him. It was too new and too wonderful to share. She wanted to savor it while it lasted and with the way things were going it wouldn't last long.

"Be that way." Gina stuck her tongue at Angie and everyone laughed.

"He really is hot." Aubrey licked her fork for extra emphasis. "And so nice. But I've always thought there was an air of mystery to him, too. He's never been super open about his background, almost like he's hiding something."

From everything he'd told Angie, he'd had a tragic childhood. A father who was murdered when Tuff was only a kid and a mother who was an alcoholic. It wasn't stuff people typically liked talking about.

"Jace likes him a lot," Charlie said. "And I've always been a fan. But, Angie, your love life is yours and yours alone."

Angie could feel her face heat. "It's not like that with Tuff and me. We're friends, that's all."

"And look, there's your friend now." Gina bobbed her head at the window with the hutch display.

Tuff was standing in front of the window with his hands stuffed in the pockets of his down jacket, checking out Aubrey and Charlie's creation.

"Last I looked, your friend wasn't working today." Gina hitched her brows.

Tuff had employed Ava's cousin to handle the shop on weekends, so he could have a day off or spend it working on projects without the interruption of customers.

"Maybe he came by to get something," Angie said. "You ever think of that?"

Before Gina could respond, he walked into the store. He took one look at their picnic spread and broke into a grin. "You move the restaurant in here?"

"Not the restaurant." Angie couldn't stop the flutter in her chest. "But we're talking about installing a deli counter. Sandwiches, salads, soup, that sort of thing."

"Yeah? This a test run?" He gave their lunch a thorough perusal. "Whaddya got there?"

"Tri-tip and all the fixings." Gina handed him one of the paper plates. "Dig in."

"Don't mind if I do." He helped himself to some of the meat, beans and potatoes.

Gina took a quick glance at her watch. "I've got to get back to the restaurant. Come to dinner tonight, Ange. Sawyer says you don't want to stay with us, but you know you're always welcome."

"I know." And Angie did. Since she'd arrived, Gina had treated her like a sister. "I'm going to skip dinner, but I'll stop by tomorrow."

Charlie and Aubrey helped Angie clean up and revert the table back to a kitchen display while Tuff ate at the cash register. A few customers came in to browse. One of them bought a brownie and stood by the counter, picking at the frosting and flirting with Tuff. She was an attractive blonde in her mid-thirties. Angie gave Tuff credit for not flirting back. Instead, he kept glancing over at Angie, silently begging her to save him.

That's what you get for being too good looking.

Charlie and Aubrey took off to make sure Taylor didn't need help at Refind with the promise to check in on Angie throughout the day. It was sweet of them, but Angie regarded the store as her safe zone. Too much foot traffic by the big glass windows for anyone to try anything.

Besides, Tuff was here now. She didn't know how long he'd stay but he didn't seem in any rush to leave.

The blonde finally got the hint and left with her brownie.

"Busy day?" Tuff got off the stool so Angie could sit in her usual spot by the register.

She motioned for him to stay put. She'd been sitting all day. "Not bad. We sold eight steaks and a chuck roast."

"Nice."

"What did you do today?"

He kept his voice low. "Got my window fixed and helped Sawyer install a half dozen cameras around both our cabins."

"This has got to suck for you." She hated the idea that the tradeoff for her safety meant invading Tuff's privacy.

"Worse for you, I suspect. I left Buddy at your place before I came over."

"You didn't have to do that, Tuff."

Tuff shrugged. "I think he likes your cabin better anyway."

Their conversation was interrupted when a scruffy-looking group of men came in. Tuff watched them browse. Angie got the impression he was memorizing their faces. They looked like your typical outdoorsy types. Men up from the city to fish or camp at the state park. They'd probably had a late lunch at Gina's and wanted beer to bring back to wherever they were staying.

Sure enough, they grabbed a couple of six packs of local microbrew from the refrigerator case and a bag of Nevada City ground coffee from the shelf where Angie planned to put the coffee bar. Tuff continued to watch them. And when they left, he trailed them to the parking lot.

"What was that about?" she asked when he returned.

"Got a picture of their license plate."

"Why? They were just tourists. Probably campers from the way they were dressed." One of them had had a backpack and they all wore REI gear.

"Maybe. But it doesn't hurt to pay attention."

She couldn't argue with that but wanted to talk about something else. It bothered her that everyone had been sucked into her drama. And if anything happened to Tuff or her family, she'd never forgive herself.

Tuff surprised her by sticking around until closing time. She called Sawyer to let him know that Tuff was seeing her home. Her brother didn't object, which was another surprise. He was still coming over later, though, to give her a tutorial on the new cameras he'd installed. If she'd just stayed in Portland none of this would be happening.

Tuff opened the door of his pickup for her, and she scooted in. He shut the door and just stood there, staring across the parking lot. She followed his gaze to a black SUV. From this distance and with only the glow from a lamp post she couldn't tell for sure, but it looked like a Chevy Tahoe. It was the only car parked on that end of the lot.

Tuff got in on his side.

"What's wrong?"

"Just checking things out."

"Do you recognize the vehicle?" There were a lot of SUVs that looked like that.

"Nope. But it's late and the only thing open is the restaurant. They're parked pretty far away from it." He tugged his phone out of his pocket, started his engine and slowly cruised by the SUV.

No one was in the vehicle. Tuff hung out of his window and snapped a couple of pictures. "I'm sure it's nothing but it doesn't hurt to be vigilant."

He was starting to remind her of Earl. "I guess not." But what a way to live?

When they got home, Tuff slid in next to her Mercedes and scanned the area before opening his door. "The place could use a few more motion lights. I'll pick some up at the hardware store tomorrow and put them in."

"Come in and I'll make you dinner."

He put his hand on his stomach. "I'm still full from lunch." But he followed her inside anyway.

Buddy greeted them at the door, his tail wagging back and forth. He jumped up on Tuff, demanding a good head scratch, then jogged down the porch steps to do his business.

Tuff took a quick walk through the cabin. "I'm going to head home. But I'll check on you in a little bit."

She grabbed his arm as he headed out. "You don't have to stand guard. I can take care of myself."

He looked at her, really looked. And she could tell that he saw her in way no one else had.

"I know you can." He pulled her into his arms and kissed her. It was soft and sweet but at the same time more. So much more. It was a yearning so strong that he fairly vibrated with it.

When he was finished, she stood there, shaken.

"Don't hesitate to call me or to push that button." His eyes moved to the watch on her wrist. "I'm serious, Angie."

She waited for him to cross the creek and disappear behind his cabin door. Then, still in a bit of a haze over the kiss, she got her phone, curled up on the couch, and called Earl.

"It's me. Did you find Kari?"

There was a long pause, then, "She's gone."

Chapter 20

Tuff sent his license plate photos to Jace with a quick note that said, "These are just for safekeeping. I'm sure they're nothing."

He checked the app on his phone to make sure all the security cameras were up and running and scrolled through the history to see if they'd gotten any hits. Just birds, a couple of deer, and a fallen tree branch. The cameras were sensitive, he'd give them that.

He leaned back on the sofa and stretched out his legs, trying to decide whether to make a fire. But he already knew the answer. *What the hell am I getting myself into?* He was longing for something that could never be. But he couldn't seem to stop himself. It was as if he was careening down a mountainside without any brakes.

His phone rang. Jace's number flashed on Tuff's phone screen.

"Tell me about these pictures," Jace said in lieu of a greeting.

"I'm sure they're nothing. The Jeep was four guys who came into the store, bought a few things, and left. I didn't like 'em. But it was probably my own personal bias." They'd been openly ogling Angie, which pissed him off. And they smelled of privilege, which probably didn't fit the mold of militia types. But what the hell did he know? "They looked like hikers or campers but posers. All shiny and new, like their boots had never met the dirt."

Jace laughed. "If I had a dollar for every one of those, I'd have enough cattle to retire. Welcome to the foothills, where every flatlander thinks he's a mountain man. What's the second one, the Chevy Tahoe?"

"Again, probably nothing. It was parked at the outer edge of the lot, a perfect vantage point for watching Daltons. It struck me as odd that in an empty lot at the end of the day it was parked so far away from the shops, especially the restaurant. But for all I know it had been there earlier when the lot was full. Angie said the store was busy today."

"It's never so busy that the lot's full but who knows. I'll cruise by and see if it's still there, run the plate. How's everything at the cabins?"

"Quiet. I just checked the cameras. Nothing."

"Yeah, I've been monitoring them throughout the day. Sawyer sure went to town."

"Was there anything from Dry Creek Village's cameras?"

"Cash is still going through the history but nothing that stands out from yesterday. We'll have to continue to keep our eyes and ears open." Jace paused, then said, "Thanks for having our backs on this. I know it's not what you signed on for. But we appreciate it."

"Just being a good neighbor."

Jace didn't say anything. Tuff wasn't stupid enough to underestimate him. The sheriff could smell bullshit a mile away.

"Okay, then, let's hope yesterday was a one off," Jace finally said.

But they both knew it wasn't.

For the next hour, Tuff played with the camera app, setting up various alerts. Buddy sniffed around the cupboard where Tuff kept the kibble. It reminded him that he'd forgotten the dog's bowl at Angie's.

He peered out the window and saw Sawyer's Range Rover in Angie's driveway. Tuff got down two dishes and filled one with dog food and the other with water. Buddy went to town on both. The dog had a bottomless stomach and seemed forever hungry. Tuff knew what that was like.

For the Christmas rush, he'd planned to spend the day making wallets. But he'd never gotten around to it. It was a good way to keep busy, so he retrieved the bolt of leather he'd brought home from the studio and laid it out on the kitchen table. He cut out a large piece to work with and put the bolt back in the closet.

The wallets had been something he'd been doing since the early days. Over the years, he'd perfected them with stylish tooling and fancy stich work. He preferred making saddles, but the wallets brought in a steady income and dressed up the shelves of his store. They also made excellent gifts.

He began cutting the first one from a pattern he knew by rote, but it quickly became apparent that his heart wasn't in it. Not today. He finished cutting all five wallets, stacked them in a neat pile, and rolled up the scraps.

His phone chimed with a camera alert and he ran out the door. Sawyer's taillights vanished down the driveway. The camera that faced their driveways must've caught him leaving. But just to make sure, he crossed the creek and tapped on Angie's door.

She peeked out the peephole, then he heard the click of the deadbolt. "Everything okay?"

"The camera went off. I assume it was Sawyer leaving but I wanted to check in."

She opened the door. "Come in. Where's Buddy?"

"Let me go get him." He went back for the dog and at the last minute grabbed his toothbrush.

* * * *

"Is there a chance your friend got gone on purpose?" Tuff asked. From the minute he'd walked into Angie's cabin, he could tell something was wrong. Her friend, Kari, was still missing. "From everything you've told me she has an independent streak." He couldn't say he blamed her. As far as he was concerned the feds hadn't done enough to keep Angie safe. So maybe Kari was smart to go her own way.

"That's what Earl's hoping. But in the past, she's always kept in touch with him loosely or left a way for him to find her. Given the weirdness with her phone number I'm petrified that something has happened to her."

Tuff could tell Angie had been crying. He pulled her into his embrace and sat on the sofa, holding her. For a long time, they didn't talk. She just clung to him like he was a life raft.

"What else did Earl say? You told him about the rat, right?"

"Yes," she murmured into his chest.

He stroked her hair, wishing there was a way he could fix everything. Experience, though, had taught him that life didn't work that way. That sometimes it threw everything it had at you and then came back for more.

He remembered the days after his father died. How as a young boy he thought nothing could be worse than losing the man he loved and idolized. He'd been wrong. Things with his mother spun so out of control that there were times he used to pray that he could join his dad in heaven.

"Ange, sweetheart, what did Earl say?"

"He thinks it could be a lone wolf, someone who followed the Liberty Fighters on the Internet and somehow found out about me and is out for revenge."

It seemed like a longshot to Tuff. How would some idiot wannabe militia type find out about Angie without having first-hand knowledge or at least access to one of the members who'd been on The Farm with her?

"Are you mentioned in any court records?"

"Not by name. I'm just known as 'Witness X.' But Earl thinks that before Burt, Zane, and the rest of them were arrested they'd started recruiting. For all I know one of these recruits came to The Farm, saw me, figured out that I was working with Jet, and has made it his mission to create havoc for me. First thing in the morning, Earl's contacting the US Attorney's Office and the Department of Justice."

Okay, now they were getting somewhere.

"I assume you told Sawyer all this, right?"

"Uh-huh." She sounded exhausted. Last night they hadn't gotten much sleep. "I don't want to talk about it anymore, Tuff. Can we please talk about something else?"

"Yep. What do you want to talk about?"

She lifted her head. One look at her big blue eyes and his heart nearly came out of his chest.

"I've worked out a situation with this community organization that helps the needy and homeless in Mill and the surrounding counties. They're going to come every week to pick up Daltons' soon-to expire food. We're not allowed to sell stuff past its due date but a lot of it is still good. Now it won't go to waste."

He kissed the top of her head. Her life had been thrown into chaos and yet, she was worried about food waste and the poor. This is what he found so remarkable about her. So damned attractive.

"The kind of stuff you were made to do," he whispered into her ear.

"The kind of stuff I'd planned to do with the rest of my life. But instead, ran home to my family and let them carry me." She buried her face back in his chest.

"Hey." He gently cupped her chin so he could look at her. "Where's this coming from?"

"Look at what a mess I've made." She welled up. "I ran off to save the world, spent my family's money on a criminal enterprise and here I am, bringing my bad decisions back to haunt the entire ranch. And you. You didn't ask for any of this. Yet here you are. My rock." She sobbed.

"You didn't bring this on yourself. No one blames you, Angie. From where I'm sitting, you're the apple of your family's eye. They love you. They'd do anything to protect you."

"I don't know why. My whole adult life I've been a flake, flying around the world, making bad decisions."

"You wanted to help people, do good. There's nothing flakey or bad about that. It's admirable. I'm freaking blown away by it. By you."

She wiped her nose with the back of her hand.

He reached into his back pocket and handed her a handkerchief.

"It's so admirable that I've probably gotten three people killed, including two of my dear friends."

"You can't think like that, Angie. These are dangerous people. They're also nut jobs. How were you supposed to stop them?"

"By not being so goddamn trusting and stupid. By not being such a coward."

"A coward?" Tuff jerked his head back. "Jesus, you're the bravest person I know. You put yourself in danger, helping to build a case against these morons. You could've had that ATF agent get you the hell out of there. Instead, you stayed and gathered intelligence for the police, all the while putting yourself at risk. I'm in awe of what you did. If it wasn't for you, who knows what damage these people would've caused. How many people they would've killed?"

"I wasn't brave. I was scared every second of every hour of every day. If it wasn't for Jet, I would've run the first chance I got. But these people had to be stopped. They had to be taken down. And after all that. After everything we did, they're still out there somewhere, causing more pain and more trouble."

"We're going to get 'em, Angela."

"It kills me that I brought this here. What if something happens to Gina, Aubrey, or Charlie because of me? Sawyer and my cousins would never forgive me."

"Nothing is going to happen to anyone. We've got this."

"I don't want you involved in this. If you got hurt or anything bad happened to you...I couldn't bear it."

"Nothing is going to happen to me. And I thought we said we weren't going to talk about this anymore."

She reached up and traced his face with her hand. "You're such a good man, Tuff Garrison."

If she only knew how wrong she was.

"You have any of that meatloaf left?" He got up and reached out his hand to pull her up off the sofa.

She took it and tugged him into the kitchen. "I do. I'll reheat it. Are you tired of potatoes? We can have those too."

"Never tired of potatoes." He set the table while she made them up two plates and warmed them in the microwave. "So tell me about this deli counter of yours."

"It was while we were eating lunch. This cute couple came in, saw our setup and asked if we served deli foods. I got the feeling that if we'd invited them, they would've joined us. I think it was the way Charlie and Aubrey spread everything out on the table. They know how to make everything look so amazing. Anyway, that's when the idea hit me. I think it came to Gina at the same time."

He leaned against the counter while they waited for the timer to go off. "How will it work?"

"I don't have all the details worked out yet. But I have noticed that people want a place to sit and eat a little something before hitting the road again. I was already adding the tables for the coffee station. But why not do more with it, right? And if we use the Dalton beef for sandwiches and salads, maybe even do hot dogs and burgers, it might save the butcher shop. Because right now we're bleeding money."

For a woman who'd settled to work in her family's grocery store instead of the career of her dreams, she was damned enthusiastic about it. She was lit up like a Christmas tree.

"Another thing we're talking about is packaging our meat in dry ice, so people traveling can take it home without worrying that it'll spoil. We're thinking of cute cooler bags or baskets with recipe cards, seasoning packets, maybe some barbecue sauce."

She let out a breath, like a deflated balloon.

"What?"

"It would've been a great day if not for...Kari."

"Your friend?"

"Yeah. You're not supposed to know her name. It slipped out before."

"Your secret is safe with me."

"I know. After Zane I never thought I'd trust another man again who wasn't a relative. But I trust you."

Though he should've, he couldn't bring himself to say, "Don't trust me with your heart because I'll only break it."

"What if something terrible happened to her?"

Tuff didn't want to be the one to confirm her concerns, but something probably had. At the very least, he was convinced someone had her phone. The fact the US Marshals couldn't find her...well, it didn't bode well for Kari.

"Will the feds look for her?"

"Earl said they would. But there's only so much they can do."

"Does she have any family members or friends you could call?"

"Earl told me not to. That I should leave it to him."

"Then that's what you should do."

The microwave dinged and Angie replaced the plate inside with another one. "Start. I don't want yours to get cold."

He took the plate to the table but waited for her. She joined him a couple of minutes later and they ate mostly in silence. Buddy got up from his spot in the living room and found a new place under the table.

In the past, Tuff had always avoided domestic situations like this one. But here in the cabin...with Angie...it felt natural. Even good. It should've scared the hell out of him but all it did was make him want to tell her the truth about himself and the things he'd done.

Chapter 21

The days passed quietly. No more dead rats hanging from Angie's door. And no strange phone calls. Cash hadn't found anything suspicious on the camera footage from the center. And Earl still hadn't found Kari. At least the FBI was working on getting search warrants for her phone and bank records. They were also closely monitoring Burt and Zane's phone calls from jail.

Despite the lack of activity, her family closed in on her like a protective shell. Between them and Tuff, the only time she was alone was in the shower. And half the time, Tuff joined her there as well. Tuff had become the silver lining to her life being turned upside down. No matter how hard she tried not to, she was falling for him. Head over heels.

Neither of them had made their feelings known. Her life was still too transitory to make any commitments. And Tuff…well, Tuff was a mystery. Despite him standing guard over her like a secret service agent and them spending every night in each other's bed, he remained emotionally distant. She knew he cared about her, but he seemed incapable of letting himself embrace whatever it was they had together.

None of that, though, was going to dampen her mood. Today the bistro tables were finally coming and she, Aubrey, and Charlie were spending the morning reorganizing the store. Early next year, they hoped to have the deli counter up and running. She'd already ordered cooler bags with the Dry Creek brand and a delivery service to keep them in dry ice. It was an investment to be sure, but Angie believed it would pay off in the end.

While she waited for the girls, she unpacked the new restaurant grade coffee machines and urns that Gina had helped her purchase. Charlie was bringing over a lovely farm buffet table where they would set up the station.

Angie had indulged by ordering cases of ceramic mugs with the Dry Creek Ranch logo, convincing herself that the small cost would be worth it in the end. The mugs had come out so cute that she planned to sell them in the store. In addition to the ceramic ones, she'd found a source for heavy duty biodegradable cups customers could take to go.

"You want me to get the machine going in the back, so we're ready to fill the urns when everything is set up?" Nina asked.

"That would be great." Truth be told, Angie was dying for a cup.

At about nine, Charlie pulled Jace's pickup up to the loading zone and together they hauled the table in. Aubrey wandered in a few minutes later with a wine bottle drier rack they could use to hang the mugs from.

"I love it." Angie jumped up and down. This was her idea, and it was coming together so perfectly she wanted to pinch herself. If it wound up making money for the store, she'd be overjoyed.

Over the next hour, they moved things around, making room for the bistro tables. It required a lot of squishing but that's where Charlie came in. With Aubrey's help, they disassembled a few displays, then rebuilt them in other areas of the floor. Somehow, they managed to make the store look even larger.

Nina brought them all fresh cups of coffee made with beans from a local roaster and they stood around sipping, admiring what they'd accomplished so far.

"This is freaking good coffee." Aubrey warmed her hands on the cup. "You better order more bags of this stuff because I have a feeling there's going to be a run on them."

That was the plan. Not only would they sell it by the cup but also by the bag.

"I love the mugs." Charlie turned the cup in her hand. "The Dry Creek brand looks so cute against the brown and turquoise. We should sell some of these in Refind, too."

"That's a brilliant idea. I ordered tons, so I'll send you back with a box."

"How are you going to wash all of these?" Aubrey asked.

"We're putting a dishwasher in the butcher shop."

Gina had helped with that too. Together, they'd ordered an industrial dishwasher specially for mugs. It was the kind of thing Starbucks probably had.

"I'm so excited." Angie couldn't believe it was all coming together. "The guy is installing it at the end of the week."

They finished their coffee and got back to work. Nina transferred the coffee to the giant urns and started fresh pots while Charlie laid out everything on the table. With the stirrers, milk, cream and sugar it was a tight fit, but Charlie made the spread look like something out of a magazine.

"The bottle rack was a good idea," Charlie told Aubrey.

It really did give the station a little something something.

Charlie finished off the arrangement with a hand-painted price sign and dropped a few sprigs of holly here and there. It was a nice holiday touch.

Aubrey stood back to give it her final designer approval. "Looks great. Now all we have to do is wait for the bistro tables to be delivered."

"You guys want me to call you when they get here?" There was no sense in them waiting when they had their own store to tend.

"Good idea." Aubrey topped off her coffee and added a little cream.

Charlie swatted Aubrey's arm. "Don't mess up my beautiful display." She moved the cream dispenser so it lined up perfectly with the milk one. She was a little OCD.

"Can we take these back to Refind?" Charlie held up her mug.

"Of course, I've got tons. Which reminds me, let me get you a box of them to sell." Angie swiped the key to the storage shed out of the drawer and shrugged into her jacket. "Be right back."

On her way, there was a man leaning against the side of Daltons, away from the windows. He was smoking a cigarette and nodded to Angie as she walked by. He looked familiar. She racked her brain to remember where she knew him from but couldn't place him.

For a moment she considered saving her trip to the storage unit for later but told herself she was being ridiculous. The man was obviously a local. He probably worked for Gina and was on break. Either that or he was a delivery guy who Angie had seen countless times but hadn't paid enough attention to commit him to memory.

She continued to the storage room, surreptitiously looking over her shoulder. The man was staring at his phone, puffing away on his cigarette, his knee bent with one booted foot planted against the wall. He appeared completely unaware of her presence.

She popped into Dalton's storage unit, wishing she'd organized the shelves better. The Halloween decorations were still in a jumble next to the Thanksgiving stuff. She put coming back and tidying up the space on her mental to-do list and searched for the mug cartons. They were of course at the bottom of a stack of empty boxes that needed to be broken down for recycling.

She tossed the empties aside until she got to the mugs. Then she rearranged the cartons so the next time she'd have better access.

She hefted the box into her arms and with one hand locked the storage unit. Angie turned around and spotted the smoking guy across the sidewalk, just a few feet away. He shielded his eyes from the sun and stared out over the parking lot as if he was waiting for someone.

Something churned in her gut but again she told herself she was being silly. There was nothing about the man remotely threatening. He dressed like everyone else in the foothills. Jeans, down jacket, work boots. And he wasn't paying any attention to her, seemingly wrapped up in whoever he was waiting for.

She readjusted her box of mugs and walked back to the market. When she got inside, Aubrey motioned at the coffee bar. There were already a few customers, standing by the urns, drinking from the Dry Creek Ranch mugs.

Angie waited until she was out of sight of the customers and pumped her fist in the air. It was going to be a good day.

She spent the rest of the morning, refilling the urns as there was a steady trickle of traffic. With only a week until Christmas, it seemed as if the entire state of California was trekking up the mountain to the ski resorts. Angie wondered if Tuff's shop was doing as well as Daltons.

Around noon, a big truck came with Angie's bistro tables. She quickly sent texts to Charlie and Aubrey. In the meantime, she had the two delivery guys stack the tables and chairs near the coffee station. It was a lot of furniture. Angie questioned whether she'd ordered too many, fearing that the tables and chairs would monopolize the store's real estate.

"They're bigger than I thought they'd be." Nina confirmed Angie's worries.

"I know, right? I suppose we don't have to use them all. Maybe put some outside."

"You could do that." But Nina didn't look optimistic. The truth was the tables would block the sidewalk and wouldn't go with the rustic picnic tables that dotted the grounds.

One of the delivery men stuck a clipboard under Angie's nose. "Just need you to sign."

She scribbled her signature but was tempted to tell him to take half the furniture away.

Tuff wandered in a few minutes later. "Saw you got your delivery."

"Yep." She started unstacking the chairs and removing the plastic. "I think it's going to be a disaster."

"Why?" He lifted down one of the tables and began unwrapping it. "You've been waiting for this."

"They looked so much smaller in the pictures."

He hitched his shoulders. "They look okay size-wise to me." He surprised her by pulling her in for hug.

Tuff was never demonstrative in public. Though her family liked to tease her about him, she doubted they knew the depths of their intimacy. Because he was so private, Angie tried to follow his lead.

"You think? Because they look huge to me. I'm worried it's going to look like a furniture factory in here."

"Let's see." He returned to unstacking the tables like they weighed nothing and removed all the cellophane wrap.

"Charlie and Aubrey are coming over to help arrange them."

He glanced over at the coffee bar. "That worked out well."

"They did a great job. Hopefully, they can fix this." The more she saw of the tables the more she realized what a mistake she'd made.

"I have a feeling it's not as bad as you think. It just looks cluttered when they're all stacked up like this." He began spreading out the tables and putting the chairs around them. "The three of you will do better with the arrangement. I'm no interior designer. This is just to give you an idea of the scale."

Nina pitched in and soon they had the tables laid out in a semi presentable fashion. Tuff was right. It wasn't as terrible as she'd originally thought. But it wasn't great. It felt tight, like people would be bumping their chairs into one another.

"Who's watching your shop?"

"No one. I closed up for lunch with you." He winked.

"When we get these right, we can figure out something to eat here. And take these babies on a test run."

His lips tipped up and her heart did a little dip.

Both their camera app alerts went off on their phones at the same time. She rolled her eyes. "What do you think it is this time? A leaf? A squirrel? A shadow from one of the trees?"

She appreciated Sawyer's vigilance where the cameras were concerned. But when this was all behind her, she planned to take down each and every camera. The endless alerts were driving her nuts.

Tuff ignored her and checked his phone, scrolling through the history. She stood next to him, staring at his screen over his shoulder, tapping her toe.

"Nothing, right?"

"Nothing that I can tell. But I have to go over there anyway and let Buddy out." He'd been keeping him home ever since the rat incident, hoping the dog would scare off any further attempts.

"By the time you get back, I will have scared us up something for lunch."

"Sounds good."

It wasn't until he left that she realized that while she'd made light of the cameras going off, there might actually be something going on. Something dangerous. And Tuff was walking right into it.

She started to call Jace, but it would take him twenty minutes to get to the ranch from the sheriff's department in downtown Dry Creek. Luckily, Cash was working from home and she got him on the phone.

"I got it too," he said about the alert. "It didn't look like anything, but I'll go over and back Tuff up."

"Thank you."

Unlike Tuff, Cash was a trained law enforcement agent, who was armed to the teeth. She was sure it was nothing. But like Earl always said: "Better safe than sorry."

Aubrey and Charlie arrived and took one look at Angie and Tuff's table arrangement and started moving things around.

"Did I screw up?" Angie chewed on her bottom lip. "They're huge."

"They're the right size." Aubrey assured her. "It's the layout that's wrong."

In no time at all, they had the tables rearranged. Aubrey was right. Spread out the way they were now, they looked like they'd always been there.

"You guys saved the day. Oh my gosh, they look so good. It's like a little restaurant," she squealed.

Charlie couldn't help herself and tidied up the coffee station. "We sold two mugs. It was to Laney, but it was still two mugs."

"I would've given them to Laney." Angie laughed.

"I've got to get back for a conference call with a pain-in-the-neck client." Aubrey pulled a face. "The woman is a demanding biotch. But she owns three homes and pays her bills on time."

"Go." Angie shooed her away. "You guys are amazing." She blew them kisses as they left the store.

Angie walked around, admiring the new setup. "How did we ever doubt ourselves, Nina?"

Nina peeked out from the aisle where she was stocking shelves. "I was scared there for a while. But it looks good. Maybe I'll start bringing my lunch."

"Me too." It reminded her that Tuff hadn't returned.

She got her phone out of her purse, took it to the back of the store, and called him. He didn't answer and she started to panic. Next, she tried Cash, who also didn't pick up. She was about to call in reinforcements when Tuff came in the door.

"Everything all right?"

"Yep. False alarm."

"Did you run into Cash?"

"Yeah," he said, suppressing an eye roll. "Thanks for sending him." His sarcasm wasn't lost on her. Men were so touchy.

Nina called out that she was taking off for lunch.

Angie scanned the store for something more nutritious than coffee and donuts, which had been their top sellers that day. "What are you in the mood for?"

He raised his brows and gave her dress a slow perusal.

"Not that." She laughed. "At least not in the store."

"No?" He winked. "Then I guess we'll stick to food. I'm game for anything."

"How 'bout cheese and crackers and veggies and dip."

"Sounds good."

She went around the store, collecting the items she would need to make her charcuterie board. There was a nice jar of quince jam she added to her basket as well as some spicy mustard and cured olives they got from a farmer in Grass Valley. By the time she was done laying it all out, the spread looked similar to something they served at the restaurant she'd worked at in Portland.

She brought it to one of the tables and found the paper plates Gina had left the last time they'd had a picnic lunch in the store.

"What would you like to drink?"

"Water's fine." He fetched two bottles from the refrigerator case. "This looks great."

They were the first to christen the new setup, eating their cheese and crackers at the table closest to the cash register. It was a fine meal made on the fly. And Angie couldn't think of one person she'd rather spend it with than Tuff.

"So, was it just a bird?"

"Don't know," he said between bites. "Those cameras are incredibly sensitive. But everything was quiet as a rabbit. Buddy was asleep on your sofa when I got there."

"He has the fanciest dog bed in California and yet he prefers the couch, the little scoundrel." Her mouth curved up and for a few seconds he just stared at her face with a warmth so profound that Angie felt the heat of it from where she was sitting. Then he quickly looked away.

"You want to get the tree tonight?"

"Tonight? It's only a week until Christmas." With everything going on and Kari missing, it had taken the merry out of Angie's holidays. She'd completely given up on getting a tree.

Her parents were coming the morning of Christmas Eve for a crab fest at Cash and Aubrey's later. Christmas was opening gifts and dinner at the ranch house. Both homes had giant trees, decorated to the nines.

"Sure, why not?" Tuff popped another cracker with some of the quince jam in his mouth.

"I doubt there are any left." She'd driven by Home Depot in Auburn the other day to do some Christmas shopping and the lot was down to two scrawny trees. By now, even those were probably gone.

"Cash said he cut his down on the property, up in the hills by the south pastures. I know one of the owners of the ranch. I bet if I asked her, she'd say go for it."

She beamed because she never thought of herself as one of the owners of Dry Creek Ranch.

"We could do that," she said.

"What time do you want to go?"

"Any time after work, though it'll be dark."

"That'll be the fun of it," he said, his intonation suggestive.

He picked her up at the store at six. Daltons was open until seven—their new holiday hours. But Nina offered to close. They went home first so Angie could change out of her dress into jeans, a warm jacket and boots for mucking around in the hills.

Tuff ran over to his house to get the appropriate tools. When she was a kid, getting the tree had been a family adventure with Grandpa Dalton. On the day after Thanksgiving, they would hike through the forest on the outer edges of the ranch and chop down the biggest fir they could find. All the grandkids would pile in the bed of Grandpa Dalton's pickup and they'd tow the tree to the ranch house in the back of a trailer. The whole ride, they'd drink hot cocoa from thermoses Grandma Dalton had packed for them.

The memory had Angie searching the pantry for chocolate to make cocoa for the outing. By the time Tuff loaded his truck, she had a thermos and cups ready to go. They hit the road, the last half of it up a bumpy fire trail into the hills.

Every time Tuff hit a rut in the road, Angie giggled. She couldn't help herself. Tuff reached across her seat and put his hand on her leg. She scooted closer. His scent, a combination of leather, soap and aftershave, filled the cab and she luxuriated in its familiarity. It was a scent that both stirred and comforted her. In the past, she'd never found excitement and safety in the same man. And the truth of it was she'd never been particularly drawn to safe.

Maybe she was now because of her circumstances. Or maybe she'd simply grown the hell up.

"What are you thinking?" he asked her in the dark.

"About you."

"What about me?"

"That you smell really good."

He barked out a laugh. "That's the first time I've gotten that one."

"And that I've never felt safer putting my heart in a man's hands."

He pulled up to a copse of trees, letting her words hang in the cab of his truck like a hangman's noose. "Don't," he finally said and cut the engine. "I care about you, Angie. But I can't be that man for you."

He slid out of his seat and grabbed the ax from the back. She followed him to a circle of mature fir trees that had been illuminated by his headlights, wishing she'd kept her mouth shut. They'd been having such a lovely time and she'd broken the mood with her confession.

But instead of letting it go, she pushed. "Why? What happened to you, Tuff?" She wasn't asking for his hand or a solid commitment. She wasn't in a position to give those things, let alone demand them. Angie just wanted him to acknowledge the time they shared together had been special. Maybe even life changing.

"Which one do you want?" He focused on the trees, avoiding her gaze and her question.

"Nothing too big." There wasn't a lot of room in her cabin. "How about this one?" Honestly, she didn't care anymore. The spirit of the evening had been broken.

"This one it is. Move back." He swung the ax, hitting the bottom of the tree's trunk.

It only took a few more hacks to topple the fir to the ground. With a cordless chainsaw, he trimmed off the excess branches. Then he tossed the tree, which only stood about five-feet tall, into the bed of his pickup. There wasn't even a need to tie it down as it fit with room to spare.

He opened the passenger door and ushered her in, then got behind the wheel. He turned off his headlights and for a few minutes they sat in the dark with only the sounds of the night filling the air.

He shifted in his seat, turned so he faced her, and said, "I killed a man."

Chapter 22

At first, she thought she'd either misunderstood or heard Tuff wrong. "Excuse me?"

For a long time, he didn't respond. And then in a soft voice he said, "He was my mother's boyfriend and I bludgeoned him to death with a baseball bat." He described it so plainly—so bluntly—that if Angie didn't know him for the good man he was, she'd be frightened by his coldness.

She swallowed hard. He'd always been hesitant when it came to talking about his background.

"Why? Why did you kill him?" She couldn't fathom Tuff as violent, let alone a murderer. He'd never been anything but gentle and kind.

"He was beating my mother. I tried to stop him, and he knocked me into the wall. When I came to, he was on top of her, his hand around her throat."

"My God, Tuff. How old were you?"

"Fifteen."

Fifteen. He'd been a mere child.

Angie could only imagine the fear and the horror he experienced that day. The man could've killed Tuff's mother. "So it was self-defense."

He let out a mocking laugh. "Yeah, except I took the time to crawl to the closet and get my bat. Some would call that pre-meditated murder. I don't care what you call it, I just wanted the son-of-a-bitch dead."

"Had he done it before? Beat your mother?"

There was the laugh again. This time, it was sad rather than mocking. "Only when he was drunk, which was every day. And when he was done beating her good and bloody, he turned his fists on me. Floyd wasn't the first. She had a string of abusive lovers after my father died. None of them bothered with me. But Floyd was a special kind of asshole and the one my mother stuck with the longest."

"Oh, Tuff. I don't even know what to say." Except, what kind of mother let a man abuse her child? "Did you go to prison?"

"No," he said. "The sheriff and DA never filed charges."

She was still reeling from "*I bludgeoned him to death.*" At least he hadn't been sent away for protecting his mother and himself.

"Look," he said, "I'm only telling you this to explain why I can't...Just don't expect more than this. It's all I can give."

Didn't he understand that what he'd given had been beyond enough? Joy, safety, happiness. And in his own stoic way, his heart. Never with words. But she'd had the words before from other men, and they'd turned out to be empty. Just platitudes with no meaning. Tuff gave with himself. And that was more than enough.

"I only told you this, so you'll know who I am and where I come from," he finished.

"I know who you are, Tuff. You're a good man. A kind man. A caring man. An honorable man. A man my brother, cousins and I are proud to call a friend. A man I wish my grandfather was alive to know."

Unmoved, Tuff started the engine. "Let's get the tree home."

The drive to the cabin was a blur. All she could think about was what Tuff had told her. How at fifteen he'd been thrust into the role of protector and here he was doing it again. No wonder he and his mother were estranged when she died. She should've been his protector.

He pulled up next to her Mercedes. But before he could hop out of the truck, she caught his sleeve. "I'm sorry, Tuff. No little boy should have to go through what you did."

"I wasn't a little boy, Angie. I was forced into manhood the day my father died. I'm not whining about it. It's just the way it was." He twisted in his seat. "And if I had to do it all over again, I would. I'd kill Floyd Barrows as soon as look at him, which doesn't make me a good, kind, or caring man. Just a flesh and blood one. So save the poetry for someone else, please."

He slid out of the truck, hefted the tree over his shoulder, and carried it inside. "How 'bout here?" He set it in the corner in the exact spot she had intended it to go, though she no longer felt like decorating it. The fact that he was even going through the motions at all was sort of surreal.

"That's fine." She took his hand and led him to the sofa. "Tuff, what happened with you and your mom after Floyd died?"

"She kicked me out of the house and told me to never darken her door again." He said it so matter of fact that she questioned whether he was being snide.

"What do you mean?" She tilted her head to one side. "He was beating her. You probably saved her life."

"Yeah, well she didn't see it that way."

"But you were only a kid. You couldn't even drive." Her voice shook with anger. "Where were you supposed to go?"

"Anywhere but near her."

The story just kept getting worse and she was having trouble controlling her rage.

"Where did you wind up?"

"I got the hell out of Montana. Hitched a ride to Wyoming and got a job wrangling on a ranch in Jackson Hole."

"You were only fifteen." What kind of place hired a kid? Someone should've called child protective services. "You didn't have any relatives? No one would take you in?"

"My father's parents were dead and my mother's…well, let's just say she was the grand champion of the lot. So not a possibility. Look, Angie, it's fine. Not everyone grows up the way you did."

No. And yet, the benefits of being loved, nurtured and growing up with wealth in a good home hadn't stopped her from making mistakes. He, on the other hand, had risen from nothing to become a successful businessman and a person of substance.

"Of course not," she said. "What happened to you was wrong. But look at all that you have accomplished. So why let the past define you?"

"I haven't let anything define me. I'm exactly the man I want to be. But I think you should ask yourself the same thing, Angie. Not a day goes by when you don't question your own accomplishments or the fact that you're a good person who wanted to make the world a better place. Instead, you blame yourself for everything those lunatic Liberty Fighters did. So instead of trying to fix me, fix yourself."

With that he walked out the door and into the darkness.

* * * *

Maybe some of what Angie had said was right on the mark but Tuff didn't want to think about it now. He'd spent his entire adulthood hiding that part of his life away. He'd only taken it out and exposed it to show

Angie he wasn't the man she wanted him to be. That he'd given her all he could give. And if she was looking for more, she'd have to go elsewhere.

He'd never be a husband or a family man or someone who was completely dependable. It wasn't in his DNA.

Just the simple pleasure of hunting for a Christmas tree had taken everything he had. But he'd wanted to make Angie happy. These last weeks had been hell for her and the tree was a good distraction. Yet, he couldn't even pull that off without ruining the outing.

He was no better than his mother in that regard. After his father died, all the traditional trappings of Christmas had fallen by the wayside. No tree, no stockings, no turkey dinners. Just a bottle of Tanqueray she bought for herself and whatever gift she could scrounge up for him at the local liquor store. When he was thirteen, she pulled her act together long enough to get him a baseball glove and a Louisville Slugger. Back then, he'd been a fanatic, memorizing MLB stats like one did his own address.

The bat had been the same one he'd used to smash Floyd's skull in.

What he didn't tell Angie was how Mary Garrison had begged the police to arrest him and send him away. Her own son. She'd chosen a useless woman-beating bastard over her child.

If it wasn't for the fact that Sheriff Strong had been to the house a hundred times, responding to calls of domestic violence, he might've arrested Tuff. But he knew Floyd—he'd arrested him countless times on drunk and disorderlies—and what he was capable of. And there were Tuff's and Mary's bruises to prove what had happened that night.

Often, he wondered if Darrel Strong had secretly thought Tuff had done him a favor. One less piece of shit in his jurisdiction to deal with.

That first night, Tuff had slept curled up in a railway car, crying himself to sleep. The train took him as far as Cody, where he hitched a ride with a rodeo cowboy, who told him about the Big Horn Ranch. What Tuff had known then about horses and cattle he'd learned from TV. But the cowboys at the Big Horn had taught him how to ride, how to hold a rope, and how to take care of himself. They were the first in a long line of ranch hand families.

From there, he traveled the West, picking up work wherever he could find it and entering every rodeo on the way. It hadn't been a bad life. Just a hard and lonely one.

A few times, he'd sent his mother money when he had enough to spare. Lord knew why. She never once tried to contact him at any of his return addresses. Finally, he gave up.

He went into his kitchen and searched through the refrigerator for something to eat. Since staying with Angie, he rarely brought groceries home anymore. The cupboards were bare.

There were lights on Angie's tree. From his cabin he could see them blink red and green. He leaned his forehead against the glass, staring at them, feeling the cold against his skin.

Buddy whimpered, dancing in a circle to be let out. Tuff opened the door for him and stood on the porch, listening to the rushing water of the creek. It was a peaceful night, lots of stars in the sky. He could see Angie's shadow through the window as she finished decorating the tree.

He shouldn't have left, but she'd touched a nerve and he needed space to think it out. Things had been moving fast between them. Too fast. And it was better that he be up front with her about his limitations.

"Hey, boy. Where'd you go?" Buddy had disappeared.

Tuff went in search of the dog and found him rooting in the dirt on the corner of the property in a grove of trees.

"What do you got there, boy?"

The dog answered with a whimper. As Tuff got closer, he could make out what looked like a pile of rags. He hadn't brought his penlight with him and jogged back to the cabin to get it. It was so cold outside he could see his own breath.

When he got back, Buddy had dug up what appeared to be more cloth and was growling. Tuff pointed his light on the area. Not rags but clothes.

"Buddy, come here." The dog trotted over to Tuff's side. "Sit. Stay."

He swept the light over the pile and moved closer. It looked like camouflage, like fatigues. He'd never seen Cash wear anything like that, mostly just Western wear. And Gina was the last tenant before Tuff. No way in hell were they hers.

He dug around for a tree branch and used it to lift the shirt for a closer look. It was your basic military-issue battle wear. Hunters weren't above poaching on private property, but these weren't a hunter's clothes. He put the shirt down and lifted the pants up. They appeared to be around his size. The last person who'd worn them had definitely been a man.

He took a few pictures with his phone and checked to make sure they were readable. His phone camera's flash was only so good in the dark. When he was done snapping pictures, he called Jace.

Forty minutes later, Jace, Cash, Sawyer, and a few sheriff's deputies surrounded the spot where he'd found the fatigues. A crime scene investigator took pictures with a better camera than Tuff's. Then, with a pair of latex gloves, he bagged each article and stored them in his van.

"It's probably nothing, right?"

Jace looked at Tuff like he'd grown a second head. "It's something. I'm glad you didn't touch anything."

Angie stood off to the side, bundled up in a jacket, hugging herself from the cold.

"You should go inside," Sawyer told her.

"I don't want to go inside." She was shaken but holding her ground. "My guess is he stood behind that tree"—Angie pointed at a hulking blue oak—"where he had a perfect view of both cabins."

"Yep." Jace slapped the trunk of the tree. It was broad enough for good cover.

"Why would he leave his fatigues, though?" It seemed strange to Tuff.

"It was a sloppy move, though we probably won't get any DNA off the stuff unless the guy cut himself and we find blood on the clothes. You never know. More than likely, he wanted to blend when he left here and changed into street clothes. Then he buried the fatigues because he didn't want to carry them out with him. But it's only a hunch."

"I went through all the camera history," Cash said. "Didn't catch a thing. I'm betting that he was here before we installed them. Maybe it was the rat incident."

That was Tuff's initial thought. "The fatigues seem a little overkill, don't you think?"

"These guys like to think of themselves as paramilitary." Cash turned to Angie and she gave a short nod. "To me it's more confirmation of what we're dealing with. I think we can eliminate kids or pranksters."

Tuff had never considered them.

"I'll call Earl in the morning." Angie looked as if she was going to throw up.

He went to her and wrapped his arm around her shoulder. "I'm not a cop but finding the fatigues…It'll help us find them." Tuff caught Jace's gaze for affirmation.

Jace nodded. "It's definitely more than we had before. We're going to get this guy, Ange."

The deputies packed up their lights and equipment. In the last hour, the temperature had dropped close to ten degrees. Tuff gazed up as the Big Dipper climbed the northeastern sky. Somewhere in the distance a coyote howled. Other than that, the wilds of Dry Creek Ranch were still. It was the silence that made the hairs on his arms stand up. Danger lurked; he could feel it in his bones.

Chapter 23

Angie laid beside Tuff in her bed. He'd stayed the last two nights despite their small falling out. Finding the fatigues had snapped them out of their complacency. With the multitude of security measures they'd taken, she'd convinced herself that it was over. That she was safe. But now she was looking over her shoulder again, seeing shadows where they didn't exist.

Kari was still missing, and the feds had stepped up their jailhouse surveillance of Burt and Zane. But they were no closer to solving the mystery of the rat and odd phone calls than when they'd started.

Angie rolled over to watch Tuff sleep. They'd made love during the night. It had been frenzied and desperate and intense, like it always was. Still, she could feel him slipping away. Ever since he'd told her about his mother's abuser, he'd been emotionally distant. Here for her in a physical and protective way but absent for anything else.

She missed him. But didn't think he was coming back.

"Everything okay?" he whispered in a scratchy, sleep laced voice.

"Mm-hmm."

"What time is it?"

"Early. Maybe six."

He rolled over to check her bedside clock, then got up. She admired how easily he went from sound asleep to wide awake. For her it was a gradual thing, requiring a lot of *five more minutes* before her feet touched the ground. But he'd spent most of his life working on ranches. Early to bed, early to rise.

"I'll make coffee," she said as he headed to the bathroom.

She shrugged into her robe and headed for the kitchen. They'd left the heat off during the night and it was freezing. She turned on the thermostat and the tree lights. Angie liked looking at it all lit up before she went to work.

Buddy wanted out, so she opened the door and watched him from the porch. It was still dark outside, but a hint of daylight peeked out over the sky. Two deer stood by the creek, drinking. Buddy barked at them and they went bounding across her driveway. He started to give chase, but Angie called him back and they both went inside.

The water was running in the shower. She could hear the old pipes squeak and groan.

She put on a pot of coffee and searched her fridge for the eggs. The water went off and she could hear Tuff dressing. He came into the kitchen a little while later, carrying his boots.

"Omelets okay?"

"I'm going to skip breakfast this morning. Are you okay here by yourself until you go to work? Or you want me to call Sawyer?"

"I'm fine." It would be daylight soon and she had the panic button and enough security cameras for Fort Knox. "Do what you need to do."

He sat in one of the kitchen chairs and put on his socks and boots. She wanted to ask where he was going but didn't. As he walked out the door something in her cracked. She thought it might be her heart.

Her phone rang. She raced to the bedroom and swiped it off the nightstand. "Hey, Earl." She prayed he had good news. "Anything on Kari?"

"Nope. But I've got something on your situation and it's not good."

Her stomach sank.

"Zane had an interesting visitor yesterday. You recognize the name Jesse Klingman?"

"No. Should I?"

"Not necessarily. Look, these guys know they're being recorded so they're careful about what they say. But the FBI is nosing around this Klingman guy. They're trying to get a warrant, which won't be easy because there's nothing illegal about visiting a guy in jail. His social media, however, shows he's sympathetic to the Liberty Fighters' cause."

Angie had to laugh at that. Their cause as far as she could tell was blowing up innocent people.

"Do you think he's involved with what's happening here?" She'd told Earl about the fatigues they found. Jace had been in touch with the FBI, and they had sent the discarded clothing to their lab for analysis. No one had definitively decided this was a clear case of witness intimidation, but they were taking it seriously.

"That's where things get interesting. Klingman has a California address. Agents are going over there today to see if anyone will talk to them. It seems more than likely that it's an old address. But it's worth a shot."

"Where is it?"

"Riverside County."

Angie sighed with relief. Riverside was in Southern California, more than eight hours away by car.

"Angie, my gut tells me this isn't good. Too many coincidences, which in my mind adds up to not really a coincidence at all. You get my meaning?"

"Yes. You think Klingman is somehow connected to what's been going on here."

"Exactly."

She sat on the side of her bed, trying to steady her nerves. "When will you know what the agents find out?"

"I'm hoping today. But, Angie, it's not going to be anything revelatory. If he still lives there, no one in his household is going to talk. And if he doesn't, the new occupants aren't going to know anything. Our best bet is that they find him and get a warrant. And even if they can get one, it'll take time."

She squeezed the bridge of her nose. It was too early in the morning for this. She hadn't even had her coffee yet. Buddy must've sensed her distress because he came into the room and cuddled at her feet. The whole thing sucked. All she wanted was to enjoy Christmas with her family. The first one in six damned years.

"Ange, I think it's time for me to come get you."

"What?" It was as if someone had dumped a bucket of ice water over her head. "Go back in?"

"That's what the US Attorney wants. The trial isn't that far away. Afterward we'll reassess."

They needed her testimony and would do anything to secure it. She had no delusions that it was anything else. Earl cared. But to the rest of them she was just a tool to bring down the Liberty Fighters.

Angie felt safest with her family...and Tuff. But what about their safety? Kari had gone it alone and now she was missing. Her head spun and her hands shook. She knew the answer before it left her mouth.

"When?" was all she said.

* * * *

Tuff stuck his hands between the rails and scratched Muchacho*'s* nose. "I've been neglecting you, haven't I boy?"

He'd won the gelding in a poker game while wrangling at the Gridley Ranch in Pocatello. Muchacho—and Idaho—had brought him a good stretch of luck. He'd lined his pockets with a couple of purses from bull dogging at the Snake River Stampede and at a rodeo in Fort Hall.

The horse had been his constant companion ever since. Tuff had bought a used stock trailer with some of his ranch hand earnings, and they'd traveled the rodeo circuit in between wrangler jobs. Most of the spreads where he'd found work had room in the barn.

Tuff sometimes wondered why he didn't miss his nomad lifestyle more. The road had been his friend and a never-ending adventure. It had also been his accomplice, helping him run from his past and anything behind him.

Then one day, he just got tired of it. Tired of sleeping in a bunkhouse on a hard cot. Tired of living paycheck to paycheck. Tired of changing addresses as often as his tires. So, when Cash told him about Dry Creek Village and the opportunity to lease retail space, Tuff said why not give it a try?

And here he was at one of the most beautiful places on earth, making more money selling one saddle than he'd typically saw in a year wrangling. He had good friends, fine neighbors, a loyal dog, and a safe place to keep his horse. Yet, he was feeling itchy. Uprooted. Ready to run. Which didn't make a lick of sense.

If he thought about it long enough, he knew it was fear more than wanderlust. Angela Dalton had gotten into his blood. And the only way to get her out was to leave this place. Pack up, hit the road, and don't look back. Just like he'd done twenty-five years ago. The loss of Mary Garrison's love had nearly broken him. Angie had the power to obliterate him.

Muchacho's ears twitched back, and Tuff heard the crunch of a footstep. He whipped around.

Cash held up his hands. "I come in peace."

Tuff let out a chuckle. "I guess I'm a little on edge."

"We all are." Cash frowned and Tuff got the feeling he'd come to deliver bad news. "I was on my way to the cabins and saw your truck." Cash joined him at the fence and hung his arms over the top rail.

"How's Angie doing?" he asked, clearly working up to whatever it was he came to say.

"Okay. She's tougher than she looks."

"Yep." Cash's lip tipped up into a half smile. "That's the way we Daltons roll."

"Any news?"

"That's what I came to tell you. The feds are looking at a guy who's been visiting one of the Liberty Fighters in the joint. He's got a So Cal address, though they're not sure he lives there anymore. They're hunting down a recent picture of him to send us. He uses an AK-47 on all his social media profile pics." Cash rolled his eyes.

"Do they think he's our guy?" This sounded to Tuff like an actual lead. If it wasn't this dude maybe it was one of his associates.

"Don't know. But it's something. Meanwhile, they're waiting on the results from the fatigues you found."

"What do we do while we wait?" Because that's all they'd been doing, and he was tired of it. He wanted Angie to breathe free again. And he wanted these yahoos behind bars.

"Just what we've been doing." Cash scratched Muchacho on the forelock. "Stay vigilant."

"You think whoever did this is done?" It had been weeks and there'd been nothing. "Maybe they just wanted to scare her."

"I think that's a strong possibility. But there's no way to know for sure. All we can do is keep our eyes peeled. And if I haven't said it before, thanks for being there for Angie and having all our sixes. You've been clutch, man." He slapped Tuff on the back.

"You guys would do the same for me."

Cash hitched his boot onto the bottom rail and stared out over the horizon. It was cold but clear. In the distance, you could see the snow-capped mountains of the Sierra. They were below the snow line in Dry Creek but occasionally got a light dusting. Frankly, Tuff didn't care if he never saw snow again. He'd had enough of it in Montana and working on ranches in the Mountain States.

"If it's none of my business feel free to tell me to pound sand, but what's going on with you and my cousin?"

Cash sounded less hostile than Sawyer. But Tuff wasn't deceived. This was a family that was protective of its own. He wished he could tell Cash that he had good intentions where Angie was concerned. But he didn't. He was going to cut and run like he always did.

"We're friends." Tuff left it at that.

"Friends, huh?" Cash smirked. "That's what I used to say about Aubrey." He gave Tuff a friendly punch in the arm. "Keep telling yourself that, buddy." He pushed off the fence, walked back to his truck, and drove away.

Tuff went in the barn, threw Muchacho a flake of hay and headed to his shop. It was early enough that he hoped to get some work done before customers started trickling in.

He parked his truck and took a circuitous route past Daltons. Angie was already there, preparing the store for the morning coffee rush. She didn't see him, so he walked on by.

The UPS guy was waiting when he got to his door. "*Wah Gwaan*, leather *mon*?"

"Fair to middling, George. You're early today."

"Christmas."

"Yep. Guess it sucks to be you."

George, a jovial fellow with a Jamaican accent, laughed.

Tuff unlocked the door and got his packages from the back. He'd spent the better half of the previous day boxing up orders to go out.

"This is nice." George ran his hand over one of Tuff's wallets. "What is it?"

"Italian leather. You like it, it's yours. Merry Christmas."

"I can't accept this, mon."

"Why not? Is there a rule about it?"

"No, but it's expensive."

Tuff took the wallet off the shelf and handed it to him. "It's my gift to you. Don't offend me."

George laughed again. "*Thenk yuh.*"

They shot the bull for a few minutes, then George loaded up Tuff's boxes on a handcart. "*Lata.*"

"Later." Tuff locked the door behind George, turned on some Sturgill Simpson, and got started on the show saddle his client wanted by February.

He'd been working it out on paper ever since he got the order and was anxious to see the picture he had in his head translated to leather. It was an intricate design and would take hours of tooling. The piece of leather he planned to use had been tanned with oak and spruce bark. It was softer than other leathers and would develop a rich patina over time.

He liked working on all kinds of projects but this one particularly interested him. It gave him room to try some things he hadn't done before. And it was a little over the top, which wasn't his personal style. But as a craftsman it gave him room to stretch.

He laid out the leather on his table and started to reach for his head knife when there was a tap on the door. Annoyed, he put the knife down to see who it was. Ava. He unlocked the door but didn't open it all the way, hoping she'd get the message. He didn't have time to hear about her boyfriend today.

"What's up?"

"We got ripped off."

He jerked back in surprise, then ushered her in. "What happened?"

"This woman has been coming in, buying flowers nearly every week. Turns out she's been paying for them with a stolen credit card. We just got a call from the bank."

"Are they going to make good on it?"

"We don't know yet. I hope so because it was like six-hundred bucks."

Tuff scrubbed his hand through his hair. "Ah, jeez. I'm really sorry, Ava."

"Yeah, well, shit happens. I just wanted to warn you in case you see her around here. I plan to tell Laney, Angie, and Gina, too. Aubrey and Charlie already know. I think they may have also gotten hit."

"Did the bank cancel the card?"

"Ours didn't. But apparently the card's real owner's bank did. It took them long enough."

Tuff had never gotten a stolen credit card before. Not even a bad check. He supposed he'd just been lucky. "My guess is she won't be back once she figures out she's been made. But just in case what does she look like?"

"Blond, brown eyes, medium build, about my height."

That described half the female population. "Anything more distinguishable?"

"That's the thing, there's nothing memorable about her. She just sort of blends into the background. Winter and I wrote up a description for Jace and couldn't come up with one thing that wasn't generic about her. But you should check with Aubrey and Charlie. They might remember something."

He planned to. He figured she must be local if she was a repeat customer, which was a shame. It was a small county and word got around. Chances were if she used a bad credit card at Dry Creek Village, she'd ripped off merchants in town too. It was only a matter of time before everyone knew who she was.

"Thanks for letting me know. Things good otherwise?"

"Crazy busy." She hopped up on the counter, clearly planning to stay awhile. "How 'bout you?"

"Pretty busy, too."

"There's a rumor going around that you're seeing Angie Dalton," Ava blurted. "She's really pretty. And nice too. I hope it works out for the both of you. You're a good couple."

Tuff wondered if she was being catty but saw no signs that she harbored any hard feelings. He supposed it was his turn to ask about Bryce, but he didn't want to get her started. He had work to do, and the truth of the matter was he wasn't in the mood to get caught up in her sideshow. Nor did he want to discuss Angie. He'd already had to sidestep that topic once today with Cash.

"Well, I better get going." Ava jumped down. "Spread the word, okay?"

"Will do."

"See you at the party."

There was another holiday gathering at Gina's. It was generous of her to host but Tuff wasn't much in the mood.

He saw Ava out, locked the door, and returned to working on his show saddle. At nine, he put out the open sign. From then on, there was a steady stream of shoppers, folks looking for last minute gifts. He sold a couple of pairs of gloves, three wallets, an overnight duffel and a belt. Not a bad haul.

At lunchtime, he turned the sign to "Be back at 12:30" and walked over to Daltons. He hadn't had his morning coffee fix and could use one. Besides, he wanted to make sure Angie and Nina knew about the woman with the stolen credit card. Who knew? She might have a pocket full of them.

There were at least a half dozen people sitting at the bistro tables, eating and drinking. It appeared that Angie's idea was working.

She waved to him from behind the check-out stand and went up on tiptoes to kiss him when he got there. He held her a little longer than he should've, but she felt good. When he tried to let her go, she clung to him as if…he didn't know. It just felt different, like she was sad.

He bobbed his head at the crowd. "Wow."

"I know, right. It's been like that all morning. I wish the deli counter was here. I'm almost tempted to set up a barbecue in front."

"What are they eating?"

"Mostly bakery stuff. And lots and lots of coffee. Have you been busy too?"

"Yep. I haven't been able to get much done on the saddle. But I guess I shouldn't complain. Did Ava come by and tell you about the woman with the stolen credit card?"

Angie nodded. "Poor Ava and Winter. Six-hundred bucks is a lot of flower money. I talked to Charlie. She said they only got stuck with a twenty-five-dollar charge. The woman bought a decorative pillow from Refind."

Tuff filled himself a mug of coffee.

"Are you hungry?"

"I could eat. What do you have in mind?"

"I brought a couple of chicken salad sandwiches and could run over to Gina's and get some soup. It's beef minestrone."

"I'll get it."

"Let me call it in, so it'll be ready when you get there." Angie asked Nina, who was stocking the refrigerator case, if she wanted soup.

"I'll grab something while I'm running my errand in town."

Angie phoned in their order and Tuff crossed the center to the restaurant to pick it up. There were quite a few people out. Jace had been talking about adding a few more retail spaces. The new merchants would have to have some kind of an agricultural bent to stick with Dry Creek Village's theme. But it seemed like a good idea to Tuff, given the crowds they were seeing.

He scanned the faces of the tourists. Skiers and day trippers. Families and couples. It made him think of Angie and how he should probably start weaning himself off these impromptu lunches. He remembered the way she'd held on to him back at the market and wondered if she might be thinking the same.

Wrapped up in his thoughts, he wasn't paying attention to where he was going. One of the tourists accidentally shoulder checked him.

"Pardon me," Tuff said. "Should've been paying more attention."

"No worries." The guy kept going but something about him seemed familiar.

Tuff tried to recall where he'd seen him before but couldn't place him. Probably a local who worked in the area. When he arrived at Gina's, the hostess got his soup. He was halfway to Daltons when he suddenly remembered who the guy was.

Tuff leaned against Laney and Jimmy Ray's kiosk, juggled the to-go bag in one hand and dug his phone out of his pocket with the other. He scrolled through his picture gallery, then remembered the license plate number he was looking for was back at his shop on a post-it note. He took a detour on his way to Daltons and rummaged through his junk drawer until he found what he was looking for, snapped a picture of it, and sent it to Jace.

"It's probably nothing," he texted. "But could you look into it?"

Chapter 24

Angie pretended to have a good time at the center's Christmas party. Gina had gone to a lot of trouble to make it festive and of course the food was divine. Everyone was dressed up, even Tuff, who had on one of his bolo ties and his Sunday boots.

There was no question now that she'd fallen deeply in love with him. No question that he saw her in a way no one else did. He'd made her feel like a hero, like the person she'd always wanted to be.

"I'm in awe of what you did. If it wasn't for you, who knows what damage these people would've caused? How many people they would've killed?"

But tomorrow she was leaving. Earl was coming to take her away without a return date. Leaving Tuff, her family, the ranch, and the store… well it made her throat close up. In the short time she'd been here, she'd felt like she belonged.

No one had been more surprised by that revelation than Angie herself. Making the store profitable and helping to preserve her family's legacy was more rewarding than she ever would've imagined. But the biggest surprise of all was that she was good at it.

It took every ounce of willpower she had not to break down in the middle of the party and cry.

"What are you doing over here all by yourself?" Sawyer handed her a glass of bubbly.

"Just taking a minute to watch the party. Gina did a lovely job."

"Yep." He let out a low whistle. "My wife knows how to throw a shindig." He glanced across the room to where Gina was talking to Laney. The love she saw in his eyes punched her in the gut. Her big brother was over the moon happy.

"Mom and Dad are planning to get here early tomorrow. You want to spend the night? We could all have breakfast together."

She was tempted to say yes but she wanted to spend her last night on the ranch with Tuff. Besides, if she stayed with Sawyer and Gina, she'd be tempted to tell them that Earl and two deputies were coming to get her. That she'd be gone by Christmas morning.

Angie knew that Sawyer would try to talk her out of leaving. But she'd made up her mind. For everyone involved it was the right thing to do. At least until the trial was behind them.

"Nah, it'll be easier for me to just come over in the morning." That's when she'd make her final goodbye.

Sawyer glanced over at Tuff, who was drinking a beer with Cash and Jace, and with a knowing smirk on his face asked, "Is he treating you right?"

"Treating me right?" She couldn't help but laugh. "I didn't realize we were in the nineteenth century."

"Give me a break." Sawyer pulled a face. "You know what I mean."

"Yes, he's a wonderful friend." He was the best thing that ever happened to her. She only hoped that in some small way, she'd also made a difference in his life. God, she was going to miss him. "You have nothing to worry about." She kissed Sawyer on the cheek. "Have I told you recently how happy I am for you and Gina and how much I love you both?"

He took a long appraisal of her. "Is there something you want to tell me?"

She playfully socked him in the arm. "Nope." She walked away, fearing that he'd see her heartbreak. She'd already missed his wedding and now she would miss the baby coming, too.

Life wasn't fair.

Tuff caught her by the arm. "I'm taking off. I'll see you when you get home." They'd come in separate vehicles.

She wanted to ask why he was leaving so soon but the party had been going for two hours. It had been a long day.

"I'm leaving soon, too." She planned to tell him that night that Earl was coming for her. She had no idea whether he'd be sad or relieved. Probably the later, judging by the way he'd been pulling away from her for days.

It was for the best, she told herself. It would make this easier for both of them.

"Honk your horn and I'll come over."

She watched him walk away. Then she made the rounds, saying goodnight, which wound up taking more than an hour. Sawyer insisted on walking her to her car.

"I'll see you as soon as Mom and Dad get here." They hadn't told Wendy and Dan about the rat or the odd phone calls for fear that they would freak out. Angie could only imagine their shock when she told them she had to disappear again.

The whole way home her stomach hurt. She should never have left the program in the first place.

She pulled into her driveway and decided not to toot the horn, almost hoping she'd come face-to-face with her tormentor so she could punch him in the nose. Angie got as far as the porch when she heard footsteps and spun around, ready to use her purse as a cudgel.

"You were supposed to wait for me."

She let out a breath. "I figured by now you'd have cleared out all the bad guys."

Tuff didn't think she was funny because he scowled. "Come on, Ange."

"Sorry. I'm just tired."

He opened the door for her. Buddy was sleeping comfortably on the couch. "I let him out a few minutes ago and went home to change."

Suddenly, she didn't want to tell him. Not now. She wanted one more night with him. One more unmarred memory to keep her warm on those lonely winter nights in Portland or wherever Earl was taking her.

She went up on her toes and kissed him. Her hands gripped his shoulders, afraid he would turn her away. But he pulled her into his arms and took over the kiss, kicking the front door closed with his foot.

She ground against the hard bulge in his jeans, wanting him inside her, wanting him to erase all the bad and give her nothing but pleasure.

He rucked up her dress, slid her underwear down her thighs, and touched her between her legs. She was already wet for him and she heard him take in a breath as he discovered it for himself. He unzipped the back of her dress and let the silky fabric slither down her waist and puddle on the floor. The cold air in the cabin made her skin prickle. Or maybe it was the way he was looking at her standing there in nothing but a see-through bra. He made quick work of that too.

There was something about being naked while he was fully clothed, something erotic. Then there was the way his eyes heated at the sight of her. It was enough to take her breath away.

She bunched his shirt in her hands and dragged it over his head. Pressing her breasts against his bare chest, she went for his belt. But he pushed her hand away, opened his buckle, unzipped his pants, and freed himself. Then he lifted her up and took her hard against the door.

She yelled out when he entered her, and he stopped moving. Angie wrapped her legs around him and urged him on. It was hot and fast.

She clung to him as he plunged into her over and over again. He cushioned her back with his arms and spread a trail of kisses down her neck, chest and breasts. Angie called out his name as he brought her to the peak of pleasure. Tuff followed her down the mountain. She could feel his body shudder as he thrusted into her one last time. He staggered back to keep from dropping her from his arms.

Tuff rested his forehead against hers as they gathered their strength. Then he carried her into the bedroom and tumbled with her onto the bed. They lay there for a while, her head resting on his chest, listening to his heartbeat. The light from the moon floated in through the slats in the blinds, bathing the room in a warm glow.

At some point, he got a second wind and rolled her under him. It wasn't long before he was hard again. This time, he took her slowly. She traced his face with her fingers, trying to memorize every chiseled feature. Every crease. And every angle.

He took her wrist and kissed each finger one by one. Then he held her arms over her head as he moved inside of her with long, leisurely strokes.

She felt hot salty tears slip down her face.

"Hey," he whispered and wiped his thumb across her cheek. "What's wrong?"

"Nothing." She turned her face to the side and thrust up, feeling his back muscles bunch underneath her hands.

He kissed her eyes and her hair, murmuring sweet words of approval in her ear.

She didn't want it to end, knowing this would be the last time. There was no telling when she'd ever see him again. And if and when she finally did, everything would be different. She made it last as long as she could, storing every moment of their time together in her long-term memory. And when she could no longer hold back, she whispered, "I love you."

* * * *

Tuff spent the morning riding the back forty on Muchacho. Angie had gone to Sawyer and Gina's for breakfast with her parents. He was supposed to join her in the evening for dinner but planned to bag out. Christmas Eve was for family. And he wasn't a Dalton.

He reined in Muchacho, who wanted his head on the way back to the barn. But he was in no rush. He didn't have to open the store for another two hours and wasn't expecting too much traffic. People would be doing their last-minute shopping at the malls in Roseville, not at the center. Most of the shopkeepers were closing early. Refind wasn't reopening until after the new year. Aubrey and Charlie wanted the time with their families.

He was thinking about cutting out early today if business was completely dead. Maybe go on a hike with Buddy. The dog had refused to join Tuff on his ride and was sacked out in the barn when he got there.

Tuff removed Muchacho's saddle and brushed him down with a curry comb. When he was done going through his post-ride routine, he led the gelding to the pasture and gave him a slap on the rump.

"You ready to go, boy?" He whistled to Buddy.

The dog sprang up, wagged his tail, and jumped into the bed of Tuff's truck.

Tuff was about to get in the driver's seat when Jace pulled up alongside him and hung his head out the window. "Just the guy I wanted to see. You got a second?"

"Yep. What can I do you for?"

Jace threw his emergency brake on, cut the engine and motioned for Tuff to come around to the passenger side. Tuff told Buddy to stay and climbed into Jace's cab, figuring he needed help with a fence or a horse.

It was cold and Tuff subconsciously rubbed his hands together. "Whaddya got?"

"A picture of Jesse Klingman." When Tuff gave Jace a blank stare he said, "The guy Cash told you about who was visiting the Liberty Fighters in the joint. The one from So Cal." Jace turned to the back seat of his king cab and showed Tuff a grainy copy of a mug shot of a man in an orange jumpsuit. "He did time in CMC, The California Men's Colony in San Luis Obispo for assault with a deadly weapon. You can have this." He handed Tuff the copy. "I have no reason to believe he's been here but keep your eyes open for him."

"I've seen him." Tuff stared at the image, positive that it was the guy who'd shoulder checked him the other day. The man in the picture looked younger, harder and cleaner cut. But it was him. Tuff would bet money on it. "He's the guy I sent you the license plate for."

"The Chevy?"

"No, I think it was a Ford. I texted you the other day. It's a picture of a post-it with his license plate number."

Jace snatched his phone from his cup holder and scrolled through his texts. "Here it is. Shit, I must've missed it. It's been crazy. Between work and the holidays. Why'd you take down his license plate? You're sure it's the same guy."

"Pretty sure. He came in my shop weeks ago. Said his name was Jim… no, John. John Black. And that his wife was buying flowers over at Ava and Winter's for her hair salon. I thought he was local. He seemed perfectly normal, except Buddy got weird. Growling, his tail straight out, and his ears forward. I've never seen him that way around people. He definitely didn't like the dude. I've always thought animals were good judges of character, so when the guy left, I wrote down his license plate number.

"I saw him again just the other day. Bumped into him on my way to Gina's to pick up lunch. That's when I remembered the license plate and sent you the text."

Jace held up his phone. "I'll run it right away. If it's him…Damn this is a good lead. You should've been a cop, Garrison."

Tuff laughed to himself. Mary Garrison's son wasn't cop material.

"I'm going to loop Cash in on this, too. Have him check the center's security camera footage for this guy. If he's really been here, I think we've got our guy."

It sounded like it to Tuff. What made him nervous was that John Black or Jesse Klingman was still coming around.

"Should I talk to Angie about him?" Tuff asked. "She's over at Sawyer and Gina's to see her folks."

"I'll handle it. For right now, we're not telling Wendy and Dan. And if it's this guy and we nab him there's no reason to ever let the cat out of the bag. My aunt and uncle have been through enough."

Tuff gave an affirmative nod. If this was the guy, he'd like to catch him himself. Put his fucking head through a wall. "I'll keep my eyes open for him."

"Tuff, you see him again and you call me. You hear?"

"Yep."

Jace glared at him. "I'm not fooling around, Tuff. No cowboy shit. As far as I'm concerned, you're a hero for making this guy. Now leave him to the police." Jace slung his arm around Tuff's neck and pulled him in for a brief man hug. "Damn, my cousin's lucky to have you."

Tuff cringed at the words, remembering his night with Angie. *I love you.* He was so damned broken he couldn't even say the words back. Hell, he didn't even know what love was anymore. He'd buried it with his father a long time ago.

But that hadn't stopped him from taking all she had to give, including her body. It was selfish. But he'd become addicted to her. Addicted to the way she filled a hole in him. Addicted to what life could be like if he wasn't empty inside.

Now that she'd said the words, he couldn't do it anymore. It wasn't fair to keep on taking. She deserved a man who could return her love. Not a hardened cowboy who was too damaged and proud to give her everything she needed.

"Take care of her, Jace." Tuff got out of the truck, crossed the dirt to his Ram, and drove to his shop.

As he'd suspected the center was dead. He waved to Ava and Winter, who were loading a van with floral arrangements. Probably their last delivery before Christmas. He unlocked his shop, put out the open sign, and powered up his laptop to check for new orders. Just a few inquiries and a picture of a little boy with special needs, sitting atop a pony on a saddle he'd made. It brought a smile to his face.

He deliberated on whether to start a fire in the wood-burning stove or simply turn on the damned heat. He settled for switching out his fleece for his shearling jacket, which hung from the rack in his studio.

He wondered if Angie would be working at Daltons or spending the entire day with her folks before the gathering at Cash and Aubrey's. He'd seen Nina's beat-up Civic in the parking lot, so he knew the market was open.

The bells chimed, pulling Tuff from his thoughts. He walked up front to find Laney rooting through his shelves.

"Jimmy Ray got me a gold chain for Christmas just like Tiffany's. I'm not supposed to know, so hush your mouth."

"How do you know what he got you?"

"Because I opened it." She continued to make a mess of his displays, presumably searching for something to get Jimmy Ray.

"What do you mean you opened it?"

She looked up. "What do you think I mean? I found it hidden where he always hides his gifts, unwrapped it, and put it back together like brand new. I do it every year."

"That kind of sucks, Laney."

"Yeah, well it's a good thing I did. Otherwise, all he'd be getting was some Carhartt socks and a couple of sweaters. I need something special."

"Kind of late." He joined her at the wallet rack. "What about a toiletry bag?"

"He never goes anywhere."

That ruled out a duffle or a boot bag. A wallet seemed lame. "What about a monogrammed case for his chef knives."

Her head jerked up. "You got one of those?"

"No."

She swatted his arm. "Then why'd you get me all excited?"

"I can improvise." He grabbed one of the brown leather satchels he sold like hot cakes and took it to his cutting table. Then he did a quick search on the internet. "Something like this?" He turned his laptop so Laney could see the picture he'd called up.

"Ooh-we, that's fine. Jimmy Ray would love that."

He grabbed a couple of belts from the front of the store and trimmed them down to make straps. Then he sliced open the satchel to turn into a case that could be rolled when knives were placed inside. With some quick work he made a few strategic stiches with his heavy-duty sewing machine. He added the straps to the outside and boom it was one hell of chef's bag. Maybe he'd make one for Gina as a gift, too.

He freehanded Jimmy Ray's initials on the top of the case with a sharp pencil. With a branding tool, he followed his rough sketch and burned in the monogram.

Laney sat on one of the stools, watching. "You've got good hands. Steady and strong."

He had good hands, just a shitty heart.

"What do you think?" He held up the newly constructed knife case. Not bad for a last-minute job. Actually, it was damned good.

"I think Jimmy Ray's gonna feel like a real chef. It's gorgeous." She pulled his head down and kissed him on the forehead. The kind of kiss a mother would give. A real mother. "You saved my bacon, sweet pea."

"You've got to wrap it, I'm afraid." He couldn't wrap for shit. "But I've got a bag and some tissue paper."

"I'll take it."

He went behind the cash register counter to pack it up when he heard a commotion outside. Laney heard it too because she opened the door and stuck her head out. "What in tarnation is that child yelling about?"

Tuff came around the counter to see what Laney was talking about. Ava was standing on the sidewalk outside the floral shop, screaming at the top of her lungs.

A woman came running toward them at breakneck speed. Tuff didn't think twice. He moved out in front of her. And when the woman tried to cut away and jet through the parking lot, he gave chase.

"Stop her! Stop her," Ava shouted. "She's the one."

Tuff grabbed the tail of the woman's jacket. She spun around, kicking and scratching at him like a cornered cat.

Ava ran at them, swinging her purse at the woman. "She's the one who was using the bad credit card," she said out of breath. "I called 9-1-1."

Laney, who'd watched from the sidelines, swooped in and held the woman back. It was then that Tuff got a good look at her. That's when he recognized her. She was the woman who'd been with John or Jesse or whatever the hell his name was the day they'd come into Tuff's shop.

Shit. It hit him like a wallop to the stomach. She was the look out.

"Give me your phone." He pried it out of Ava's hand and called Sawyer. "Is Angie with you?"

"Not yet. My parents just got here. Why?"

"Call Jace and Cash and get over to her cabin now!"

Chapter 25

Angie was running late as usual. Last she'd spoken to Sawyer, their parents hadn't arrived at the ranch yet. Crazy LA traffic. It was still faster to drive, even if it was across the state. Otherwise, they'd have to contend with the long lines at LAX, then at Sacramento International Airport. Someone would have to pick them up and drive the hour to Dry Creek Ranch. At the end of the day, it was simply easier to make the trip in a car.

She got out of the shower and threw on a pair of jeans and a sweater. She'd already packed her bags and whatever essentials she would need when she left Dry Creek Ranch. This morning, after Tuff left, she'd tearfully written out instructions for Nina on how to proceed with the new deli counter at Daltons. Earl was scheduled to get here this evening. Enough time to tell everyone she was leaving.

It was unorthodox to be sure. Entering the Witness Protection Program was supposed to be done in secret. But given the circumstances, Earl's supervisor had agreed that she could tell her family without divulging her new location. Angie didn't even have the location. She'd know when she got there.

There was a noise in the kitchen. She'd become so desensitized to the camera alerts that she didn't even hear them anymore.

"Tuff?" He was the only one with a key.

Good. Before she went to Sawyer's, she wanted to tell him that she was going away. Otherwise, she'd lose the courage. Even though he hadn't said it back, she was glad she'd told him she loved him before she left. Tuff needed love and she had plenty to give.

"Is that you?" She went inside the kitchen in her bare feet and her wet hair wrapped in a towel.

An arm came around her neck and a hand covered her mouth. "'Morning, Angie. We meet at last. Zane sends his love." His voice was deep and unrecognizable.

Her heart stopped.

For a second, she was paralyzed with fear. Then her fight or flight instinct took over. She tried to kick him, but he pressed her against the counter and she couldn't land a blow. Her panic button watch was on the dresser next to her phone. Fear welled up inside her. The man was twice her size and judging from his arm, which was as thick as a tree trunk, he had significantly more strength than she did.

Her only hope was that the security cameras had alerted the cavalry. She tried to bite his hand and he slapped her. The sting made her eyes water and her ears ring.

"Don't do that again, you little bitch."

She recognized him instantly as the man who had been smoking in the center's parking lot the day she'd gone to the storage unit for the extra Dry Creek Ranch mugs. "What do you want?"

"What do *I* want?" He laughed. The sadistic sound of it scared her more than the slap. "I want you to shut the fuck up and do what you're told. If you'd done that in the first place, we wouldn't have to have this little talk, now would we?"

She didn't respond and furtively grasped for what she could use as a weapon.

He yanked her chin. "I asked you a question. I expect an answer."

She squinted at him defiantly. He slapped her again, this time with the back of his hand. She felt her head snap before falling to the floor.

"Get up!"

When she didn't immediately do as she was told, he kicked her in the stomach with his steel-toe boot. She retched from the pain.

"I said, get up."

She tried to hoist herself up and fell to the floor again, dizzy. Angie reached up for the edge of the counter and managed to pull herself to her feet, afraid he'd kick her again if she didn't.

"I'm still waiting for an answer. So, let's try this again. Are you going to do what you're told this time?"

"Screw you," she said under her breath.

"What was that? I can't hear you." He back handed her so hard she saw an explosion of light behind her eyes.

Her nose was bleeding. She used her hand to staunch the flow.

"Jesse, what the hell's taking you so long?" A man in fatigues, a goatee and some kind of assault rifle strapped over one arm came into the kitchen. "The cameras have all been rigged. Lorna will be here any second and you're in here dicking around." He took one look at Angie and let out an expletive. "Jesus Christ. No one said to tune her up before we ice her. It's supposed to look like an accident."

It was in that moment that Angie realized that this wasn't merely a game of intimidation. They planned to kill her.

"Let's get the hell out of here," gun guy said, then turned to Angie and gave her a thorough once over. "Get some shoes on the bitch."

"Come on." The guy called Jesse grabbed her by the neck of her sweater and dragged her into her bedroom. He clearly was familiar with the layout of the cabin. "Put on some shoes." He shoved her at the closet.

She was less than two feet away from the dresser where the panic watch sat. She was afraid that if she even looked in the direction of the dresser, he would guess her intentions.

"Move it!"

She stumbled into the closet, knowing that once they got her away from the ranch she was never coming back. There were a pair of tennis shoes on the bottom shelf. She calculated how long it would take her to get from the shoes to the watch. But Jesse dashed any hopes of that happening when he blocked her way out of the closet.

"Put 'em on." He dragged her to the bed and shoved her down.

She tried to stall, which wasn't difficult. She was so scared her hands shook and she couldn't tie her laces. It was less than four feet to the dresser. All she had to do was get to the watch and press the panic button. The only thing standing in the way was Jesse, who towered over her, watching her every move.

By now, Tuff was at the barn. And clearly the other guy had done something to the cameras to keep them from alerting anyone that she was in trouble.

"What did you do to Kari?" She knew now that these guys were cleaning house and getting rid of anyone who could testify. Her question was merely a stall tactic.

Get to the watch. It's my only hope.

"Who the hell is Kari?"

Angie looked up from her half-tied tennis shoe. Either Jesse was giving Robert De Niro a run for his money or he was truly clueless about Kari.

"I asked you a question, bitch."

"Zane's sister." Zane didn't have a sister.

Jesse scowled, then grabbed her by the neck. "Get up."

Without thinking, without breathing, without even considering the consequences, Angie threw her elbow back, catching Jesse in the ribs. In the time it took him to rebound from her surprise attack, she rushed to the dresser. Before she could reach the watch, he grabbed her and slammed her against the wall. She crumpled, using the edge of the chest of drawers to hold her up.

"You want to play rough?" Jesse's grin was mean, filled with a mouthful of tobacco-stained teeth. "I like it rough." He cut his gaze to the bed, leaving her no doubt about his intention.

"Jesse, what the hell is taking you so long?" Gun man came into the bedroom, took one look at Angie slumped against the dresser and turned to Jesse. "I give you one job to do and here you are fucking it up!"

He pointed his gun at Angie and jabbed the barrel towards the door. "Let's go. We've wasted enough time."

This was her last chance. Once they took her away, she was at their mercy and they'd made it clear they had none to give. She pretended to hoist herself up, using the dresser. The watch called to her like a sign of hope. Out of choices, she inched her hand closer, trying to be as surreptitious as possible.

Jesse had slunk off to keep watch, while gun man scanned the room. The bench at the foot of the bed where her purse sat had caught his attention. She used the opportunity to cover the watch with her hand. Her thumb searched for the small panic button on the crown as she desperately tried to keep her hand from shaking. The trick was to shove the watch in her pocket without being caught. She prayed that Jace could use the watch's tracking device to find her before it was too late.

"What do you got there?" Gun man, who was more observant than he looked, came closer and pried her hand open. "What's this?"

Tears streamed down her face. No way could anyone come in time to rescue her. Once they got on the highway there was no telling where these men would take her. There was countless quiet roads and secluded backcountry spots where no one would find her for days, even weeks.

He took the watch from her and quickly looked it over. "This might come in handy." He stuck the muzzle of the gun between her breasts and grabbed her purse. "Move it."

Angie wasn't sure whether she'd managed to press the alert button, but gun man wasn't likely to hang around to find out. She'd screwed up her one shot.

"Come on." He poked her in the back and she stumbled, only to be yanked up by her hair. The pain sliced through her like a sharp-edged knife and she cried out. "Don't dally and it'll go easier for you."

But there was a gleam in his eye that told her he intended to toy with her before he put her out of her misery.

* * * *

Tuff pulled over to the side of the road. It took every ounce of self-discipline he had not to floor it to the cabins in his pickup, horn blaring. But he knew sneaking in on foot would give him an advantage.

He was sure the woman back at the center was Jesse Klingman's lookout. Until Jesse heard from her, he wouldn't make a move, leaving Tuff time to take the man by surprise. He jumped down from his truck and at a run headed for the cabins through the woods. He'd hiked this part of the ranch so often he knew it like he did his own backyard. It was a longer route to the cabins than taking the road, but it would get him to the thicket of trees behind Angie's house.

He kept a hunting rifle at home but didn't have time to get it, even though he suspected Jesse was armed. Judging by the fatigues Buddy found in Tuff's yard, the guy liked playing soldier and was probably loaded to the teeth. Tuff would have to improvise.

When he got to the thicket, he crouched down behind a large tree to suss out the situation. It was too damned quiet. There were a couple of lights on inside the house, but he didn't spot any movement through the windows. He duckwalked until he was hugging the exterior logs of the back of the cabin and listened. The building was so well insulated he couldn't hear a thing.

He knew for a fact that all the windows were locked. Sawyer had spared nothing to chance when it came to security measures. The only way in was to break the glass and that would make too much noise.

The screen door creaked and for a second Tuff feared that he'd been detected. Then he heard voices on the porch.

"Where the fuck is Lorna?"

Tuff made his way around the side of the cabin, careful not to make any noise.

"She should've been here five minutes ago."

"She might've seen someone on the road and is waiting until the coast is clear."

Shit, there were two of them. Tuff wished he had his phone to check the cameras. See what he was up against.

He crawled on his belly to the side of the porch and lay against the base of the cabin, hoping like hell it would camouflage him from sight.

"Change of plans because I'm not waiting here like a sitting duck for her to show up. Knowing Lorna, she's buying shit at one of those stores. We'll figure out a ride when we get to the site."

"Your keys in here?"

Tuff heard something rattle.

"Cat got your tongue again, bitch? I need the keys to your Benz."

"If I give them to you, will you let me go?"

Tuff's chest squeezed. It was Angie's voice.

The two men laughed.

"Sure, sweet cheeks, right after we get done having some fun."

Tuff rolled to his side and crawled back around the house toward the driveway. It was a good ten yards to Angie's car. But if he could beat them there, he could launch a surprise attack. He'd nearly come out of his skin at the "fun" remark. The asshole who made it was going down first.

The screen door opened and closed again. Tuff knew that Angie kept her keys on a hook in the kitchen, which bought him a couple of minutes. He fought himself from looking back to make sure Angie was okay. His sole focus was to get to the car and come up with a plan, knowing that Angie's captors were intent on leaving the ranch before they got caught.

By the time he reached the Mercedes, he was out of breath. But he didn't waste any time. He managed to get his pocketknife out of his jeans and with as much stealth as he could muster moved around the car, puncturing the tires.

Lorna's not coming, boys, and the only way you're leaving is in the back of a police van.

In his haste, he didn't hear them approach until they were only a few feet away from the passenger side of the car. He quickly rolled under the vehicle for cover. It didn't leave him much room to maneuver but it was the best he could do.

"Get in." The door squeaked open and Tuff could see Angie's tennis shoes peeking through the undercarriage of the car.

Hang tight, baby.

He flipped onto his belly and waited; his knife poised to do as much damage as he could.

"You drive." A set of car keys rattled and a pair of combat boots came around to the driver's side.

The door scraped open and Tuff made his move, ramming the knife into the man's calf as hard as he could. The dude bellowed like a cow stuck in barbed wire.

"What the hell?"

Tuff rolled to the other side and tripped the second guy as he attempted to get into the back seat behind Angie. The man fell to the ground. The surprise attack was just enough of a distraction to throw both men off their game and give Tuff a small advantage.

He acted fast, reaching for the guy's throat, while catapulting himself on top of the man.

"Gun!" Angie screamed. "He's got a gun."

Tuff saw the AR-15 in the dirt, mere inches away from the guy's hand. They struggled for it. Tuff's opponent matched him in size, but he was a nimble SOB. Jesse had rallied from his knife wound and came around the front of the car, racing for the rifle.

Tuff shoved his knee into the face of the guy he had on the ground. But Jesse was gaining on him.

Suddenly a succession of blasts went off in the air. This was it. Tuff was no match for a semi-automatic.

"Get back!"

Tuff shoved the side of goatee boy's face into the dirt. He wasn't going down without a fight.

"I said, get back."

It was then that Tuff realized it was Angie's voice. He looked up to find her holding the rifle and Jesse coming at her.

"Shoot," Tuff yelled but could see indecision written across her face. She couldn't do it.

Well, he sure the hell could. He jumped up and ran toward her, but Jesse had the lead.

"Angie," Tuff shouted.

She screamed and shot off another series of rounds into the air. "Don't make me shoot you."

Jesse must've seen something in her eyes because he stopped short. Goatee boy floundered in the dirt, trying to get up. Tuff kicked him back down.

A siren rent the air. Jace's SUV barreled up the road, followed by a pickup and a Range Rover.

What the hell had taken them so long?

Chapter 26

Angie sat on Cash and Aubrey's sofa, staring into the Christmas tree lights. Her mother insisted she eat and Gina brought her a plate of food. But Angie didn't have an appetite.

Tuff had passed on dinner and she was worried about him. What he'd done this afternoon had been nothing short of heroic. If it hadn't been for him, Angie had no doubt she'd be dead in her car somewhere.

Earl and two other deputies from the US Marshals Service had gotten rooms at a hotel in Grass Valley. Angie felt terrible that they were spending Christmas Eve away from their families.

Cash had insisted they stay for dinner, but all three men declined the offer. Tomorrow, they would conclude their reports and catch flights home.

Jace was still at the sheriff's department, going over the case with a cadre of FBI and ATF agents from the Sacramento office. Angie and the rest of the family were waiting for him to come home and give them the details.

Despite being interviewed for much of the afternoon by law enforcement, Angie knew little about either of her attackers. She'd never seen Jesse Klingman before that time in Dry Creek Village's parking lot. And the other guy—Randy Joost, according to Earl—was not familiar to her. The woman, Lorna Zemanski, had come into Daltons a few times but had never stayed more than a few minutes.

Cash's theory was that they were lone wolves, who'd connected with the Liberty Fighters online and forged a relationship with Zane and Burt while they were incarcerated. But they hoped Jace would know more after his meeting with the feds.

"Honey, eat," her mother cajoled.

"I will." Angie wrapped the throw blanket tighter around herself. Even with the heat and fire blazing, she couldn't seem to get warm.

Sawyer plopped down next to her and placed the pack of frozen peas that had been sitting on the coffee table back on the right side of her face. She'd refused to go to the emergency room, though her entire body throbbed with pain.

"Tuff said you're a badass with an AR-15." He was trying to lighten the mood, but Angie didn't find anything about what had happened this morning funny. Tuff could've been killed.

"Why do you think he didn't want to come to dinner?" she asked.

Sawyer sighed. "My best hunch is that he thought you needed time with your family."

Tuff was part of her family as far as she was concerned. Even if he didn't love her back, he'd always be an integral piece of her new life. And an integral piece of the Dalton clan.

"We'll pack him up a dinner and Sawyer can run it over to him," Wendy said.

"I'll bring it to him."

"Oh, honey, it's best if you stay here tonight. Or over at Jace and Charlie's. We'll all be together."

Cash and Aubrey's house was already full. Angie's aunt and uncle were here. Besides, she wanted to stay the night with Tuff. "We'll see, Mom. I have to go home sometime." Everyone but Earl had been opposed to her going back into WITSEC.

A child's shout went up in the other room and Jace came in with Grady and Ellie hanging off each arm. Travis trailed behind.

"Can we open our presents now?" Grady begged.

"Tomorrow morning, kiddo."

"Just one? Please."

Jace put Grady in a headlock. "Let me talk to the grownups first and then we'll discuss it."

Grady groaned. Uncle Jed threw Grady over his shoulder like a sack of potatoes and called to Ellie and Travis to follow him into the kitchen.

"What did you find out?" Sawyer got up off the couch.

"I'll tell you as soon as Tuff gets here. I asked him to be part of this." Jace held Angie's gaze. "How are you holding up?"

"I'm fine."

"Are those two men locked up?" Angie's father had been pacing in front of the fireplace all evening.

"Oh yeah." Jace sagged into one of the leather club chairs. "Klingman was out on parole. He's going away for a long time. And Joost…he's squawking like a bird, desperate for a deal. Even with a plea bargain, he'll be doing some serious time."

"What about the woman?" Cash asked.

"She's got a couple of priors for check kiting. And now this…she won't be seeing the light of day for at least a few years. If they charge her with conspiracy to witness tampering and get a conviction, she could be looking at much more."

Uncle Jed returned and took a seat next to Cash. He was a retired San Francisco police inspector, which was the same as a detective. But inspector was what they called them at SFPD. Uncle Jed was forever railing at the television whenever cop shows got it wrong.

There was someone at the door. Angie heard a couple of whoops and hollers and Tuff's voice, wishing the kids a Merry Christmas.

"We're in here," Cash called.

The great room was just off the large entryway. The house, which had been completed last summer, was fashioned after Jace and Charlie's ranch house. Rustic and bold with open beam ceilings, large iron trusses and huge windows that let in the views and the light. Aubrey of course had put her own touch on the place, giving it a more modern vibe than the one Angie's grandparents had built. But it still conjured the same feeling of hominess, family, and ranch life.

Tuff came in, handed Aubrey a bottle of wine, and pecked her on the cheek. He locked eyes with Angie, silently asking if she was okay. She nodded. He took the chair closest to Jace and stretched his long legs in front of him.

Grady ran in, holding up a gift bag. "Tuff gave us presents. Can we open them?"

"You didn't have to do that, Tuff." Charlie said. "It was very sweet of you." She turned to Grady. "You can open them if it's okay with Tuff."

"Go for it." Tuff winked.

"How 'bout you, Ellie, and Travis open them in the kitchen?" Charlie told Grady. "And when we're done talking, you can show us all what you got. And thank Tuff for his generosity."

"Okay." Grady shot out of the room like a dog who'd seen a rabbit.

For the first time that night, Angie smiled. Despite everything that had happened, the kids would still have Christmas.

Jace glanced over at Charlie with such adoration in his eyes it made Angie's heart sing. Then he shook Tuff's hand. "Thanks for coming. I figured you'd want to hear this and it made sense to only do it once. Plus, we have enough food for an army."

"Don't keep us in suspense, son." Uncle Jed threw another log on the fire and returned to his place besides Angie's aunt.

"Randy Joost met Burt Randolph while the two served in the Marine Corps together. They kept in touch over the years. But unlike Randolph, Joost made good for himself. After his time in the marines, he went to night school, took computer science classes, and landed a job as a technical support engineer with a defense contractor in San Diego. A year ago, he got laid off. The company lost its contract with the government and had to downsize. Joost apparently took it hard. His social media from that time exhibits signs that he was growing more and more angry and disenfranchised. About that time, Joost said he started flirting with a couple of militia and survivalist groups, including the Liberty Fighters. But it took him two years to become fully radicalized. By that time, Burt Randolph was in jail."

"Let me guess," Cash said. "Joost contacted Randolph in the joint and Randolph told him to take up the cause and finish the work the Liberty Fighters couldn't get done."

"Yep." Jace reached for the cup of coffee Charlie had brought him. After all that had happened that day, he had to be exhausted. "But first they had to clean house." He looked over at Angie and sighed.

"What was Klingman's role?" Angie's father asked.

"He was your basic militia groupie. Became enamored with the Liberty Fighters on the internet and became Zane White's pen pal and biggest fan. Eventually, the two men forged enough of a relationship that Jesse started showing up on visiting day at the jail. Zane hooked Klingman up with Joost with instructions to get rid of any and all witnesses."

Angie shuddered. "What about Kari?"

"According to Joost, he broke into her house a month ago to lie in wait, but she never came home. The FBI suspects she knew she was being watched and went into hiding."

"What about her phone and the calls?"

"Joost admitted he stole the phone and made the calls to spook you."

"Jesse said he didn't know anything about her when I asked him. He seemed genuinely clueless."

Jace shrugged. "Jesse was nothing more than a foot soldier who took his orders from Joost, who was marching to Randolph's drum. It doesn't surprise me in the least that he knew nothing about Kari. The FBI and the ATF are looking for her. As soon as I know something, I'll tell you, Ange."

"Thank you." It was the first good news Angie had heard all night. Perhaps Kari was okay. Her friend had always been a survivor. If Kari thought someone was after her she would know how to disappear. She'd been doing it for years without the feds' help.

"How did they manage to pull this off without us seeing anything on the security cameras?" Sawyer wanted to know.

"That was my question, too." Tuff shifted in his chair.

Angie could barely look at him. He'd been living a quiet peaceful life until she'd come along, bringing a band of thugs on her tail. Tuff had already suffered enough violence without her bringing this to his door.

"Joost told us he rigged the cameras. Basically, he wound the clock back. The only images we were getting were the ones he wanted us to see."

"I guess his computer training came in handy for that," Cash said.

"Yup." Jace took another sip of his coffee.

Charlie got up to pour everyone refills. Angie would've preferred a stiff drink.

"I wish I would've paid more attention to my gut—Buddy's gut—that first time Jesse came in my shop." Tuff looked down at his boots.

Angie scooted to the other side of the couch and took Tuff's hand. "If it wasn't for you…" She couldn't even say it.

But Jace didn't hesitate. "We wouldn't be sitting here right now in front of cozy fire and a lit-up Christmas tree. You saved the damned day."

"Ava deserves a lot of the credit." Tuff looked away and stared out the big picture window into the darkness. "If she hadn't chased down Lorna, I never would've put everything together the way I did."

"We all owe a debt of gratitude to Ava," Angie's mom said. "But Tuff, what you did…" She choked up.

Sawyer went around the coffee table and hugged Wendy. "It's okay, Mom."

Tuff seemed embarrassed by the attention. Angie squeezed his hand and he squeezed it back. He glanced up at her and held her gaze. There was so much sadness in his eyes that Angie wanted to hold him.

"It turns out Jesse and Lorna had rented a place in the neighboring county, so they could stay close and watch our every move, while reporting back to Joost," Jace continued.

Angie told them about the day Jesse had followed her to the storage unit. "At the time I didn't think anything of it."

"None of us would've." Sawyer sagged back into his seat.

"She told us she owned a hair salon in Colfax," Aubrey said. "We had no reason not to believe her."

"Are there more?" Angie had been dreading asking the question. She didn't want to live in constant fear and the idea of leaving Dry Creek Ranch made her stomach hurt. She'd always loved it here, but the place had come to mean so much more to her in the last couple of months. Security, family, purpose. But most of all it's where she'd found love. Real love, even if Tuff couldn't return it.

"The feds don't think so," Jace said. "And that's after a thorough examination of all of Zane's and Burt's correspondence, phone calls, and jailhouse visits. The fact is no one other than their attorneys, Jesse Klingman and Randy Joost have visited. Both men, now facing charges of conspiracy to murder two federal witnesses, have been moved to solitary confinement and have been denied any visitation other than their lawyers. The other members of the Liberty Fighters have all turned on one another, hoping to make deals."

"What about Rich and Diana?" she held her breath, knowing in her heart of heart the answer before Jace could respond.

He was silent for a while and Angie could feel the tension build around the room.

"I'm not at liberty to say."

"What?" Angie pushed away the frozen bag of peas her mother kept pushing on her. "What do you mean you're not a liberty to say? Are they alive, Jace?"

"I'm not at liberty to say."

"That means they're alive, doesn't it? Oh my God, they're in WITSEC, aren't they?" How could Jet, and then Earl, not have told her? All those nights she cried herself to sleep, wishing she'd done more to save them.

"If they are, Ange, they won't be for long. So let it go." Jace gave her his stern cop face, which wasn't all that stern, given that the two of them had played in diapers together.

Cash ignored Jace. "It makes sense, especially because we know that the feds had been watching the complex before they sent in their undercover agent."

Knowing that Kari, Rich and Diana were alive was the best gift Jace could've given her. The day had started out worse than any nightmare but the resolution... Angie squeezed her eyes shut as a flood of relief momentarily rendered her speechless.

Tuff reached over and touched her leg as she exhaled a deep breath. "I think what everyone is trying to say is that it's over. You and your friends are safe."

Chapter 27

Tuff went home, leaving the Daltons to celebrate Christmas. Angie was staying the night with her family, which he was torn about. After the events of the day, he wanted—needed—to hold her through the night. Yet today had only cemented all the reasons why he couldn't give her all she deserved.

Tuff could never be that man.

His cabin was cold and dark. Instead of building a fire, he turned on the heat and sat on his sofa, staring into the darkness. There was no Christmas tree, just a sad looking Ficus Tuff had tried to nurse back to life. It was hanging on by a thread. Perhaps if he'd remembered to water it from time to time, the plant would be doing better.

He let Buddy out and fed him an extra biscuit when the dog finished his business. "Merry Christmas."

The hound stretched out at Tuff's feet and together they went back to staring into the dark. The cabin grew warm to the point of being stuffy. Tuff started to shrug out of his shearling jacket when he felt his mother's envelope weighing heavy in his pocket. He ignored it the same way he had when Sheriff Strong had handed it to him at her funeral.

Hanging the coat up, he hunted through his refrigerator, even though he'd eaten at Cash and Aubrey's. A bad habit, he supposed.

The scrimmage with the Liberty Fighter wannabes played through his head on a constant loop and he tried not to think about what would've happened if Angie hadn't taken control of the gun. Later, when the police came, he discovered that Klingman had also been packing.

He could've lost her. In the blink of an eye, he could've lost the one person who mattered the most. The knowledge of that haunted him.

He closed the fridge and searched through the cupboards for the Maker's Mark he'd stashed there so long ago the bottle was dusty. Tuff took a glass down and gave himself a healthy pour. The bourbon burned its way down the back of his throat.

He took the drink with him to the sofa and turned on the side lamp. He didn't even remember where the table lamp had come from, whether he'd inherited it from Gina when she'd moved into the cabin or if he'd bought it secondhand. For the first time, he noticed how ugly it was. A white misshapen resin cowboy boot and a mismatched shade with a burn mark from a hot bulb.

He finished his bourbon and went to the window. Except for the porch light, Angie's cabin was dark. Tomorrow, he'd let himself in and clean up whatever mess those sons-of-bitches left. He didn't want Angie to have to see the carnage.

Buddy whined as if he could feel Tuff's discontent and the melancholy that had settled over him like an old coat. It was just the trauma from the morning, he lied to himself. Deep down inside, he knew it was his past catching up with his present. It was about his inability to let the darkness go. To forgive and forget.

He wandered into the kitchen, considering the wisdom of a second drink and looked at the clock. Midnight. Christmas morning. Another shitty holiday alone.

He thought about Cash and Aubrey's house, about all the gifts under the tree, about the aroma of a homecooked meal, about happy and well-adjusted kids. But mostly he thought about the love he'd witnessed in that house, how it emanated off the walls.

He thought about his own Christmases as a boy after his father died. About his mother passed out on the couch, barely coherent. About his shame. About his loneliness.

How long would it go on like this? As long as he let it, he supposed.

He drifted back into the living room, took his jacket off the rack, and rifled through the pocket. The envelope. He warred with it as he touched it with his hand.

Throw it away. Better yet, burn it.

He stood there for what seemed like a long time, rubbing the edge of the worn paper. Finally, he removed it, wiped the lint away and took the envelope with him to the sofa. He placed it on the coffee table and stared at the swirly cursive of his name. Theodore. The "T" looked like a leafy tree and the "d" a flower. He traced the letters with his finger as if they were three dimensional.

Buddy lifted his head, dropped it on Tuff's boots and went back to sleep.

Tuff gingerly picked up the envelope as if it might scald him. There was a small bump in the corner, like a penny had been tucked inside, hidden in the folds of a piece of paper. He turned the envelope over and stared at the seal, then quickly sliced it open before he changed his mind.

He unfolded the top third of the notebook paper to find his father's St. Christopher medal buried in the bottom seam of the letter.

Mary hadn't sold it after all.

His eyes blurred as he touched it, holding it between his fingers, the warm medal smooth against his hand. It had been Tuff's grandfather's, passed down to his father when he joined the marines. The police had given the medal to his mother with the rest of his father's personal effects after the convenience store shooting. The chain was gone but the bail was still there. His mother's perfume and the faint smell of cigarette smoke clung to the pendant. It was a familiar scent, flooding Tuff with memories of the singlewide trailer in Fontaine.

He found a leather cord in his work box, strung it through the bail, and tied it around his neck. He would be the third Garrison to wear the St. Christopher medal, the last vestige of his father. The last vestige of Tuff's heritage.

He settled into the couch to read the letter. Like the envelope, it had been scribed in his mother's floral handwriting.

Dear Theodore,

Countless times I wanted to reach out to tell you how sorry I am. But I was afraid the words would sound empty after all this time. And I didn't want you to think I was looking for a handout.

I know about your saddle shop—I saw your website on the internet—and your success. I am so proud of your accomplishments. I know your father would've been too. Despite my deplorable actions as a mother, you pulled yourself up by the bootstraps and made something of yourself. Of course, I'm not surprised. You were always a special child. Your father's son. Too good, too smart, and too honorable for someone like me. I've always known that about you, even when I was too drunk to walk.

As I write this, I am sober. Twenty-four hours and eighteen minutes. For me, sobriety brings clarity. The stark clarity of the terrible things I've done and the despicable way I treated you. I turned my back when you needed me the most. You probably saved my life that day. But the sad truth of the matter is that I wanted to die.

I love you, Ted. For years, I've been sorting through the old pictures, wondering what life would've been like had I not been the awful person I turned into after your father died. You were better off without me. I only would've let you down over and over again.

You will always be the good and kind man your father was. I go to my grave heartened that someday you will marry and carry on your dad's legacy, not mine.

I'll say it again. I love you, Ted.
Sincerely,
Your mother, Mary Garrison

He read the letter three times, needing time to process each word, each sentiment. He wasn't sure how to feel about it. Anger, sadness, guilt, or acceptance. In the end, he decided she hadn't been asking for anything. Not for his love, not for his understanding, not even for his forgiveness. She simply wanted him to know how she felt about him before taking her own life.

He slept on it, letting his mother's words dominate his dreams. When he woke, he felt lighter. Freer. And for the first time in twenty-five years, he forgave Mary Garrison and released the self-inflicted shackles that had held him hostage from living a full life.

He removed the photo he'd snatched that day from his mother's trailer from the nightstand drawer where he'd tucked it. It was of him as a small child and his parents in front of a roadside diner outside Missoula. They looked happy. They looked loved.

He swung his legs onto the cold, hardwood floor, slid into a pair of jeans and went to the kitchen where he stuck the picture to his refrigerator with a magnet.

Then he called to Buddy. "You want out, boy?"

Buddy loped out of the bedroom and shot outside to the creek, sniffing his way along the shoreline. Tuff gazed across the water at Angie's cabin. No sign of life there yet.

Forty minutes later, he was out the door.

Breakfast was in full swing at Jace and Charlie's. Though Tuff had invited himself, they welcomed him like he was part of the family. He made his way around the piles of torn wrapping paper and boxes of strewn gifts to find Angie.

She was in the kitchen, alone, washing out the coffee pot. She did a little double take when he wrapped his arms around her waist.

"You sleep okay?"

She put down the pot, turned so she faced him and waggled her hand from side to side. "In fits and spurts."

"Can I take you away from all of this for a little while?"

"Uh, sure." She worried her bottom lip. "Is everything all right?"

"I read my mother's suicide note last night."

"Oh, Tuff."

"It's okay. It was actually good that I read it."

She held his gaze, ostensibly to see if he was telling the truth. "Let me grab my coat."

They walked through the dining room to curious stares. "I'm borrowing Angie. We won't be long, I promise," he said.

Angie grabbed a jacket from the coatrack in the entryway and led him out the door. "You want to take a walk?"

"Yeah." He took her hand and headed for the creek.

They followed it for a while, letting the sounds of nature fill the silence between them. They came upon a large oak. Tuff pressed Angie's back against the massive tree trunk and kissed her. He'd missed her. They'd only been separated a night and yet he'd felt like a piece of him had been lost.

She caught his face in her hands and kept him from taking the kiss deeper. "Tell me about the note."

"Not much to tell. She apologized and basically said she couldn't live with what she'd done."

Angie's eyes grew moist and she pulled him toward her. "I didn't know she'd left a note."

"Yeah. The Fontaine sheriff gave it to me after her funeral. I wasn't going to read it but..."

"What?"

He lifted his head and stared up at the sky, not knowing how to put his thoughts into words. "After yesterday...after nearly losing you...I guess I needed to close the door on some things."

"Did it help, reading your mother's note?"

"I think so." He took a deep breath. "It helped me let go of the anger." A lot of the pain, too, he supposed. "It helped me re-evaluate my life...the things I now realize I want and out of fear denied myself."

"Fear of what?"

He swallowed hard. Tuff had never been one to express his feelings particularly well. Half the time, he went around hiding them from himself. Talking about them out loud? Well, he was just a cowboy. A proud cowboy.

When he didn't answer, she looked at him. Really looked. "Did you fear being rejected because of your mother?"

"Maybe," he finally said. "But that's not what I came out here to talk about."

"Oh, God, you're leaving." Angie tipped her head back and closed her eyes.

"Why would you think that?" Though if he was being honest with himself, he'd thought about it. He'd considered bolting the moment he knew he was in too deep with Angie. "My business is here...you're here. That is if you're planning to stay."

She opened her eyes and he stared into their blueness, mesmerized. Wholly smitten.

"I am," she said. "My family is here. And I love it. Everything about it." She held his gaze, making her implication clear.

"Good," he said. "Because I love you." The words slipped off his tongue easier than he'd expected. The last time he'd told anyone he loved them was his mother when he was only thirteen years old.

He pulled Angie into an embrace and held her, basking in how right she felt in his arms...in his heart.

"Tuff," Angie reached up and pulled his face down for a kiss, "I love you too."

"You think we can make this work?" he said against her lips.

"It's been working." She giggled into his shoulder. "Don't you realize that our hearts were locked together, even before you said the words?"

He let that float around in his head for a while. "I want more."

"Okay. Tell me what more looks like to you."

He walked her over to a fallen-down log and tugged her down to sit next to him. She stuck her hand in his jacket pocket and he pulled her tight against him to keep her warm.

"A commitment," he began. "Maybe a family at some point."

"Yeah?" A smile split her face. It was so bright it was radiant. "I'd like that."

"Is this going to be enough for you?" He stared past the creek, over the mountain tops. "I know your career plans didn't include this ranch. I'll go wherever you want but I believe we could have a good life here."

She leaned her head against his neck. "Me too. Are you sure you're ready for this?"

It was a big step for him, and he'd be lying to himself if he didn't say he was swamped by fear. By doubt. But he loved Angie Dalton beyond all measure, and he couldn't imagine life without her.

"I can't give you a fraction of this." He waved his hands to indicate the vast wealth of a ranch the size of Dry Creek. "I was raised in a singlewide trailer in Fontaine, Montana. It's a million miles from where you came from. I don't have a fancy college education or a corporate job. And I grew up one of the hungry folks you wanted to feed. But I love you and I'll always take care of you, even though you're perfectly capable of taking care of yourself. Damn, woman, you took on an entire militia group and won." He kissed the top of her head, inhaling the scent of her shampoo, wanting to hold onto her...protect her...forever. "You're my everything, Ange. Until you came along, I was a lost soul."

"Me too," she whispered, then moved into his lap, twining her arms around his neck. "I traveled the world, looking for something I couldn't find, only to come home and find the love of my life just next door. This ranch was my solace as a child. A wonderous place, where my brother, cousins, and I roamed free. But I never thought of it as a place where I would settle. Funny, how I went in search of my future when it was right here all along. But, Tuff, wherever you are is home."

He looked at her, love shining in her baby blues like a beacon in a storm. And whatever residual resentment he harbored toward his mother and the ugly hand he'd been dealt all those years ago melted away.

"I'm good here." He put his hand over her heart. "With you...always."

Epilogue

Angie couldn't make the picnic baskets fast enough. It seemed that everyone wanted to take advantage of Dry Creek's spectacular spring weather. They'd even added more picnic tables to the grounds. Dry Creek Village had become such a hot spot for dining al fresco that there were waits to snag a creekside table.

The deli had been a runaway hit. The baskets—Angie's idea—had been inspired if she did say so herself. Instead of buying à la carte, customers loved getting a full meal and drinks all wrapped up in a pretty, portable cooler basket embroidered with the Dry Creek logo, the ranch's brand. They could eat in the center or take it to go.

She'd begun using similar packaging for Dalton steaks, ribs, and roasts. Between that and the deli, their meat sales had skyrocketed.

"Angie, Tiffany's on the phone." Nina called from the front of the market.

Angie took the call in her office alcove. "Hey, Tiff. I hope you're calling to say you'll do it." She had asked Tiffany to serve on the board of the new Dalton Foundation, an extension of the program Angie had started to distribute food to women's and homeless shelters.

"I'm onboard," Tiffany said. "This is such a wonderful thing you're doing for the community." Besides using Daltons' waste to feed the hungry, Angie's plans included an agricultural program that would help low-income families learn how to grow their own food. Tuff had suggested the idea and Angie had run with it, getting the rest of her family to sign on.

"Yay!" Angie jumped up and down, clapping her hands. No one made things happen in the Sierra Foothills like Tiffany. She was a one-woman machine. If anyone could help get the plan off the ground it was her. "Our first meeting is at the coffeeshop tomorrow at noon. Can you make it?"

"I'll be there."

Angie hung up and practically skipped to Tuff's studio to tell him the good news. She found him in the back, working on a new saddle. Buddy was in his usual spot underneath the cutting table, snoring away.

"Hey." He stopped what he was doing, wrapped his arms around her waist, and pulled her in for a kiss. "You on a break?"

"Tiffany agreed to be on the board. It's real, Tuff. The foundation is real."

"It was always real." He kissed a trail down her nose.

"But now we have two non-family members participating. It makes it more legit."

He laughed. "Okay. I'm glad she signed on. The woman is a little nutty, but she's connected. Between her and Laney, they know everyone in three counties."

"I know, right? I'm so excited about this." She rubbed her hands together, grinning from ear to ear.

"I'm excited about us," he whispered in her ear.

"You didn't tell anyone yet, right? I want my parents to be here when we make the big announcement." She and Tuff were going to San Francisco for the weekend to buy the ring. Tuff's spontaneous proposal had shocked them both.

They'd been eating take-out from Gina's in Angie's cabin when he suddenly blurted that he wanted to make them official. "Let's get hitched," had been his exact words. Without a ring, he'd improvised with a piece of braided leather.

Despite his lack of planning and dearth of flowery words, Angie thought it was the most romantic proposal she'd ever heard. She'd cried and he'd taken her in his arms, his eyes shining with so much love she felt it all the way to her marrow.

"Not in my wildest dreams could I love anyone more than I love you," he'd said. "I want us to be together forever."

"Me too," she'd soaked his shirt with happy tears. "When?"

"Whenever you want. We can go right now, find a preacher, a justice of the peace, a ship captain, whoever has the power to make it official."

She'd laughed. "As much as I love the idea, I'd like to have a real wedding for the sake of my mother." And for her own sake if she was being completely honest. Before, Angie had always considered the expense of a wedding silly, especially when people were homeless and starving. Now, she admitted she wanted the white dress and at least a small party. Marriage to a man as wonderful as Tuff was something to celebrate with her family and friends. "And I think we should wait until after Sawyer and Gina have the baby. That way he or she can be there too."

"You give me a date and I'll be there with bells on."

"Oh no, buster, you're helping me plan this thing."

They'd spent the last few nights playing around with ideas ranging from a barn dance to an intimate dinner at Gina's, finally settling on a creekside ceremony and a mid-sized party in Jace and Charlie's backyard. They didn't know they were hosting yet, but Angie had no doubt that her cousins would be delighted. That was the thing about the Daltons, they were all for one and one for all.

"I haven't told a soul." Tuff danced her to the corner of the room and pulled out a stool for her to sit. "But there's only so long I can keep news of this magnitude secret." He grinned and those not-quite dimples came out to play. They never failed to slay her.

She leaned forward and gave him a peck on the lips. "Soon. My folks are coming next week. You think you can make it that long?"

She still couldn't believe he'd popped the question. Angie knew how much he loved her. He showed it every day in big and small ways. But he was still learning how to trust…how to believe that the people he loved wouldn't let him down.

She supposed they were both learning new things about themselves. For her, the biggest lesson was that she could still accomplish her hopes and dreams from right here on Dry Creek Ranch with the people she loved most in the world.

"Maybe," he teased. "Or maybe I want to sing it from the mountaintops."

She brushed a lock of hair off his forehead. "I've heard you singing in the shower. You might want to hold off."

"You don't like my singing?" He winked.

"I like everything about you, including your retched rendition of 'Hey Good Lookin'." It had been one of Grandpa Dalton's favorite songs—and now hers.

"That's good." He leaned into her. "Because I like everything about you, too. Want to go home early?" He waggled his brows. "My boss is cool with it. How 'bout yours?"

She glanced at her watch. It was only two. "I'll be docked pay but you're worth it."

"You bet your sweet behind I'm worth it." He hooked her around the waist, whistled to the dog, and locked up.

They walked home, holding hands, brimming with love and optimism for the future of Dry Creek Ranch.